"What do you have in mind?"

Heather stepped closer, and Garrett breathed in her subtle citrus scent.

"A contest. If I get more strikes out of twenty pitches than you do, you stay. If you have more, then I'll release you."

He stared at her. Processing. She couldn't be serious. Sure, he had control issues, but he was still better than a college-level player. She was making this easy. But if she was foolish enough to offer him this out, he'd take it.

They eyed each other for a long, tense moment before he jerked his chin at her.

"You're on."

Dear Reader,

Growing up, I sported scraped knees instead of bows, spent my days prowling through the woods playing "war" rather than dressing up dolls, and learned to shoot BB guns before mastering the art of mascara application. Never a "girlie girl," I still fell head over heels for Harlequin romance books in my preteen years and am thrilled to write for this wonderful company. I've never questioned those different sides of me, and accept that I'll always be as excited to watch a ball game as I am to watch *The Bachelor*.

A League of Her Own is dear to me because Heather embraces her competitive, sports-loving side, as more and more women are doing today. When I watch or attend games, I hear women cheering as loudly as the men. I enjoyed writing a romance for female sports enthusiasts, like me, who have sentimental hearts—even if we yell for blood when our team loses a run/basket/touchdown/goal. I'm excited to showcase strong female characters like Heather, and give readers a different kind of romantic heroine that they can relate to and root for in the story.

I would love to hear from you about your favorite sports experiences and teams as well as your thoughts about the novel. To contact me, email karenrock@live.com.

Thanks!

Karen

HEARTWARMING

A League of Her Own

—

Karen Rock

H HARLEQUIN® HEARTWARMING™

Recycling programs
for this product may
not exist in your area.

ISBN-13: 978-0-373-36703-0

A League of Her Own

HARLEQUIN®

Printed in U.S.A.

™ www.Harlequin.com

KAREN ROCK

is an award-winning YA and adult contemporary author. She holds a master's degree in English and worked as an ELA instructor before becoming a full-time author. Her Harlequin Heartwarming novel *Wish Me Tomorrow* has won the 2014 Gayle Wilson Award of Excellence and the 2014 Golden Quill Award. When she's not writing, Karen loves scouring estate sales, cooking and hiking. She lives in the Adirondack Mountain region with her husband, daughter and Cavalier King cocker spaniels.

www.KarenRock.com

Books by Karen Rock

HARLEQUIN HEARTWARMING

13—WISH ME TOMORROW
37—HIS HOMETOWN GIRL
59—SOMEONE LIKE YOU

Visit the Author Profile page
at Harlequin.com for more titles

This novel is for all "sports moms" and especially my wonderful mother-in-law, Bernice Rock, the greatest, most dedicated of them all. Your seven sons and daughter are blessed to have had your unfailing support as you cheered them on at games and worked hard behind the scenes to keep their hectic lives running smoothly. Most important of all, you gave them your unconditional love. They couldn't have had their amazing childhoods without you.

CHAPTER ONE

IF HEATHER GADWAY'S cell phone hadn't already been dead, she would have killed it.

She peered at the blank screen, then squinted at the sun overhead, picturing her frowning father getting sent straight to her voice mail… again. Ever since she'd moved to California, he'd insisted they speak every morning. He'd probably left his version of a warm-and-fuzzy message, one she imagined sounded like this:

"Heather. For Pete's sake. Charge your phone. Next time put the cord next to your makeup. Then you'll actually remember the darn thing needs juice."

After a silence punctuated with grumpy noises, he'd end with, *"Call me back so I know you're alive."*

She grabbed another softball from a nearby bucket and tossed it to her rookie Morro Bay University pitcher. If she asked to borrow her player's phone, she could probably shoot off a text to her father, but a part of her rebelled at

the thought. She hadn't remembered to charge
the phone again, but it wasn't the end of the
world. In fact, it was possible that she'd been
ducking her cell lately, and half-forgetting to
charge the battery, because she wanted a little
breathing room from her dad's too-frequent
check-ins. She was twenty-seven, not seven.
She'd earned the right to go twenty-four hours
without a call.

"You're spraying the ball," she pointed out
to Alicia as other girls in bright blue uniforms
stretched or ran plays around the wide green
field outside the chain link bullpen. A few
lined up near the plate, taking hitting practice with their batting coach. "Watch that release point."

Heather took off her visor and swiped a hand
across her wet brow. It seemed as if they'd
been at this for hours, and she was melting
right along with the ice in the cooler. But she
wouldn't give up on Alicia, even though her father needed reassuring. As the pitching coach,
Heather realized the team's newest recruit depended on her. She'd been in those cleats nine
years ago and knew how nervous the first-year
student felt.

Alicia pulled off her sunglasses and squinted

at Heather from the mound. "Too early or too late?"

"Depends on the pitch. Stay consistent." Heather smiled encouragingly despite her unease. Ideally this phone lapse would earn her only a lecture for missing their daily check-in, an important routine her father had stuck to since nearly losing her fourteen years ago.

She twisted her wrist sweatband. With twenty minutes left in this session, Dad would have to wait. Not exactly his strong suit. As the owner of a Triple-A Minor League baseball team, he almost always got what he wanted. Few said no to Dave Gadway. Definitely not Heather.

"We need to replicate that point of release every single time," she added, forcing her attention back on Alicia. "Feel where the ball is coming off your fingertips." She pantomimed a pitch, arcing her arm back and then sweeping it forward, her fingers unfurling at her waist.

The girl's blond brows came together. "Am I going to be ready for tomorrow's game?" She tossed the softball to Heather.

After snatching it from the air, Heather twirled the familiar sphere of white, seamed leather in her palm, loving the feel and the good memories that came with it. For much of her life, playing sports had been her escape. The one place in her chaotic childhood she'd had some control. But as a former Red Tails pitcher herself, she knew that pitching was a high-pressure position.

Heather pasted a confident look on her face. Instilling self-assurance in her players was important, especially with the young ones like Alicia.

"Of course. We'll keep pitching until we get it. Let's slow it down a little. Put you back in the strike zone. We need to get the feel back for the release point." She flipped the ball to her player.

"Got it." Alicia's shoulders lowered, and the first smile of the day ghosted across her lightly freckled face.

Their bullpen catcher, Bucky, stood and waved from the opposite end of the fenced-in area. He might be over forty feet away and wearing a mask, but Heather could picture the older man's scowl. "We playing catch or pitching? Haven't got all day here."

Heather cupped her hands around her mouth. Despite years on the field, she'd always been soft-spoken, her words clinging to the back of her throat before she forced them out. It was a holdover from time spent tiptoeing around her volatile mother. "Sorry, Bucky. All set now."

Bucky swatted the air with his mitt and crouched again, pounding his fist into the leather's center. "Let's go, girlies!"

Alicia's brow furrowed and her fingers gripped the ball as she peered down the line. Good, thought Heather. She wasn't letting well-meaning but crotchety Bucky get to her. Sports were as much a mental game as they were a physical one. Alicia had to focus, or no amount of speed—and the first-year student was fast at nearly seventy miles an hour— would help her win games.

With a breathy grunt, Alicia wound up and released the ball off her fingertips. Slower this time, waist-high, perfect form, Heather observed before she heard the satisfying crack in the catcher's mitt.

"St-eee-rike!" hollered Bucky, jabbing the air with his fist before hurling the ball back toward the mound. "Keep it there, sweetie pie!"

Heather bit back a smile. Bucky worked with nationally ranked athletes, but it didn't stop him from using endearments that made some of the girls blush. If there was a "sweetie pie" in the bullpen, it was crusty Bucky. The Red Tails were lucky to have this veteran assisting and warming up pitchers during practices and games.

"Way to go, ace!" Heather exclaimed as she scratched her eternally peeling nose. No matter how much sunscreen she slathered on it, she resembled Rudolph year round.

Alicia nodded without turning her head, her eyes on Bucky. The low buzzing of a lawn tractor grew louder as it neared, mowing diagonal green lines in the outfield, where it wouldn't interfere with the infield practice. The smells of freshly cut grass and the honeysuckle growing up the fence mingled in the soft spring air. Heather hoped Alicia noticed none of this and was, instead, zoned in on getting another strike…not preoccupied with issues off the field like Heather was. Argh. Even thousands of miles away in North Carolina, her father still stirred the pot of her life.

She gnawed the inside of her cheek. His letting go was about as likely to happen as her actually wearing makeup, something he'd know if he paid attention to more than her mistakes.

Alicia wound up and released the ball, snapping Heather out of her thoughts. She grinned before she heard the catcher's mitt pop. Nice! Right down the middle.

"St-eee-rike!" roared Bucky, and he winged

the ball back at the mound. "You split the plate in half with that one, doll face!"

Alicia's mitt folded around the ball, and she brought it back to her chest before turning to Heather. "Same speed?"

Heather gave her a fist bump, then raised her radar gun. "No. Let's put a little something more on it."

Alicia's teeth caught her lower lip. Then she nodded and faced forward, her back straight.

A blur of white exploded from Alicia's side and smacked straight into Bucky's mitt.

"Sixty-eight." Heather glanced up from the digital display and gave a thumbs-up. "Excellent control and speed. Let's get a few more over the dish, and then we'll go for the corners."

"Sounds good." Alicia grabbed the ball Bucky winged at her and began again, her determination exactly what Heather had hoped to see when she'd brought her out for this one-on-one session.

The young woman had the makings of a standout athlete: a strong work ethic, a positive attitude and talent. It was why she'd lobbied for Chris, Morro Bay's director of softball operations, to recruit Alicia, despite her small size and inconsistent arm. Growing up around her father's team had taught Heather a lot about spotting potential, and Alicia had it in spades.

Twenty minutes later, Heather lowered her radar gun and waved at Bucky. "All set, thanks!" she called.

The older man pulled off his mask, his red face wet with sweat, his helter-skelter gray hair defying the laws of gravity. He headed up the line with a rolling gait and grabbed a sports drink from the cooler. After a long swig, he lowered it and pointed the bottle at Heather.

"Alicia reminds me of you. Mark my words. She's small, but she's got a big future. Might even beat that record of yours."

A gasp sounded beside Heather, and she glanced at a round-eyed Alicia.

"No one is ever going to win more than one hundred and fifty games," Alicia said reverently. "Coach Gadway's a legend."

Heather popped the top off a drink and handed it to her flushed, tired-looking player. Sometimes young athletes forgot the simplest things, like staying hydrated. "Oh. I wouldn't be sure about that. Records are made to be broken."

After Heather's sharp glance prompted her to throw back a long gulp, Alicia blurted, "Not yours. You were my idol growing up. I cut out all of your articles when you played here."

"Thanks, Alicia. That means a lot. And you—" Her throat closed around the rest of her sentence, something that happened whenever her heart spoke instead of her brain. "You inspire me, too." She returned Alicia's hug, then busied herself packing up their gear, never comfortable with praise. It touched her that she'd been a role model for Alicia. Sports were character building, especially in young women. They'd certainly saved her.

But if there was one thing she'd learned as a baseball team owner's daughter, fame was fleeting. Her real legacy, she hoped, would be helping other players, like Alicia, reach their potential.

"You're awesome, Coach," Alicia exclaimed as she grabbed the bucket of balls Heather passed her.

For a moment, Heather imagined how great it would have been if her father had heard that compliment, then shook the thought aside. If he had, he would have grumped that she should have pushed Alicia harder or some other criticism. It was his nature to point out faults, and he often found them in her. According to her childhood counselor, it was his way of showing he cared. If only it hadn't hurt more than it'd helped.

Behind them, Bucky hefted the cooler, and they headed for the exit. Sparrows took flight as they swung open the squealing gate and entered the large field, which was nearly ready for tomorrow's game. Heather paused for a moment and drank in the neatly raked and marked baselines, imagining the seats packed, the crowd cheering for Alicia and her first win. It'd be a great moment, and she hoped it came true.

Bucky snapped the padlock shut, breaking her out of her reverie. With a wave, he strode off toward the office area.

After Heather reassured the girl she'd do just fine in the upcoming game, Alicia went to the changing room, and Heather headed toward her office. She'd done solid work with Alicia today. In her gut, she knew she'd been right to recommend her, but ultimately, it all came down to the athlete's psyche. As much as she wished she could be in control, when it came to people, you couldn't count on anything. She'd learned that lesson the hard way.

Inside her small office, she sank into her flex-back chair and glanced up at the shelf holding her two USA Softball National Collegiate Player of the Year trophies. It'd been a long time since she'd felt the high of an achievement like that. As the youngest member of the coaching staff, she had a lot to prove.

She glanced at a picture of her father wearing his Triple-A Falcons team jacket and dropped her head into her hands. She wanted to show her dad she could succeed, too. It still stung that he'd vetoed her offer to come home to Holly Springs after college and work for the team, an institution that'd been in their family for three generations.

"You're not experienced enough, Heather," he'd said. "There's more to running a team than just being a great player."

And so far, without a recent division title, she hadn't proven him wrong. Although she worked with Morro Bay's head coach, helping him with roster moves and recruiting, they still hadn't put together a winning team.

With a sigh, she grabbed the landline. It was noon here, three o'clock in Holly Springs. He'd be out of the office, watching practice, no doubt.

An hour after leaving voice mail and text messages on her dad's cell, worry twisted her gut. Why wasn't he returning her call? Watching practice wouldn't stop him from getting back to her. She'd expected a lecture, not silence.

She punched in the number for Pete, the Falcons team manager. Fear fluttered inside her when the outgoing message stated that his number had been disconnected or changed. What was going on?

Scrolling through her contacts, she found Reed's cell number. Surely the Falcons hitting coach could give her some answers.

"Reed," he answered, curtly.

She relaxed at the sound of his familiar, scratchy voice. "Hi, Reed. It's Heather. I'm trying to get a hold of my—"

"Heather. We've been calling you." His voice grew louder, and in the background an overhead PA system crackled, announcing a code blue.

Her heartbeat sped as she checked her missed calls and saw his number. Was Reed in a hospital? Was her father? "What's going on? Is Dad okay? Where's Pete?"

"Pete didn't renew his contract, so he left a week ago. As for your dad, I'm waiting for the doctor, so I'm not sure. Wait. Here's somebody in a white coat."

Heather's fingers tightened around the handset. Oh. God. No. At sixty, her bull of a father had never been sick a day in his life. It had to be serious if he'd agreed to go to the hospital. Or—she squeezed her eyes shut—worse yet, there'd been no choice.

"I'm putting the doctor on, Heather. Hold on."

There was a moment of silence, and then a woman's voice came across the line.

"Heather Gadway?"

Heather's answer seemed sucked into the cleft between her collarbones. After a long moment, she gasped out, "Yes?"

"This is Dr. Freeman. I'm afraid your father suffered a heart attack today that's damaged his left ventricle."

"Is he going to be all right?" Her voice cracked. Suddenly she was eighteen again, leaving home for California, looking at a world that, for the first time, would not include her father. Back then she'd feared the distance separating them. But this...this could be permanent.

"He has stenosis—narrowing—in two of his coronary arteries that we'll treat with angioplasty and stents. However, another, smaller artery is blocked. We'll hold off on a bypass to see if he's improved after the first procedure. If so, we'll simply manage the occluded artery medically."

The doctor's words raced through her mind too fast to make sense. "An angioplasty?" A halting gap appeared between her questions, endless seconds when the words cowered against her lips. "A stent?"

On the other end of the line, the physician cleared her throat. "I'm sorry to rush through all of this, but surgery is in thirty minutes."

"Thirty minutes?" Heather repeated, peering at her watch. Her father's operation would be underway before she boarded a flight. She needed to be there. Now.

She tapped her keyboard and brought up screens with flights.

"Yes. Given the degree of atherosclerosis and his symptoms, it's best to act quickly. I have every confidence in this procedure. His prognosis looks good if he makes some changes in what I understand is a stressful life, including healthier eating, exercising and more relaxation."

Heather blinked in surprise. Her wired father never took a day off. And if Pete was no longer managing the Falcons, Dad was under more pressure than ever.

"That being said, I can't make any promises," the doctor continued. "Do you have any questions?"

Heather pinched the bridge of her nose. She knew that life didn't come with guarantees. Yet somehow, naïvely, she hadn't believed that rule applied to her father. He was her rock. Tough. Unyielding. Immune to weaknesses. Here was a chink in his armor, and it shook her to her core.

She scribbled a question on a note card, then read the question aloud: "When will he be out of surgery?" It was a speech therapy trick she hadn't used in years. She'd outgrown most of her speech issues except in the most extreme situations.

"If all goes well, two hours, then another hour or so before he's released to his room."

"Will you tell him…" Heather's words halted in her tight throat, the passage blocked. She clicked on an online ticket and noted the arrival time. "…tell him I'll be there by five? Eight your time."

"I'll note it in the chart. Your father is in good hands."

"Thank you." Heather hung up and studied her palms. No matter what the doctor suggested, Heather knew the truth from a lifetime of lessons drilled into her by a demanding parent.

Talent was no guarantee.

"LET'S DRINK TO Mr. Gadway's recovery. Two days post-op and he's already up and bossing the nurses around."

Garrett Wolf nodded in agreement then stared at the glass of Jameson his teammate plunked down on the pub table before him. His hands were clenched in his lap. He inhaled the familiar, woodsy smell of the whiskey, imagining its smooth taste on his suddenly parched tongue.

His sponsor's phone number ran through his head. He'd call if he couldn't resist those three fingers of whiskey. And he could use it tonight. Down the whole bottle until the sting of his miserable performance at the game earlier floated away. Luckily he'd attended an AA meeting this afternoon. It helped.

"Drink up, buddy. The night's young and the season's still early. Don't let tonight get you down. You'll win next time." The Falcons' starting catcher, Dean, pulled up a wooden stool and gulped an identical beverage.

Garrett's dark thoughts grew blacker. As a starting pitcher, he'd screwed up this chance to prove himself. A win would have confirmed that his past, as a Minor League player who'd squandered his potential, wouldn't repeat itself. He needed to show that the Falcons' risky decision to sign him would pay off.

But playing competitively after a three-year hiatus had rattled him, catching him off guard. Self-doubt, not booze, had impaired him this time. Ironic. Tomorrow, he'd hit the field and work on the control he'd lacked. Get his act together. If he didn't, he'd miss his last opportunity to move up to the Major Leagues. It was the childhood dream that'd gotten him through foster care, the adult goal that'd turned his life around.

"Aren't you going to drink that?" Dean asked, eying the whiskey. "Toast to Mr. Gadway?"

Garrett shoved the glass away, his fingers lingering, before forcing himself to let go. "I'll send a card."

"More for me, then." Dean studied him, then shrugged and threw back the drink.

Garrett looked away, not wanting to see the guy swallow the tempting brew. Yet all around him his new teammates were drinking beer so frothy he felt it on his upper lip, taking shots that made his own throat burn. He wanted a drink in the worst way. And with only twelve months of sobriety under his belt, he didn't trust himself to resist.

Not in this place.

Not ever.

In a couple of minutes, he'd leave. He'd already congratulated the new shortstop who'd been called up from their Double-A team. It was the reason they'd gathered here tonight to celebrate.

Dean squinted up at him. "Are you one of those devout types?" He ran a hand through his short brush of red hair. "Didn't mean to offend you."

Garrett relaxed. The guy meant well. It wasn't like the world conspired to make him relapse. Though sometimes it seemed like it.

"You didn't. And I'm not." He pulled a bronze coin from his back pocket and placed it on the table, leaving it out long enough for Dean to get a look before sliding it away again.

Without a word, Dean swept the glasses away and deposited them on another table. When he returned, his face had lost its jocular expression. "My dad was an alcoholic. It's something to earn one of those chips, and I wish he'd done it. You should be proud."

Garrett nodded. He was proud. It'd been a

hard year spent getting sober and back in competitive shape to pitch again. If he hadn't run into his old foster friend, a one-armed veteran who'd scolded him for wasting his God-given talents, he wouldn't have quit his construction job and tried again.

"Today wasn't the best debut," he murmured. He kept his hands busy shelling peanuts, his eyes on Dean instead of the rowdy beer pong game by the pool table, or the group raising their glasses every time someone hit the dart board's red center. The smell of fresh popcorn wafted from a machine by the bar while a rock song pulsed through the dark, wood-paneled room decorated with sports paraphernalia and TVs playing every MLB game in progress. It seemed as though the crowd moved to the same thrumming beat, everyone in sync, all but him.

Dean crinkled his stub of a nose and shrugged. "It wasn't all you. Sure, you gave up those walks, but if it wasn't for Jogging George, we would have tied in the eighth."

"Jogging George?" Garrett smiled at the nickname that suited their third baseman. Dean was right. If George had hustled on that play, he could have beaten the throw to first, rather than letting the runner on third score.

Dean nodded and signaled to a passing waitress. "A couple of Cokes over here. And more peanuts." He turned back and leaned in, his voice lower. "Defensively, our outfield didn't show much effort on that fly ball in the gap either. They got three runs off of that."

Garrett nodded, thinking the game through. Dean was right. He was putting all the pressure on himself. It was the same bad habit that'd led him to drink when he'd messed up in the Minors before. Although that wasn't the whole story.

Not even close.

"So what's the deal with this team?" After earning his AA chip and calling his former agent, he'd been invited to try out for the Falcons. A week later he was signed and on the field practicing with the team. And now, after another two weeks, he'd pitched his first game. A loss. One of only a few this season, he vowed.

His eyes flicked to the bottles lined along the mirror-backed shelves behind the bar. In the past, he would have drunk away his defeat until it didn't matter. Until nothing mattered. Until he hadn't mattered…eventually. Not that, as a foster child, he'd ever felt like he counted. But for a brief time, when he'd been a top draft pick known for his ninety-five-miles-an-hour fastball, he'd felt like somebody. He wanted that feeling again. Would make it happen.

"It's a decent group," Dean said cautiously.

Garrett followed Dean's glance over to a group of men. They joked around with the new shortstop, who clutched his beer like it was his first. Maybe it was. The sight made Garrett want to rip it out of his hands before it was too late.

"You can't cut it here," brayed the second baseman as he jabbed the shortstop's shoulder and laughed, making the kid flinch. "Not like Waitman over there. He got another moon shot tonight."

He leaned across the table and shouted over to the dart board crowd. "How many dingers you think you're getting this year, Waitman? Thirty?"

Their left fielder pointed his dart at the second baseman and pretended to throw it. "More than you, loser."

Another player at the table turned back to the shortstop. "You're playing real baseball now." The guy clapped the young player on the back, making him stagger forward and spill his beer.

"You'll face tough pitchers up here," warned

Jogging George. "Everyone throws ninety miles per hour, some faster, like Wolf, but more consistent. Man, we got shelled tonight."

Garrett returned their stares when they looked over at him, his face impassive. He'd had a tough time controlling his arm when he'd been drinking, a problem that plagued him sober, too. But he'd keep working on it. Straighten out his pitch the way he'd straightened out his life.

"Don't take it personally," Dean muttered, nodding a thank-you when Garrett slid cash to the waitress delivering their sodas. "If these guys would put more effort into their game, we might have a winning season."

"They don't bother me." Garrett turned sideways and leaned his arm on the table, facing Dean. "The Falcons haven't gone to the playoffs in over fifteen years, right?" He lifted his soda and drank, telling himself it tasted better without rum.

"Yeah. And now that Pete left—our manager—we'll be lucky to finish at five hundred for the season." Dean tossed some nuts into his mouth and chewed, his expression distant. "His wife told my sister the contract we offered him was at a lower salary. The Gadways can't pay more. Wonder if the stress caused Dave's heart attack."

"Could be," Garrett mused, feeling bad for the man who'd given him this break. He hoped they'd find someone good to manage the team, to take the pressure off Mr. Gadway and help the Falcons. Plus, at twenty-seven, Garrett was getting old to be considered for a move up into the Major Leagues. Without a strong, stable team behind him, one that wouldn't make errors that allowed hits or runs, his prospects of getting the stats he needed to impress their parent team were lower still.

A couple of giggling young women stopped beside their table, their voices shrill, as they eyed Garrett and Dean. Garrett avoided the blonde's come-hither look, not impressed with the blatant flirting. He had better goals than scoring with a new girl every night.

"Heard he's stable though…" Dean mopped up an overturned drink the girls spilled when they bumped into their table.

"Oops. Can we buy you another one?" purred the blonde, flipping her long hair out of her eyes. "Rum and Coke?"

"We're fine," Garrett muttered without giving her more than a brief glance. He hated to be rude, but baseball groupies, which these girls looked to be, were hard to get rid of.

"I insist." The brunette leaned over far enough to give both men a healthy view of her cleavage.

"It's not your call to make," Garrett shot back. "Now. If you'll excuse us?"

"I'm Melissa," the blonde piped up, extending her hand to Dean as if she hadn't heard Garrett's dismissal. "And this is my friend, Dana."

"Nice to meet you," Dean said, clearly torn between two good-looking women and Garrett's glare. "My friend and I—"

"Are having two rum and Cokes. Coming up!" Melissa called and sauntered away, her hips swinging in short shorts.

"So what do you two like to do for fun?" Dana trailed a fingernail up Garrett's arm and leaned close so he could smell her sharp perfume. "Whatever it is, Melissa and I are up for it."

Garrett jerked away and placed a twenty on the table. "Use this for the drinks. Have a nice night."

He strode away and heard Dean's mumbled apology before the catcher joined him at the door. Garrett pushed through the exit and plunged into the balmy night, his heart rate slowing as he gulped in the smoke-free air.

"What the heck, dude!" Dean called as Garrett hurried toward his sports car. All around them, crickets serenaded the half moon that hung low and bright in a dark sky.

Garrett wheeled around. "Go on back. Hanging out with those women, drinking… that's not my scene. Not anymore."

Dean jogged up to him. "Hey. I get it. You didn't want to be bothered. With that ugly mug of yours, getting pestered by gorgeous women must happen a lot. Poor guy."

A low laugh escaped Garrett. Dean was growing on him. Garrett had vowed to keep his distance from the other players. Avoid situations that'd tempt him to drink. But Dean seemed different from the rest. An ally when he could use one. According to his sponsor, in between AA meetings he'd need support like Dean's.

Garrett leaned against his car, one boot resting on his rims. In the distance, a rushing stream gurgled, the frogs' deep hum accompanying the violin whir of insects.

"It's quiet in Holly Springs." Strange as it sounded given his former, fast-paced life in Atlanta, he liked it.

Something about this small town settled the part of him that felt unmoored. Like he could belong here, though he knew that wasn't possible. As a kid shuttled from one house to the next before landing in a group home, he'd learned not to put down roots. Get too comfortable or close to anyone. The one time he had, it'd ended in a tragedy he did his best to avoid thinking about.

"It's a little too quiet." Dean glanced up the road toward the center of town where a few lights twinkled. "Since they shut down the last of the fabric mills a year ago, the town lost its only major employer and draw, except us. If we fold—"

Anxiety stabbed Garrett, sharp and sudden. "Is there a chance the team's going under?" Mr. Gadway was the first to give him a chance. Would there be others?

Dean looked around and stepped closer, lowering his voice. "There's a rumor that it's up for sale."

"You think that's true?"

"We're not drawing as many fans as we used to, and with another Minor League team starting up just an hour farther from Raleigh than we are…" Dean jerked his chin west, then looked back to Garrett.

Garrett rubbed the back of his tense neck. "We need to turn it around—hope the next manager is going to do that…" He'd never have a strong record if the team kept losing game after game. He needed his time with the Falcons to count—to attract Major League attention, he had to make his mark.

"Who's going to take over as manager? Not Reed."

Dean slapped at a mosquito, leaving a smear of blood above his elbow. "Hope not. He doesn't put more than three words together. These younger guys need a firm hand."

"But if they couldn't afford Pete, who are they going to get?" Garrett wondered.

When Dean shrugged, Garrett's jaw flexed. New owners would mean uncertainty and flux while they set up infrastructure, time he couldn't afford to waste. New management, if it was someone inexperienced or ineffective, could cause the same damage. He'd worked too hard to lose this second chance.

Not when it might be his last.

CHAPTER TWO

HEATHER SAT IN the Falcons' former dugout and gazed at the sky. It was purple, almost watery-looking. The moon peered back at her over the tree line, and birds called their good-nights from the spreading branches. Scout, the family's collie, bounded through the entrance and circled the bench before flopping down at her feet, exhausted from chasing who knew what...

She zipped her sweatshirt against the slight chill, thinking for the hundredth time that she should leave their old field and head home. Yet after two weeks of staying indoors, either in the hospital or by her father's side, she needed this gulp of air.

And being here was peaceful. Even the rattling cicadas in the scrub brush sounded like a lullaby. She'd always escaped here during her mother's addiction-fueled rampages. A place she could run to from home.

Heather wondered what would have happened if her mother hadn't sustained the back injury that'd hooked her on painkillers. Although it'd happened when Heather was too young to remember, she'd always wished she could have done something to prevent the muscle sprain—or seen the signs of her mother's medicine misuse, a habit that'd become a much bigger problem than her back. She glanced around at the peeling white paint on the warped walls, up at the sagging ceiling, and out at the shaggy field. Like all baseball fields, it was beautiful to her. Abandoned or not.

She stretched out on the gouged wooden bench, feeling completely alone. Scout nudged his wet nose into her palm, and she smoothed the russet crown of his head. Well, maybe not absolutely alone. But still…after enduring her father's constant stream of remarks that the soup was too bland, that the air-conditioning was too high, that his pills weren't crushed well enough in the jelly…the recriminations seemed endless…she needed this time to herself.

She brought her knees up and wrapped her arms around them. At least she'd heard that Alicia had won her second game today, the accomplishment bolstering her. It'd also felt good when her university's operations director, Chris, had said he'd be glad when she came home. Yet California would never be a place she could settle down. She was appreciated there, but it wasn't where she belonged.

This was home. She remembered the grouchy old third baseman who'd been a career Minor Leaguer. He'd bought her Pixy Stix at the snack counter after every home win. The team's bus driver came to mind. He'd let her sneak on board for a handful of away games the summer she'd turned eleven. The year her mother was worse than ever.

Being a part of that year's championship run had instilled her love for the game while helping her escape a hellish life. She and the players weren't related, but they'd always been her family. North Carolina's dense woods, distant mountains and numerous streams part of her DNA.

Like a migrating bird, flying home had settled the part of her that'd felt adrift since she'd left for college. Maybe she'd apply for a coaching position locally. Keep an eye on her father and help out with the Falcons...if he'd let her. She craved his approval, but there was as much of a chance of getting that as there was of her returning one of her mother's recent calls.

A moth fluttered by her forehead and she shooed it away, staring up at the cobweb-covered ceiling. She'd heard her mother's promises too many times to trust them again. That faith had nearly killed her when she'd climbed into her parents' car and woken up, two days later, in intensive care. It'd been her thirteenth birthday, a day marked with a lit candle stuck in green Jell-o and the news that Mom had checked herself out of the hospital and left their family for good.

She pulled up the hem of her sweatshirt and traced the raised silver scar that ran along her stomach. It was a tangible reminder of how close that trust had come to ending her life. Her mother's abandonment left wounds the surgeons couldn't stitch closed…so she'd done it herself, shutting off the part of her that could ever believe in others again.

Whomp! The loud bang of a ball hitting the backstop echoed in the still twilight. She scrambled upright and peered into the purpling light, Scout already bounding for the field. A tall man stood on the pitcher's mound, his chiseled profile outlined by the sun's last rays. His strong jaw flexed and, in a blur of movement, he wound up and let loose another fastball, his biceps tense before he dropped his arms.

He was powerfully built with broad shoulders and a wide back that tapered to a lean waist and flat stomach. When he lifted the bottom of his shirt to mop his brow, she glimpsed a hard six-pack that sucked the air right out of her. The coach in her admired the physique that promised results on the field. The woman in her... Suddenly her sweatshirt was too warm over her tank top and she shrugged out of it, her eyes lingering on the strong play of his quadriceps shifting as he changed his stance.

Male, athletic beauty like his was undeniable. The symmetry of his features and body, and the animal grace of his movements, made it hard not to stare. She wasn't in the market for a boyfriend. Needed to focus on her father and building her career. A romantic relationship would only distract her. Still, he was a pitcher, same as her. There was no harm in a little conversation about that... Besides, she needed to call off a barking Scout.

Oh, who was she kidding? It was hard to resist wanting a closer glimpse. And that's all it could be, she told herself firmly as she sat up and left the dugout. How long had he played for the Falcons? She hadn't seen him before. She would have remembered the tousled golden hair that grabbed the fading light and the intense eyes that suddenly swerved her way.

"Oh!" she exclaimed, her hands rising to her ribs as if to contain her ferociously beating heart. "Sorry to disturb you. Scout, down." She gave a silent thank-you to her unreliable tongue for not tripping up her words and watched, grateful, as her sometimes unruly pet lowered his belly and muzzle to the dirt.

A frown marred the man's handsome face, a line appearing between his slanted brows. He looked down at her over a straight nose that stopped above a pair of full lips. "This is a closed practice." His eyes stared directly into hers, causing an odd, plummeting sensation in her legs. So much so that she dipped a little at the knees.

She opened her mouth, but now her voice had run down her throat. Looking at him made it hard to think—or speak.

He gestured to the square he'd marked off with glow-in-the-dark tape on the backstop. "If you don't mind, I need to continue pitching. Alone. And this is private property."

Heather pulled words from her throat as if she was raising them from a well, determined to match his arrogant tone. Who did this guy think he was?

That was the problem with good-looking guys. They expected everyone in the world to be nice to them but didn't bother to return the favor.

"I know. It's mine. Or my dad's. I'm Heather Gadway." She strode forward and extended a hand. When he shook it, a rush of awareness exploded up her arm.

"Garrett Wolf," he drawled, his voice dark, smooth and hypnotic. "Your father recently signed me." He glanced at Scout. "Nice dog."

Words collected in her mouth and lay there, irritation weighing them down. He was the reclamation project, the reformed alcoholic who'd caused his last Triple-A team lots of trouble with the media and on the field. And she'd almost let herself be attracted to him. Well, shoot. That was not going to happen.

She dropped his hand as if she'd touched acid and stepped back, a knot forming in her throat. At five-ten, she was a tall woman, but Garrett had to be more than half a foot taller. Six-four or -five, maybe.

"Welcome to the team," Heather forced out, not meaning it at all. Why had her father signed such a high-risk player, anyway? Sure, he was easy on the eyes, but it wasn't like they were putting up billboards. Her dad, of all people, should know they didn't need former addicts on the Falcons. What if he relapsed? Always a real possibility. "I'm visiting while my father recovers from his heart attack."

The stern lines of his face relaxed, and suddenly he was the all-American boy next door, the kind who broke every girl's heart—every girl's but hers. There wasn't a chance she'd fall for his charm, no matter that his easy smile made her stomach jump and flutter. She'd seen what he'd been like *before* he'd found out she was the owner's daughter.

Garrett tossed his ball in a gym bag and scooped up his sports drink in a sleek, fluid movement that mesmerized her. When he drew closer, she could smell his pine-scented aftershave and a fresh, masculine musk. "Your father's a good man. I hope he's doing better."

Heather shifted her footing and cleared her throat. Garrett was getting under her skin in the worst way. His earlier arrogance needled her. Yet somehow, when the corners of his lips lifted and his deep dimples flashed, she had to catch herself before grinning back. *Get a grip and be professional,* she warned herself before saying, "He is. Chomping at the bit to get out more. I've practically had to tie him to the bed."

A spark ignited in his blue eyes, and she flushed. What a strange thing to say. Provocative when she meant to be anything but.

"How long are you staying?" he asked, his deep voice lowering further, his unswerving, intent gaze on her.

She scuffed the dirt, her ears ringing with the staccato *thrum thrum thrum* of her rapid pulse. "Not sure. I'm a pitching coach for the Morro Bay Red Tails. They want me back. But Dad needs me."

Garrett's eyebrows rose. "So you're a pitcher, too."

"I was. Still miss that feeling of controlling the game." She pressed her lips shut. Now why had she admitted that to a stranger? One she should be running from instead of hanging around like a groupie...

Understanding lit his eyes. "Me too. I like taking the lead. Being in charge." He stepped closer and stared down at her before he tucked a strand that'd fallen from her ponytail behind her ear. She shivered, the caress turning her inside out as his hand lingered by her cheek.

Unable to look away, she returned his stare, wishing he was anyone else. Or she was anyone else. But whatever she might fantasize, the reality was that this magnetic pull had to be severed. After a moment, she forced herself to back away.

"I'd better be going. My father probably needs me."

"Tell him I wish him well," Garrett said. "Will he be at tomorrow's game? Both of you?"

The way he said it sounded like a personal invitation. Like he wanted her there. But she had to be imagining this. Few guys dared make a move on the owner's daughter. She doubted Garrett would jeopardize his comeback by screwing up like that. And besides, her dad would go ballistic if she even considered cozying up to this guy. Time to exit. Fast. Every time their eyes met, she felt light-headed.

"Maybe. I'll be around. Let's go, Scout," she called and fled.

Just not around you, she added silently, looking over her shoulder and catching his stare.

Not if she could help it.

HEATHER SNUCK ANOTHER look at her father as they seated themselves at the boardroom table. He'd scolded her for fussing over him these past two weeks, but with the scare he'd given her, it was hard to leave him be. Sometimes it felt like if she looked away, he might just disappear. And despite her mother's sporadic attempts to contact her these past ten years, she still felt as though her father was all she had in the world.

Though lately, ridiculous thoughts of a gorgeous pitcher had also kept her company. She needed a mental fly swatter to squash them. Was he the reason she'd already laid out her outfit—a sundress and wedge sandals—for tonight's game? Usually she was content with shorts and a T-shirt that'd survived a mustard spill or two. When she got home, that dress was going right back in the closet. No way was she dressing up for Garrett Wolf.

"Mr. Gadway." A man in a fitted, expensive-looking suit entered the room and extended his hand to her father, his thick gold ring flashing under the recessed lights. "It's nice to meet you in person, though I hadn't anticipated the pleasure of meeting your lovely daughter as well."

Heather tried not to cringe visibly at the moist press of his palm against hers, still wondering what this meeting was all about.

If she hadn't overheard her father confirming the time and location, she wouldn't have known he had something important scheduled. Luckily, he'd grudgingly given in when she'd insisted on coming. Her reminder that he still needed someone to drive tipped the scales.

"I'm Sam Gowette, and this is my business partner and brother, Joe." A slightly younger man joined them. He had the same wavy brown hair as his brother, his protruding eyes lingering on her a moment too long. Gowette? Realization sizzled through her. These were the media moguls who owned their Major League affiliate, the Buccaneers. Why were they here?

"Tomas Swarez, our attorney, is here as well." Heather returned the distinguished-looking man's nod, her nerves jumping higher and higher until they reached her throat and made her swallow hard. What was going on?

The attorney passed a folder to her father and looked at her apologetically. "If I'd known you were coming, I would have prepared a purchase offer packet for you as well, Ms. Gadway."

Heather set down her mug. "Purchase offer?" Her heart raced. Were they selling the team? A sharp glance at her father showed him looking straight ahead, a slight tick appearing beneath his left eye. A sure sign he was unsettled.

The Gowette brothers exchanged a long look before the older one—Sam—faced her with a smile that didn't reach his eyes. "Ah, yes. It's an offer we've been discussing with your father. Our purchase of the Falcons."

A hot flush started in Heather's gut and burned its way up to her cheeks. "I'm afraid there's been a mistake." She turned to her father and said in a low voice, "The Falcons are not for sale."

The lawyer straightened his tie and cleared his throat after a nod from his employers. "With all due respect, Ms. Gadway, this deal has been negotiated with your father, the sole owner of this property. We'd appreciate the chance to proceed with our discussion without further interruptions."

"What is going on?" she whispered to her father.

"Heather. This has nothing to do with you," he growled beneath his breath. His brown eyes slid her way and narrowed at the edges in a way that used to make her duck under her covers.

But she wasn't a kid anymore. And this had everything to do with her. The Falcons were her family's legacy. Sure, she wasn't the son she imagined her father would have wanted. But there wasn't anything a man could do for this team that she couldn't. Her father needed to give her a chance to turn it around rather than sell. Believe in her instead of ripping everything she did apart.

She opened her mouth but closed it when her father's index finger tapped the table in front of her. Fine. She'd listen, but he wouldn't possibly sell the team without talking it over with her first. Would he?

"Shall we begin?" the attorney intoned, and all the men flipped open their folders in unison.

Heather leaned to the right and read over her father's shoulder. The Gowette Corporation was proposing to purchase the Falcons for eight million dollars, a ridiculously low price. Her heart beat so loudly she wondered if her father could hear it. But he refused to meet her eye as he scanned the document.

A knock on the door sounded when her father reached the last page. The one with the empty signature lines.

"Sorry if I'm interrupting," said Frank Williams, the Minor League's director. He was a tall man with salt-and-pepper hair clipped short around his square-shaped head. His eyes darted to Heather, and he smiled in recognition. His daughter was her high school best friend and former softball teammate. "I stopped by to check in on the Falcons and heard there was a sale meeting. Thought I might sit in if that's okay."

Heather breathed a bit easier. She knew Frank well and had always thought him a fair person. He'd never agree that eight million was a reasonable price. Not for a team that grossed half of that a year. Or at least, it used to before the fabric mills had all shut down. A lot had changed since she'd left home.

In fact, she'd hardly recognized Holly Springs when she'd driven through it the other day. Gone were the crowds bustling along the streets. Many of the coffee shops and local artisan spots were boarded up. Even the children's bookstore had shut down. Worse yet, the people walked with their heads low, as though the pride they'd once had in their formerly thriving town had left along with most of its populace. It broke her heart.

The Gowettes and their lawyer nodded and grinned at Frank as if greeting royalty. His opinion held a lot of sway, and they obviously were courting it.

"The proposal is to purchase the Falcons for eight million dollars, a price previously negotiated between my clients and Mr. Gadway," announced the Gowettes' representative. When he raised his coffee mug for a sip, she noticed his hand trembled slightly. He had to know this was a terrible offer.

Frank cleared his throat and peered at her father. "And that price is agreeable to you, Dave?"

Her father paled and, for the first time since she'd seen him in the hospital, looked defeated. "I'm out of options. And the price is fair since they're not going to use any of the Holly Springs facilities."

Heather sucked in a harsh breath. "Why? We just built the new stadium ten years ago, and the old stadium is still a decent place for targeted practices."

"Because we're relocating the team closer to Pittsburgh," the older Gowette brother cut in flatly, clearly losing patience with her.

"But the Falcons have always played in Holly Springs." Heather struggled to raise her voice, yet the more upset she got, the more her brain muted her vocal cords. She turned to her expressionless father and put a hand on his arm, feeling the thin parchment of his skin. He seemed to have aged overnight.

"Your grandfather founded the team here in the '30s. We have an obligation to this town. Its people." Sure, the growing trend was Major

League owners buying their Minor League affiliates, but she'd never imagined it happening to the Falcons. Her family couldn't give up a tradition they'd started long ago.

"Joe, Sam, Tomas," her father said, his voice filled with the gravel that came from shouting for most of his life. "I'd like a moment with my daughter. Alone."

The men shot her disapproving looks and left. Frank remained, sitting quietly after her father nodded for him to stay.

The creases in her father's broad face deepened when he turned toward her, his firm jaw showing the slightest droop. When had her dad ever looked his age? He gathered her hands in his, his familiar calluses chaffing her palm. "It's time to be a grown-up, Heather, and that means making tough decisions."

Disappointment stung her, but she wasn't surprised. Criticism was his way of caring, right? She gritted her teeth and ignored the old hurts.

"I'm listening, Dad. And I can't believe that we talk every day and something so important to you—and me—never came up. Please do bring me up to speed."

Her father sighed. "Since the fabric mills shut down and the brand new Double-A stadium went up on the other side of Raleigh, we've lost money for five years straight. I've tried to keep it from you. Didn't want you to worry, but the truth is, I can't afford to keep going."

"You should have told me. I would have come home to help instead of just visit." She squeezed his hands, wishing he'd trusted her with the truth. But open communication had never been their strong suit. Living with an addict meant keeping secrets. It was a pattern they'd never broken free of, even after her mother had left and she and her dad had attended Al-Anon meetings together. Although the group was a way for friends and families of substance abusers to share their experiences, Heather and her dad had never talked about it outside of meetings.

Her father shook his head. "You're doing just fine out there in California, and there's nothing you could help with here. Pete left because I had to offer him a lower wage. Since I can't pay the kind of salary that'd buy us a decent manager, we can't turn the team's record around and attract the fans. I'd do it myself, but with my health where it's at, that's not an option anymore."

But she could help. Sure she loved coaching

the Red Tails, but this team belonged to her ancestors, and Holly Springs was where her home and heart were. If the team left, there would be little to keep the town going.

"But you don't have to do it yourself. I'm here. I'll take a leave of absence from the university, manage the team for free and get the Falcons back on track while you recover." Although she used her most confident "coach" voice, inside she shook at the idea. Could she pull it off? It'd been her dream, but she'd always imagined gradually easing into the position with time to learn from Pete. Now she'd have to figure things out on the fly. Sink or swim time.

Her father pressed his lips together and shook his head. "You don't have the know-how for a job like this, Heather."

"I grew up with the Falcons and know as much about them as anyone here. Even you." She searched his eyes but saw only flat refusal reflected back at her. Her chin rose as she tried again. "I've worked my way up with the Red Tails and help out with their roster and recruitment. I can do this. Give me a chance."

He swatted the air with his hand. "Out of the question. Besides, who ever heard of a woman managing a men's Minor League base-ball team?"

Frank put his elbow on the table and leaned in. "Actually, the MBA's been trying to rectify that, Dave. Someone like Heather could help with that." He gave her an encouraging smile. "We need to show that we're equal opportunity employers."

Heather's heart warmed. Frank believed in her.

"But I can't afford to lose more money, or spend time teaching her the ropes," exclaimed her father. He pushed back his gray hair, his face turning red. "She'll never learn fast enough."

His cutting words threatened to shove Heather right back to her childhood and all the times she hadn't been good enough. Not for him.

But he'd also said it was time to grow up, and she'd done that. He just didn't see it. With this chance, she'd prove that she was capable and deserved his respect.

"I don't need your help," she said, forcing the dial up on her voice. "I watched a game the other day, and already have some changes in mind to improve the team."

Her father snorted, but Frank steepled his

fingers and regarded her carefully. "What would you do?"

She went through the mental notes she'd taken while watching yesterday's game. "First, George Hopson's a good hitter, but he's slow. He clogs up the bases and could have scored a run from third if he'd hustled on that long fly ball. Defensively, your center fielder, Rob Vader, is plenty fast, but he's wall-shy. He pulled up short yesterday and missed a catchable ball that hit the bottom of the wall. Two runs scored because of that. We need more effort on those kinds of plays. Finally, that new pitcher, the tall, blond-haired one..."

"Garrett Wolf?" her father asked, looking slightly stunned at her rush of words. It felt good finally to have the floor. To share her opinion. To be listened to. Taken seriously.

She nodded, trying to appear calm despite the leap in her pulse at Garrett's name. "He's a risk, and I'm not sure if he's worth keeping. I didn't see him pitch that game, but heard he's got control issues. He'll need help with that if he's going to be an asset instead of a liability."

She would definitely put the Falcons pitching coach on that task, not trusting herself to give the dangerously attractive new player the pointers he needed. That is, if she even got the opportunity to save the team.

Her father was already shaking his head. "Impossible."

"Dave. This isn't my call, but if you'd like my advice, I'll give it," Frank weighed in.

At her father's stiff nod, the man continued. "The season's already begun, and the team can't be relocated at this point anyway. This sale can be made in September if you still want it. In the meantime, give Heather a chance. I've watched this kid of yours for years. She's level-headed, hardworking and no quitter. She'll motivate these guys. Besides, as the first Minor League team with a female manager, you'll draw attention and may sell more tickets. Female baseball fans are a growing demographic. We need to get with the times."

He winked at Heather, and she glowed at the praise and support. Frank had been a good father to her friend, and now he was her champion when she'd least expected it.

Her father rubbed the white bristles on his chin, his eyes half-closed. "This is a bad idea," he grumbled after a long, tense moment.

"But you'll try it," Frank urged him.

"Won't change anything," her father sighed, giving her a pitying look beneath the unclipped hedge of his brows. "Just putting off the inevitable."

Heather ducked behind her emotional shield before her father's lack of faith wounded her further. She had four months to turn the team around and prove him wrong. And she had a few ideas of her own about how to put the Falcons back in the limelight besides wins and the novelty of her gender. One plan had taken hold when she'd fielded a request from a local group home for troubled foster kids who couldn't live with families. They were eager for tickets and she was happy to give them, along with other opportunities if her father would let her.

Ideally, with a focus on positive change, her gender would become a nonissue—for her and all women who wanted a career in baseball.

The Gowette brothers knocked and confidently strode to their seats, their lawyer in tow.

"Shall we start over?" Their attorney seated himself, then flipped to the pages where signature lines lay empty.

Her father crossed his arms over his chest. "No need. Sale's off."

The brothers sputtered, one of them protesting, "We've been putting this deal together for months."

"Then you won't mind waiting a few more.

The Falcons are going to finish their season before I revisit this sale option."

"This offer won't be around forever," warned the older brother, pointing his finger.

"No." Her father stood with a sigh. He looked down at Heather and put a heavy hand on her shoulder. "And neither will I. But we'll take our chances."

After the Gowettes and their lawyer left, Heather flew into her father's arms. "Thank you, Dad."

"Don't thank me. I was trying to save some inheritance for you instead of burning through it with another bad season, but if you and Frank think this is a good idea…well…we'll give it a few months. After that, no more arguments. The team goes."

"There won't be any more arguments," Heather whispered in her father's ear before releasing him.

He harrumphed and walked out of the room with Frank as Heather lingered.

She looked out at the empty parking lot, imagining it full again. Holly Springs deserved another chance. And after a childhood full of hearing what she couldn't do, she deserved this opportunity, too. Finally, her father would learn he could count on her, trust that she was capable. Believe in her.

She had one shot and wouldn't mess it up.

CHAPTER THREE

"ANYONE KNOW WHAT the meeting's about?"

Garrett looked up at George Hopson, who'd turned around in his foldout chair, the cherry smell of chewing tobacco accompanying his question.

Garrett shrugged when he caught Dean's subtle headshake. It was one thing to speculate in private. But this was a formal meeting. No sense in getting everyone riled up about rumors until they knew the truth. From what he'd heard, it'd been a couple of days since the franchise owners had met with Mr. Gowette and speculation was rife.

On his own end, however, he was worried. After his conversation with Dean, he'd called his agent and already had a couple of teams lined up who might be interested in giving him a tryout if the Falcons released him. He was a risk as a reclamation project who now had a 0-1 record. If he let any more time go by and his record worsened, he'd be out of options completely. He was fortunate the teams even entertained the idea of looking him over. If his current team appeared to be in more jeopardy than he'd previously believed, he needed to move fast. .

"Don't know." He lifted his foot and placed it on his jittering knee. "Change in schedule?"

"Is it true they're selling the team?" jabbered the new shortstop beside him. His hair was slicked back and wet from a recent shower, his polo shirt pressed as neatly as the crease in his pants. Garrett looked at his own wrinkled button-down shirt and jeans. He'd put in some effort at least—he'd usually be in a T-shirt and shorts. Since practice started in an hour, there wasn't much reason to get dressed up.

"Guess we'll see." He rubbed his jaw, wondering when the meeting would begin. He was as anxious as the rest, but his years of learning to keep his temper in check as a foster kid, then hiding his feelings during games altogether, made camouflaging his emotions second nature.

"They're probably announcing our next manager," put in Waitman, their left fielder. He shook a packet of raisins into his mouth and chewed as he watched the clock above the double doors at the front of the large team meeting room.

Murmurs of agreement erupted from the rows of seats around them. It was the most logical explanation. And a critical choice. The wrong manager would influence the entire season and, by extension, Garrett's prospects of a strong record that could propel him to the Majors. If the team gave up trying, it wouldn't help his stat line. He needed the Falcons to hustle, to execute plays well and get batters out. If they didn't, it would mean more runs and more hits and fewer innings pitched, all stats chronicled on his record.

A pitcher usually only got around a hundred throws per game. If the guys backing him up couldn't get the outs they were supposed to, it meant facing more batters per inning, burning through the number of throws allowed before he was pulled from the game.

With luck, the news would be good and he'd see the owner's beautiful daughter at tonight's game. He hadn't been able to get her out of his mind since they'd met. In fact, he'd looked her up online and discovered that she was one of the top collegiate softball players of all time. Impressive.

Looks and talent. She had it all.

Including a father who'd bench him if he so much as treated her to a stadium hot dog.

Not that he'd do anything that stupid. She'd be off-limits even if her father wasn't the owner. He had to stay focused on his career, not women. Even ones as attractive as Heather.

She was pretty in that natural way he liked best. She wore no makeup, but freckles and a sunburned nose brightened her heart-shape face. Her large eyes, a color that reminded him of jade stones, were set beneath golden brows that matched the strands running through her long, wavy light brown hair.

Yes, she was gorgeous, and the wary expression in her eyes made him feel strangely protective. What he wanted to shield her from, however, he hadn't a clue. Yet something about her reminded him, strangely, of himself. She seemed guarded, as if ready for whatever life was about to dish out next. Weird. As Dave Gadway's daughter, she was rich and privileged. What had she ever suffered?

He stopped his runaway thoughts. Whatever had happened to put that expression in Heather's eyes, it was none of his business. Had to stay that way. He'd watch her from afar, and if she crossed his path again, he'd take a different road.

He checked the time. Three o'clock. The meeting should have started by now.

As if on cue, the doors swung open and in walked Dave Gadway, looking pale and thinner, but still the big presence he'd always been. The hitting coach, Reed, followed him along with their pitching coach, Smythe, and their strength trainer. But the person who caught his eye was Heather.

She was almost unrecognizable in a fitted black pantsuit that hugged her long legs. With her hair back in a tight updo, her unusual eyes looked bigger than ever. Her mouth, a soft pink, was small and tilted upward at both corners. It made him want to kiss her, though that was impossible. What was it about always wanting what you couldn't have?

"What's the daughter doing here?" Dean leaned over and muttered in his ear. "It's serious if they called in the family."

Garrett's stomach twisted. Dean had a point. It was unusual for family to attend team meetings beyond the owner. Unheard of…unless… they were planning on selling. If that was the announcement, he'd ask for a release from his contract so he could play for another team that would ensure him a better record. After his dismal performance at the last game, there was a decent chance the Falcons would consider letting him go.

Mr. Gadway stood in front and held up a hand until the athletes quieted.

"There's been a lot of rumors. First of all, we are not going to sell the team this year," he began without preamble, his gritty voice carrying to the back of the silent room. He rocked up on his toes, then back down to his heels.

Dean blew out a long breath, but Garrett knew better than to relax. Life had thrown him too many curveballs. His eyes wandered to Heather, who faced her father, hands twisting behind her back. If they weren't selling the team, what was she nervous about?

"We've appointed a new interim manager for the remainder of the season," Mr. Gadway continued, and Dean nudged Garrett's side, his mouth lifting in a sideways smile. It was encouraging…only…shouldn't the new manager be here? Unless he was. Had Reed been promoted after all? If so, that was bad news. The guy was too soft, didn't give much direction. And Smythe? He looked on the brink of retiring.

Mr. Gadway coughed, and Heather strode to his side with a glass of water, looking every inch the caring daughter.

"I've picked an experienced manager," Mr. Gadway continued after handing Heather back the empty glass. "Someone I have extreme confidence in to be able to turn things around—Heather Gadway, formerly of the Morro Bay University Red Tails. I'll give her the floor."

Garrett watched, stunned, as Heather stepped forward, her expression serious and determined despite the men who lowered their heads, shook them and muttered at this shocking announcement. Heather. The woman who'd been occupying his mind ever since he'd met her, the woman whose lips tempted him even now, was his new boss?

What. The. Heck.

She stood patiently until the murmuring died down. When she spoke, her voice was low enough to make them all lean in.

"First of all, let's state the obvious. I'm the first female manager in the Minor Leagues. Most of you know that I'm Dave's daughter. I've spent the better part of my life around this game, and with the Falcons. As a pitcher, I've won four College World Series titles and two USA Softball National Collegiate Player of the Year awards. Up until now, I was a coach for the Division One Morro Bay Red Tails."

"Unbelievable," the young shortstop muttered under his breath, echoing Garrett's own miserable thoughts.

Heather bit her lower lip, and her eyes wandered over the group, stopping for a moment on Garrett. "I've watched this team for the past few days, and I'm seeing a lack of effort in places. That will not happen on my watch."

Several chairs squeaked as the players moved restlessly around him, the atmosphere tense. If he wasn't so pissed, he'd feel sorry for her. Why hadn't she said anything yesterday?

After another lengthy pause, Heather began again. "We have the talent to succeed if everyone gives one hundred percent. Playing hard makes a difference. You owe it to yourself, and the team, to do so."

Garrett caught Dean's slight nod out of the corner of his eye. She might be softening up his friend, but he'd be damned if he'd play on a team led by a manager with no actual baseball coaching experience. Sure, she knew softball, but up until now, when it came to baseball, she'd been only a spectator.

"I'm going to be meeting with each one of you over the next couple of days." Heather gave her first smile to the group, her face softening attractively. Garrett steeled himself and glanced at his watch. With forty minutes left until practice, he'd make sure he was her first meeting, though she wouldn't like his news. He'd demand his release and wouldn't leave the room without it.

"As I watch more of the games and practices, you'll receive a critique of your performances and a plan for how to reach your potential." Heather's smile broadened. He noticed a few of the guys returning her smile while others scowled and studied the floor. She'd have her work cut out for her winning over this group.

"I know some of you have your doubts. To be honest, if I were in your shoes, I would too."

"Yeah!" someone burst out from the back of the room, earning a scowl from Mr. Gadway. Heather didn't miss a beat.

"But I have confidence in my ability to teach and motivate. If you give me a fair shot, we can win, which is what we all want."

A couple of guys murmured their agreement, and he shut his mouth before he joined them. He wanted to win. But Heather wasn't the person to help him do that. He had nothing against a female manager. Just one with no real baseball management experience. Someone who'd probably gotten the job by playing her Daddy's-little-girl card.

She wasn't who he'd thought she was when they'd met at the old field. Like so many rich kids, she was the kind of privileged, indulged child he'd never liked. Was that wariness in her eyes an act to get people to take care of her? Well, it wouldn't work on him.

Heather clasped her hands. "Practice starts in forty-five minutes. See you there. Thank you."

His grumbling teammates filed out, followed by the coaches and Heather's father. Garrett, however, remained in his seat, watching the lithe young woman as she stood by the door.

At last she turned to him.

"We meet again. Garrett, right?"

He stood and strode to the door. When he stopped, her eyes widened, caution swimming in their depths.

"You mentioned personal meetings," he said, keeping his voice even, hiding the irritation shimmering through him. "I thought we'd have ours now."

She blinked up at him, and her lips moved. Though he strained to hear, he couldn't make out what she'd said.

"I'm sorry, I didn't catch that."

A bright pink suffused her cheeks, and he

forced himself not to notice how pretty the color made her.

"I said that I haven't finished my notes for you yet. I'll watch you pitch tomorrow. We'll meet after that."

He had to give it to her. Soft-spoken or not, she had a direct way about her. He didn't doubt that she could lead...just not professional baseball players. "That's what I wanted to talk to you about. I'm requesting to be released from my contract. This isn't the right place for me to advance in my career."

Her mobile face stilled. "And why would that be?"

"Look, I'll be blunt." He tapped his fingers on the sides of his legs. "This team isn't hustling, and it'll be a long time before they come around to supporting you. Things will get worse instead of better. I have a limited window of opportunity to advance. Given these factors, my bottom-line pitching won't look good with a losing team behind me. I'd like to help you, but selfishly, this is my last shot."

A speculative gleam entered her eyes. "So you're asking to be released because you think I can't help you reach your goals."

A long breath rushed out of him. She was

going to be reasonable. "That'd be great. Thank you."

She arched an eyebrow. "You're wrong, and I'll be as frank with you as you were with me."

His relief turned to irritation. So she wasn't going to make this easy. He held his tongue and waited to hear her out.

"I think you're overvaluing yourself." She nodded when his mouth dropped open. Guys talked this way to each other. Not women… especially not pretty women…to him.

"Your control isn't where it should be, and if that's not addressed, you'll also be another reason why this team isn't doing well. But you have potential, and I can help you."

"Right," he scoffed. What could a softball pitcher do for him? "No offense, but I need someone with more experience."

She tapped her chin and angled her head, her eyes flashing up at him. "If I can change your mind about that, will you drop your request and give me your support and a hundred percent effort?"

He held in a laugh. Was she for real? There wasn't a chance she could change his decision. "What do you have in mind?"

She stepped closer, and her subtle citrus scent curled beneath his nose.

"A contest. If I get more strikes out of twenty pitches than you do, you stay. If you have more, then I'll release you."

He stared at her. Processing. She couldn't be serious. Sure, he had control issues, but he was still better than a college-level player. She was making this easy. But if she was foolish enough to offer him this out, he'd take it.

They eyed each other for a long, tense moment before he jerked his chin at her.

"You're on."

THE NEXT MORNING, Garrett stretched his linked hands overhead, a familiar pull tugging his triceps. He dropped his arms and circled them, loosening his upper back and keeping his mind focused. All around him the pink-yellow sky had grown bluer, fat-bottomed clouds hanging low as if wanting a better look at his impending matchup with Heather. He adjusted his cap brim against the strengthening light, then executed a series of lunges across the field's moist grass, shorn blades clinging to his cleats. The crisp air filled his lungs and for a moment, he imagined what it would be like to put down roots here in North Carolina.

He tossed out the thought and alternated raising his knees to his chest. Once he finished the pitch-off, he'd be trying out for other teams. Moving on. Losing today and playing for the Falcons wasn't an option, no matter how beautiful their new manager. Her expressive green eyes had lingered in his mind when he'd woken, the memory of her soft, lilting voice running through him like a warm drink on a cold night.

But he needed to steer clear of those thoughts and stay centered. Winning his contract release should be easy as long as he didn't get distracted.

Suddenly, a wolf whistle sounded to his left, piercing the still air. Hanging over the dugout fence were several of his teammates—former teammates soon—he reminded himself. He swore beneath his breath. He'd guessed they'd show up, if for nothing else than to heckle him. But he was sure they were also curious to see their new manager in action. He scowled and jogged over.

"Beat it. This is between Heather and me."

George Hopson pursed his small mouth and raised eyebrows so light they disappeared into the deep furrows on his forehead. "Don't recall it being an invite-only shindig, do you, fellas?"

Several of the guys shook their heads, and Waitman, the left fielder, smirked. "What's the matter, Wolf? Thought you'd like our support. We got up early to cheer you on."

A few players laughed, and Waitman and Hopson elbowed each other.

Garrett wiped the annoyance off his face. Fine. He could play this game too. "That's good, since it'll save me from finding you to say goodbye. As soon as I win this, I'm out of here. But I'll miss you." Yeah. Okay. He laid that one on extra thick, but it'd worked.

That shut them up, and Garrett kept his expression impassive as he stared them down.

"Where are you trying out?" piped up the new shortstop. Garrett did a mental search for his name and found it—Valdez.

He shrugged and took Valdez's offered bag of sunflower seeds. "I have some options."

Technically Garrett couldn't have any meetings formalized while still under contract. But there were a few teams with a date and time ready when he won his release. In an hour or so, he'd grab his packed bags and head out. No sense lingering. He'd learned in foster care that when the time came to move on, you went. No looking back, even if an emerald-eyed beauty was in your rearview mirror.

Speaking of which, where was Heather? This whole contest was her idea.

A hushed exclamation sounded, and he turned to watch his opponent jog up the field. The strengthening sun gathered around her, setting her lithe, athletic body aglow as she drew closer. Her hair was swept off her face in a ponytail that bounced around her delicate jaw and long neck. Sunglasses obscured her eyes, but her full mouth looked relaxed and soft and incredibly kissable.

"You're going to catch a few flies if you don't shut your trap," called Hopson, but Garrett barely heard him.

She was gorgeous. Tall and slender, her clinging tank top revealing soft curves, the pink color setting off a face that'd stop a man's heart—if he let it. But his had been ripped out long ago. So why was she affecting him this way? He dragged his eyes from her long, toned legs, the tanned skin flashing beneath black spandex shorts.

Back in the day, if she wasn't the owner's daughter—heck, even if she was—he would have taken her to dinner, fixed her breakfast the next morning and moved on to the next conquest. He thought he'd had his fill of beautiful women. But looking at Heather, he sensed something unique. There was a purpose and strength about her that drew him. She posed a challenge, one he would have wanted to meet on and off the field if things were different. If she was someone else, not a spoiled rich girl whose latest whim would run his career into the ground. He was putting a stop to that. Now.

"Hey, Skipper!" called Valdez, his use of the classic manager nickname and fawning tone earning him a sharp glare from Garrett.

"Hey, guys. Nice of you to come out this morning," she said after clearing her throat several times. Maybe it was the first time she'd spoken this morning? Her voice sounded rusty, though he detected no uncertainty. In fact, from the confident smile she flashed him, it looked as if she was sure she'd win.

Not that it rattled him. He'd met a lot of over-confident athletes. Being a collegiate champion might have inflated her ego. It was one thing to watch professional athletes, another to test your mettle against one. He'd have to be careful not to best her by too far a margin. No sense in demoralizing her, especially in front of her new team.

"Are you ready?" She dropped a bag by the backstop, pulled out a blue visor and adjusted it over her head. When she swept off her glasses and peered up at him, his stomach jittered and his breath hitched. He reined in his slipping control and forced an easy smile.

"Sure. Would you like to pitch first?" He wanted her to say yes. Going last meant he could guarantee his score only topped hers slightly, just enough to make Holly Springs dust in his tire treads and Heather a dream that'd never materialize.

She angled her head so that her long ponytail slid over her smooth, tanned shoulders, and gave him a perfunctory smile. "I'd like to observe you first, if you'd don't mind."

"Observe me?" The question leaped out of him in surprise.

She finished a gulp of her sports drink and lowered it, looking him dead in the eye. "So I can finish taking notes on you."

He nearly swallowed the sunflower shell he'd just popped in his mouth. Her ego must be out of control if she thought he'd lose. He flexed his fingers and nodded curtly. "It's your prerogative."

Dean's red hair appeared in the dugout, and he jogged around the fence, pulling on his catcher's mask. "Sorry I'm late!" He dropped two bags of balls beside home plate and squatted behind it. "Who's pitching first?"

"Looks like me." Garrett sauntered toward

the red clay mound, ignoring his jeering teammates.

"Whatever you do, don't pretend you're in a
game or you'll definitely lose," heckled Hopson, whose comment earned a round of chuck-
les from the group.

"Go get 'em, wild thing," put in Waitman,
who did an impromptu dance Garrett caught
out of the corner of his eye. The rest of the
crowd joined in, laughing.

"Ignore them, Wolf." Dean punched his mitt,
his nearly colorless eyes squinting against the
sun.

Garrett shrugged. "Who? I don't hear anything but some whining gnats." This was actually going to be fun. Pitching contests meant
no batters. Nothing but mitt. And his throws
would strike it every single time.

"Ohhhhhhhhhh! That hurt," guffawed another player, and some made boo-hoo sounds.

"Knock it off, Falcons," snapped Heather,
and the rowdy bunch subsided. Even Garrett
gaped at her, surprised. Her voice might be
low, but it demanded attention.

"Sorry, Skipper," murmured the new shortstop. A few kissy noises erupted, then stopped
when she turned her head and stared hard into
the dugout.

"Thank you, Valdez. As for the rest of you, stay and act like the professionals you are, or leave before I ask you to. All right?" She leaned her defined arms on the padded top of the dugout fence, her shapely ankles crossed. But her casual pose didn't fool him. She was deliberately acting like this to make him believe her victory was a foregone conclusion. It was the oldest trick in the book. She'd need to do a lot better than that if she hoped to best him.

"Ready whenever you are," she said, her voice flippant.

Garrett took a deep breath and dug his toe into the clay, setting his stance. She'd learn fast not to play games with him. This first pitch had to be a strike. A statement. And it was. He knew it the moment it rolled off his fingers, his lifted leg lowering as he watched the ball smack into Dean's glove.

"Strike!" hollered Dean, a wide smile showing behind the black grille of his mask.

"Don't worry, honey. You've got this in the bag. He couldn't hit the broad side of a barn," hollered the first baseman. "That was a lucky throw."

Garrett caught the withering look Heather shot the dugout, and the crowd quieted, or at least Garrett imagined it did. When pitching, he usually heard only two things, his breathing and the sound of the ball hitting something—preferably the mitt.

He raised his arm overhead and let loose another scorcher, this one harder than the last.

"Strike two!"

He lifted his hat off his head, then pulled it on again, anything to keep him from feeling even a bit of excitement that he'd nailed two. That was nothing. Amateur hour. Time to show Heather what he could do.

His next three pitches were right down the middle, his speed on the safe side. He paced to the back of the mound and stepped onto the rubber-spiked cleat cleaner, drawing out the suspense. His teammates were quiet and still, his perfect pitching settling them. Only Heather paced in front of the linked barrier between the field and the players, her eyes on him. She wasn't looking so carefree now. In fact, unlike most women, she didn't seem to like what she saw… His next pitch hit the dirt, spraying Dean's shin pads.

Dean grabbed a new ball and winged it back to the mound. Garrett turned it over in his hand as he harnessed his scattered thoughts. Heather got under his skin. That had to stop. His eyes drifted toward her again, but she was busy scribbling on a clipboard. Were those notes about him? Determination had him striding to the top of the mound, his jaw tight. He squared his hips, focused on Dean's mitt and pushed off from his back foot, releasing the ball at the sweet point.

Pop!

He blew out a breath before Dean yelled "strike." There. Back in form.

"Even a blind squirrel finds an acorn every once in a while," a voice taunted him from the dugout, earning the speaker a raised eyebrow from Heather.

The words barely registered. Today, only his pitching did the talking. At least, the kind he paid attention to. Ten strikes and one ball later and he was on top of his game again. In control. Heather's clipboard swung by her side. He couldn't read her expression behind her wraparound sunglasses, but she had to be impressed. She was probably wishing she hadn't offered him this chance to get off the team. But if she'd been impulsive enough to give him the out, he wouldn't feel sorry for taking it.

When his next pitch veered low, skimming the dirt where it landed before home plate, it barely registered. He'd already gotten sixteen strikes. It was good enough to win, and he shook his arms out, getting the blood flowing in them as he breathed easier. He wound up, his eye steady on the mitt, and watched in surprise as it flew over Dean's shoulder. How had it gone that far astray?

Dean dug in the bag and chucked another ball at Garrett when he walked to the base of the mound. He snatched it out of the air and stalked back to position. He was ending this with a strike. He'd begun with a statement and he'd finish with one, too. With a head full of steam, he rocketed the ball to the center of the plate.

He grinned before it smacked into Dean's mitt. Done. Seventeen strikes, three balls. That said it all without stripping Heather of her dignity. He pegged her as high as fifteen strikes out of twenty. Max. She'd get close enough to prove she was capable, but not enough to keep him from leaving.

If only Heather didn't make him question if he really wanted to go.

EIGHTEEN STRIKES. It was all Heather needed to keep the guy. Pitcher, she corrected herself. She wasn't looking for a man. Especially not a reformed alcoholic bad boy. But after seeing his grit and ability to tune out his hecklers, she now saw the potential her father had spotted. After making the adjustments she'd suggest, Garrett Wolf would go far. She admired his wide shoulders as he strode to their catcher and shook his hand. He had lots of potential...

She gave herself a mental kick. Thinking with her hormones was not going to win the day. He might be the best-looking man she'd ever seen, but at the end of the day, he still worked for her. He was an asset, she told herself firmly. Nothing more.

After a few more stretches, she returned the shortstop's enthusiastic smile and ambled to the mound, her heart beating furiously fast. Not only did she need to keep Garrett in her bullpen, but she also had to prove she'd made the right call in challenging him. The team had to see her as a capable manager, a leader to follow, a person whose decisions could be trusted. Given the skeptical looks she'd caught, she knew she had an uphill battle.

She slid her eyes his way, taking in his powerful form and razor-sharp jaw. A thrill sputtered in her veins when he tipped his hat to her, his eyes a brilliant blue beneath the brim.

"Get 'em, sweetheart!" roared Hopson, whose mouth, apparently, worked faster than his brain, or his legs. Unlike Bucky's words, the endearment didn't feel sweet. It felt insulting. Still, overreacting to it would make her seem too sensitive—the double-edged sword all women faced.

"If we'd known he could throw that well, we would have told him he was being released before every game. Maybe we would have won one by now," added Waitman, slapping Garrett on the back as the tall man stepped behind the dugout fence.

Heather couldn't resist a slight lip curl at that one. It was true. He'd pitched better than she'd expected—a good sign that he reacted well to pressure. When Dean hurled a softball her way, she stepped neatly to the front of the mound and folded her glove around it.

Eighteen, she thought as she brought the glove up to her chest. She leaned forward, then straightened, bringing her arm up and around behind her as she took a strong stride. The ball rolled off her fingertips a moment too soon. She didn't have to look to know she'd thrown low, though she did anyway, watching the ball skip off the plate with a sinking heart. This wasn't the start she needed. Out of the next nineteen pitches, she could miss only one.

"Don't let him off the hook, hon!" bellowed

the first baseman, but Heather shut him out. In fact, she didn't hear anything at all except the slap of the ball in her mitt as she got her nerves under control.

She peered at the catcher's mitt and went into her windup, delivering a pitch so precise, Dean's mitt never moved. She'd found her release point. Sweet.

"That's a winner," Dean encouraged her before tossing her the ball. Her excitement rose, but she tamped it down. With only one more mistake allowed, she needed to stay loose and relaxed.

Six more strikes and the players had stopped talking to each other, their eyes glued on her.

"She might make this interesting," she overheard one of them say.

Out of the corner of her eye, she noticed Garrett yank off his cap and rub his brow, shielding his eyes against the intense sun splashing all around them.

He was starting to look concerned. Good. They should all take notice. She was a fierce competitor. They needed to see that in their manager. But after two more textbook pitches, the ball sailed high, making Dean reach overhead.

Darn. Only halfway through and she couldn't

miss one more pitch. She looked up at the sky, wondering how she'd put herself in this position. For the first time, she felt nervous. She might actually mess this up and lose a player, her first mistake as manager. How would she ever get the team's respect back if she didn't keep Garrett? Worse yet, she'd have to tell her father, who, since he'd been busy with follow-up medical appointments in Raleigh, didn't know about her reckless challenge. She had to pull this off.

Battle back.

Strike after strike after strike and she slowly but surely built toward her goal. She'd nailed nine in a row and, but for the birds in the trees, the field was deadly silent. She felt the team's eyes on her, their expectations, and the sharp criticism from her father if she screwed this up. She swallowed hard, despite her dry mouth, and brought up her glove, making her hand relax when it wanted to clutch at the ball.

This was it. One throw that meant so much. She mentally ran through the delivery that had earned her the last nine strikes and, in one swift move, duplicated it exactly.

The ball snapped the mitt closed.

"Strike!" Dean screamed, leaping to his feet, his glove high in the air and waving. Elation and deep relief flooded her, and she staggered slightly, having held herself in control for so long.

Yes! She'd won. Not that she'd expected to lose, but after giving up those early pitches, it had seemed perilously possible. She glanced over at the dugout and hesitated before joining the jabbering crew. Several glanced her way, their eyes speculative.

"Nice job, Skipper!" yelled Valdez. The rest of the men only nodded her way, then turned toward a grim-faced Garrett. Dean jogged over to join the group.

"I know you're disappointed, but I'm not," she overheard Dean say as she neared. "This team needs you."

"Yes, we do," she echoed, hoping she hadn't damaged their working relationship with the contest.

"That was impressive." Garrett turned to her, pulling the sunglasses off the back of his cap and sliding them on. Hiding his incredible eyes. "It looks like you have me for the rest of the year. Despite all of this, I'll give you a hundred percent."

Impressed at his professionalism, she nodded. "Thank you, Garrett. I'll see you at practice later today. We'll discuss a few tweaks in your delivery then."

Garrett nodded, his mouth tight. "See you there." He walked off with his teammates, leaving Heather feeling unsettled, despite her victory. It was her first step forward as team manager, and Garrett had promised her his best.

She pictured his handsome face.

So why, then, didn't that seem like enough?

CHAPTER FOUR

"YOU DID WHAT?!" Heather's father demanded from his seat at the kitchen table.

The knife stilled in her hand, mayonnaise dripping from it onto the turkey sandwich she'd been making. Fidgety thoughts darted through her mind like squirrels in trees. How to explain without making her father lose all faith in her? Go back on their agreement to let her manage the team?

"Garrett Wolf asked for a release, and I challenged him to a pitching contest to earn it." She dropped Scout a piece of turkey.

Her father's fist thumped the table, rattling the cutlery and making his glass of skim milk jump. Her heart leaped with it. She was in for a tongue-lashing. She knew it as surely as Reed's trick knee predicted rain. Only this would be a tempest.

"I signed him, Heather," he growled, the lines that ran from the corners of his mouth to his chin deepening, waves of disapproval rolling from him and crashing over Heather. "He wasn't yours to risk losing."

She forced her clenched hands to unfurl and smear the rest of fat-free mayo, add a piece of light cheese and close up the sandwich. While her reply ducked behind her heavy tongue, she silently cut the perfect diagonal line her father demanded, added carrot sticks to the plate and brought it to the table. When she pulled out the high-backed wooden chair opposite her father, it scraped against their tiled floor. Other than his grunt of a thank-you, it was the only noise in the open eating space.

When he bit into his sandwich, her tongue loosened. "There was no risk. I wasn't going to lose." Though for a moment, she had to admit, that had been a real possibility.

Her father forced down his bite and lifted his cup to point it at her. "You're a college-level player, Heather. These are professional athletes. You got lucky. That's it."

"It was that or he was going to ask to be released from his contract. We could have lost him either way," she insisted.

"Because of your recklessness," he blustered on, as if not even hearing her. "We almost lost a high-speed pitcher we signed cheap. You think we could have filled his spot at that price again?" He passed a bite of sandwich to Scout, who now huddled by his master's chair, tail thumping.

She clasped her hands beneath the table and rested them on her jittering thigh. "No, sir."

Her father's small eyes relaxed at the corners as he nodded and lifted his sandwich again. "That's right. Professional sports management requires a level head, calculated judgments, informed decisions...not acting on a whim. From now on, you run everything by me. Even if I am out of town. You should have called me after the team meeting when he asked for his release. I know I left right away for my appointment, but that's no excuse." He bit off a large chunk and chewed, his mouth working hard.

"So I can't make decisions on my own? Do what I think is right for the team? That's not being a manager. It's being a puppet."

Her father pointed a carrot stick at her. "You're on trial here. Frank may have faith in you, but you've got to prove yourself to me first. Got it?"

She bit back the rest of her arguments. There was no reason to get him worked up. It was obvious he wasn't budging.

"Yes. But I'll change your mind soon. The

more independent I am, the less you'll need to worry about. It'll keep your anxiety down."

Her dad snorted and shook his head. "Forget what those doctors said. Until I say otherwise, everything goes through me. You are not steering this ship by yourself, Heather." He eyed the orange vegetable with suspicion before stuffing it into his mouth.

She ducked her face and bit the inside of her cheek. Gadways did not cry. Ever.

He surprised her by reaching across the table and patting her arm. "Honey, I know you haven't had the easiest life. With your mom in and out of rehab before the car crash, and me on the road with the team, you grew up doing things on your own."

And lonely, she added silently, but she swallowed the thought and looked up. Her father might be hard on her, but he loved her. She wouldn't make him feel bad for doing what he thought he had to do to provide for them.

"I'm still with you." The edges of his lips curled in one of his rare smiles. "This old guy's got some years left in him." His eyes grew distant. "But I won't be here forever. I need to know you're taken care of—"

Heather chaffed against his old-school paternal thinking. She could make it on her own.

Didn't need to be "taken care of." Would he have said that to a son?

Still. She rushed around the table to hug her protesting father, stepping lightly over Scout. He meant well. "Dad, we're going to have a good season, and we're not losing anything. I've got some ideas." She thought of her recent exciting conversation with the group home's director. Her plan to help their troubled kids and give back to the community was taking shape.

Her father's bushy eyebrows rose. "Plans you're sharing with me."

"When I've got the details figured out."

Her father opened his mouth, and she held up a finger before continuing. "But not before I put anything in place. Deal?"

Her father stood and wrapped her in a familiar, musk-scented bear hug. "I only want the best for you." Scout barked and stood on his hind legs, pressing his front paws on their thighs, nudging his way between them.

She scratched Scout's ears, then pulled back and examined her father's wide face, the features that always seemed one size too small for it. "Then trust me, Dad. Believe that I can do this. It's all I want."

Her father harrumphed and sat back down.

"I'm not filling your head with fake promises. I won't tell you it will all work out. You've got this shot because you want it so bad. Be happy with that."

Heather squared her shoulders and grabbed her keys. She waved goodbye before heading out to the afternoon practice, Scout scooting out beside her.

She'd never be satisfied with that. In fact, his lack of faith only made her more determined. She'd prove him wrong with the best season the Falcons had seen in years. That's all there was to it. She was no longer just striving to succeed; she was going to become a legend. Someone who made her father proud.

When she reached her car, she slid inside and turned on a thumping rock anthem from one of her favorite sports movies. It lifted her chin and mirrored her spirits.

Her father's mind might seem made up, but she'd change it, one win at a time.

SHE STUFFED THE keys into her tote and flung open her car door, nearly hitting the classic red sports car that swerved into the spot beside her.

Her protest died in her mouth when she spotted Garrett behind the wheel, his head banging back and forth to what must have been some metal tune, his thick blond hair sliding around his face. A muffled, whining guitar solo sounded from behind his closed window.

At her sharp rap, he started and whipped his head around, his oceanic eyes wide when he spotted her. The glass lowered and a wailing instrument was silenced when he punched off his CD player.

"Didn't take you for a Guns N' Roses fan," she said, unable to resist leaning in a bit, enjoying his discomfiture. "Do you prefer Slash or Axl?"

His eyes slid from hers and he shrugged. "Neither. Just getting my energy up for practice."

Her eyebrow rose as she looked from the CDs scattered on his passenger seat back to him. "*Appetite for Destruction, G N' R Lies, Use Your Illusion I* and *II*…that's an impressive collection for someone who's not a fan." She glanced at his floorboards and backseat, wondering if he had empty bottles of booze rolling around. She breathed a bit easier when she saw he didn't. He was clean. For now. But she knew all too well how quickly that could change. The thought had her backing away from his car.

She had no business getting friendly with

the players. As their superior, they needed to show her respect and seek her advice. Joking around about music preferences? Uh-uh. What was it about Garrett that made her lose her good sense? As her father had said, she'd acted impulsively by issuing the challenge instead of scheduling a sit-down meeting. And here she was again, hanging around him like a groupie.

Ugh.

"Heather, wait!" Garrett's deep voice called, but she didn't slow her pace. It carried her toward the rear entrance to the stadium.

Before she got to the door, he jogged up beside her. When she reached for the handle, he put a hand on the frame.

"There's something I wanted to say before we go in." Without his cap, he looked younger, his hair mussed around his perfect face. He had the looks of a sports advertiser's dream. Too bad he also had a history of squandering opportunities.

She wiped away the frown forming on her face and stepped back. His proximity did funny things to her, short-circuiting her brain.

"A lot of the guys aren't on board with you as manager." At her steady stare, he ran a hand through his hair and shifted his weight to his right foot. "It's no secret that I'm one of them."

Her mouth tightened as she reined in her irritation. First her father, now this? Would anyone believe in her? With so many doubts, it was getting harder and harder not to question herself.

But she couldn't. Second guessing yourself stopped progress, and she intended a lot of growth for this team and, ideally, for Holly Springs.

She stepped forward and watched his nose flare and eyes sharpen. "You promised a hundred percent effort if you lost the match-up." Her finger jabbed with each word. "Which. You. Did. Remember?"

His head jerked back, a line appearing between his brows. "I'd like to erase it from my memory."

Her hands balled on her hips. She probably looked like every stereotype of a hormonally enraged woman. But she was beyond caring. "Well, you can't. A real man keeps his word. A weak one doesn't. So which are you?"

He sucked in a large breath that seemed to inflate him. Make him grow taller.

"Which do you think?" he ground out.

"Guess you'll just have to show me." She

began to pull on the door handle, then stopped and looked up at him. The anger on his face almost made her lose her nerve.

"Oh. And one more thing. Full effort means that if you have the urge to drink again, you'll let me know. No surprises. We'll get you the help you need."

Before she could yank open the door, he placed his hands flat against it on either side of her face and leaned in, dangerously close. She shivered at his proximity, fingers of fear tiptoeing up her spine.

"Don't ever insinuate that I'm taking my sobriety lightly. Not getting help. I attend AA meetings every week." His jaw clenched and his brows angled sharply together. A dull and heavy silence fell. Her heart skittered along her ribs like the wand she'd once used to play the xylophone.

"Didn't mean to suggest you were. And I'm glad you're attending Alcoholics Anonymous." *Please keep it up*, she added silently and lifted her chin. "Now, let me in before I fine you for making us both late to practice," she added, keeping the quake out of her voice. He was looking at her with the stormy expression her mother had worn when Heather had questioned her sobriety. Yet she was an adult now, not a girl to be pushed around.

He seemed to give himself a little shake, then moved back, allowing her the room she needed to hustle inside before things got uglier.

His next words stilled her hands on the door.

"I can't promise you." His words broke through the small oblivion she'd girded herself with, dropping like a dark, sharp stone.

"Excuse me?"

"I can't promise I'll stay sober. Being an addict is a life sentence, and I won't make promises I can't guarantee I'll keep. Will I keep up with my AA meetings and fight like anything not to drink? Yes. Am I focusing on becoming a better player and advancing my career? Definitely. Will I fall off the wagon again?" A shadow crossed his even features, distorting them. "I don't know. I sure hope not."

Something in his low, ragged voice pierced her armor and made her soften. At least he was honest. Not giving her the false assurances she'd heard growing up. Still, it didn't quiet the unease shimmering through her at what could happen in the months ahead with Garrett.

Her eyes met his and she struggled to speak, the words straining against her ribs and becoming lost. He meant everything he'd said; it was obvious. But was it enough?

He blew out a long breath and moved restlessly. "Look, I don't know what you have against alcoholics, but if you had any experience, you'd know—"

"My mother was addicted to prescription painkillers. She nearly killed me when I was thirteen in a car accident. I've had more than my share of experience with addicts, thank you very much."

Her hand rose to her mouth, but it was too late to stuff her family's secrets back inside. Why, oh why, was it impossible to control her words? First they wouldn't come, then they burst from her with a will of their own. Now she'd revealed too much. She didn't want Garrett's pity. She needed his respect.

Yet when he looked at her, she didn't spot sympathy. Surprise, yes. Understanding, it was there too.

"Sorry to hear that," he said at last, peering straight into her eyes.

She nodded brusquely. Personal sharing time was over. "Well, that's in the past, and I'd rather focus on the present. Shall we?" When she pointed to the door, he swept it open and waited for her to precede him.

They passed through the cool, dim, narrow space that led to the field, their shoulders brushing, hands bumping into one another. A peaceful quiet kept pace. It was a fragile presence that neither seemed willing to shatter, a jagged truce they didn't want to break.

An hour later, Garrett threw hard and watched in frustration as his pitch veered left of home.

"Ball!" called Dean. "That batter would have walked. Bases would have been loaded."

"Great," Garrett snapped and grabbed Dean's tossed ball. "Coach Smythe, any suggestions?" he asked, seeming to startle the older man leaning against the wire fence of the bullpen.

"I've got one," said a familiar female voice, and he tightened at the sound of it. Heather. Her revelation about her mother touched him; it explained that haunted look in her eyes. But it didn't change the fact that she was his manager and the obstacle that stood in the way of his having the winning season he needed.

"Whaddaya got, Skip?" the pitching coach drawled, his wrinkled elbows fitting neatly into the fence's metal diamonds.

Heather opened the gate and walked in,

bringing the clean, citrusy smell he associated with her.

"Garrett, you lost the pitch-off with me because you were tiring and lost your arm slot."

He glanced at Smythe, who shrugged, neither denying nor confirming Heather's observation. But his arm hadn't dropped down. He would have noticed that. In fact, after all these years of playing and struggling for control, wouldn't someone have mentioned it before? And who was some college player to point out what he did wrong?

The one who whupped your butt this morning, a voice reminded him. He shut off his protest with a jerky nod and let her go on.

"Your angle has to be the same every pitch."

He shrugged. "It felt identical every time."

She raised her eyebrows, a know-it-all look that annoyed him to no end. "There was a slight variation."

He tossed the ball in the air, biting back what he really wanted to say. In the parking lot, Heather had seemed approachable. But now, she acted as if she knew better than everyone else. And while that was expected for a team manager in the Minors, she lacked the experience he required to trust her. "I threw seventeen out of twenty strikes."

Heather nodded, looking impressed, and he relaxed. Things would be easier between them if she understood that she had a lot to learn. "Yeah," she put in, "but I threw eighteen out of twenty, which doesn't make me happy. It should have been twenty out twenty. That's the difference between us. I don't settle for great. I want perfection. That's the way you win games."

He reeled back, feeling the slap of her words. Was she suggesting he didn't care? Wasn't motivated? He had everything on the line here. "Look, Skipper," he said evenly, an edge of frustration clipping his words short. "I want to control my arm as much as you do. Even more. And how is it that you detected a variation in my arm angle when no other coach or manager has ever said a word about it?" He tried to keep the accusation out of his voice, but he had to say what he felt.

Heather, however, looked as cool as the light wind that ruffled the grass by their feet. "I can't speak for what other people saw, only what I picked up. If you get your arm angle corrected, you're capable of twenty out of twenty. Now that I'm your manager, I'm recommending a throwing program for you to get your flaw corrected. Since you're pitching tonight, we'll start tomorrow here at noon."

He nodded, his mind in turmoil. He'd planned on practicing more himself anyway. But following a softball pitcher's advice about his overhead throwing angle? That was crazy.

"And Smythe." She paused in the open gate, her eyes on him. "Work on making sure Garrett recreates that angle every pitch. When he drops his arm, let him know and have him do it again correctly. It's the only way he'll get the feel for when he drops out."

Smythe nodded, his rheumy eyes making Garrett wonder if the guy would notice a fly ball before it smacked him in the face. If Heather was right, would Smythe be able to spot the supposed flaw?

He watched her saunter away, wishing she'd stayed, but glad she'd left. His feelings for her were all over the map. If he was irritated with her on the field, why was he so intrigued and attracted off it? He needed to stop thinking about Heather as anything more than his manager.

HEATHER LEANED ON the glass counter of Mr. Ferguson's crammed baseball card shop later that afternoon, inhaling the familiar scents:

cherry chewing tobacco, strong coffee and old leather from autographed gloves lining the walls. Beside them hung classic jerseys mixed among snapshots of World Series–winning teams and signed bats. In a corner, a seat from the Dodgers' old stadium still held court, a black cat snoozing on it.

"Hey, Babe," she crooned, crossing over to stroke its soft fur.

"Heather!"

An older man with a florid face and white hair bustled from the back office, his smile wide. "It's good to see you. Guessed you might be in town. Sorry to hear about your father. Is he feeling better?"

She gave Babe a final ear scratch and joined Mr. Ferguson by the cases. "He's full of salt and vinegar."

His grin matched hers. "So he's back to his old self."

"And then some."

"How are things in California? You running that team yet?"

She laughed. "Not that one. But I've been named the Falcons interim manager." Pride swelled her voice, filling out each vowel.

Mr. Ferguson thumped his hand on the counter, rattling the balls in their clear cases.

"You don't say. You've always had talent. Runs in the family."

She kept her ironic smile to herself. If only her father could hear this. "Thanks. I see you still have that Mickey Mantle rookie card."

A separate spot showcased the rare card with the baseball legend. Mickey held a bat over his right shoulder, his eyes roaming the sky, his blue cap stark against the white background, his looping autograph on the bottom. It was hard to believe this simple shot was worth six figures. Then again, it was Mickey Mantle. She sighed. What she would give to add that to her collection.

Mr. Ferguson nodded, his raised eyebrows a thin, white line. "That's my 401K. And it's a good draw for the store. Don't know if you noticed, Heather. Things are a little quieter in Holly Springs these days."

She sighed. It felt like a ghost town. "I have. You're not in danger of closing, are you?" This sports memorabilia shop held such fond memories for her, and Mr. Ferguson was a sweetheart.

"Nah. Still hanging in there. Was thinking of—"

His words cut off when the chime above the door sounded. To her surprise, a tall, familiar pitcher sauntered in, one who got her pulse leaping.

"Mr. Wolf. What an honor." Mr. Ferguson hurried to the door and extended a hand. For a moment, Heather wondered if he might bow. Sheesh.

Garrett's dimpled smile flashed, making her stomach jump. "Nice to meet you. Mr. Ferguson, I assume?"

The owner nodded so hard his glasses slid off his nose and thudded against his chest, held, at least, by their chain.

Heather must have made some sound, because Garrett's eyes leaped to hers. The light in them faded, and she raised her chin. Today's practice had been rocky, but she'd given him important pointers. If he didn't appreciate her advice, tough.

"Skipper." He nodded, his friendly expression now shuttered. Cautious.

"Hello, Wolf." She turned to Mr. Ferguson. "I'll come back another time. We'll catch up then." When she moved toward the door, he cleared his throat, stopping her.

"Not before I show you something I know you'd be interested in. A card you've been after forever..."

Intrigued, she tore her eyes away from the golden-haired athlete and turned.

"Willie Stargell's 1963 rookie card?" she breathed, following Mr. Ferguson's march to the counter. She had many cards of her favorite player, but this one had long eluded her.

"The very one," pronounced Mr. Ferguson, producing the plastic-encased rarity with a flourish.

Heather's hand rose to her chest. Wow. Mr. Ferguson was very connected, traveling far for trade shows, but this—this was amazing.

She ran her fingers along the smooth, hard edge. Oh, how she wanted it!

"Davis, Gosger and Herrnstein are on that too, right?" Garrett's arm brushed against hers as he joined her at the counter. "Topps made it."

She looked at him sharply. Players sometimes stopped in to sign things for local owners. She hadn't met a lot who were serious collectors like her. Interesting.

"Right. Have you seen it before?"

"Only in magazines," he said, his eyes on the card, the naked want on his face matching hers.

"This is the first time I've seen it in person, too," she admitted, meeting his eyes but quickly looking away.

"What's it graded?" Garrett's deep voice seemed to move through her, shuffling her insides around.

"PSA three, Very Good. There's a hairline crease in the upper corner. That's it. Otherwise, it's a find."

"I'll say." Garrett's awed voice echoed her feelings. "And how much will you take for it?"

"Two hundred and fifty if Heather's interested," Mr. Ferguson replied, looking at her fondly.

She felt Garrett's frown at being cut out of the sale. Frantic to whip out her debit card, however, she wouldn't focus on him. Too bad. She and Mr. Ferguson went way back. How many times had he let her sweep up the place in exchange for cards? Countless. And she was sure he'd given her a far better deal than her cleaning warranted.

"Thank you! I can't wait to add it to my collection." She watched the proprietor run her bank card, anxious to have the collectible in hand.

"We could compare collections sometime. Trade duplicates."

She turned to Garrett, surprised. "You brought your cards with you?"

"Got in the habit while growing up in the foster system. Moving from place to place. I never travel without it." He raised an eyebrow and that crooked smile appeared again, dimples denting his cheeks. Despite her resolve, she warmed to him. She never let her cards out of her sight, either. How sad that he'd grown up without parents. Without a real home. That must have been rough.

"Guess we have that in common. I brought mine to California, then back to North Carolina." They stared at each for a long time until Mr. Ferguson cleared his throat.

"Am I interrupting something?" the owner asked, the knowing laugh in his voice making Heather squirm.

"No!" they both exclaimed too forcefully to fool anyone, especially themselves.

She replaced her bank card and grabbed the brown bag Mr. Ferguson handed her. Time to go before she discovered other interests they shared. More ways that would make her relate to the man rather than the athlete. As his boss, she needed to know only his performance stats.

End of story.

"See you at tonight's game."

He nodded, his eyes briefly dropping to her mouth before rising again.

"Bye, Mr. Ferguson. Thank you!" she called, then quickly made her escape.

With her mind full of Garrett, however, it wasn't a clean getaway.

IT WAS THE bottom of the sixth, and Garrett paced to the back of the mound, rubbing the baseball in his hands while the crowd chanted in the early evening air.

"Get 'em outta there!" a voice pierced through the waves of noise rolling through the stadium. Garrett wasn't sure if the spectator was talking about him or the batter who had a full count on him. With runners on first and third and two outs, this pitch would turn the tide. A strike ended the inning and maintained their one-run lead. A ball or a hit meant a score that'd tie up the game and put his chances of winning at risk.

And he needed this out.

He glanced over at the dugout and noticed Heather, looking cuter than he could have imagined in one of their uniforms. She caught his eye, and their conversation at practice earlier came back to him.

He'd dismissed it at the time, sure he'd handle this game better than the last without her supposed "help." Yet now here he was, on the edge of a precipice that could finally get his season off to the right start.

The hitter before him stepped back from the plate and circled the air with the tip of his bat. Garrett glanced at first base, and the runner trotted back a few steps to safety. With his body sideways, he thought about his arm angle and read Dean's signal, three fingers, then a leftward swipe with his index finger. A fastball. Outside. He took in a long breath through his nose and pushed it out through his diaphragm, his glove on his hip.

No more stalling.

He wound up and lit up the air. Instead of the cheering crowd heralding a strikeout, he heard a smack and watched the ground ball split between short stop and third base. Valdez and Hopson nearly collided as they stretched, too late, for the catch. The runner on third scored easily. Waitman charged fast, scooping up the ball and hurling it toward home plate. He needed to prevent the go-ahead run from scoring from second.

Garrett lined himself between home plate and Waitman, ready to grab the outfielder's throw and cut off the ball in case the throw was late.

Dean yelled, "Cut, hold!"

Garrett reached up, grabbed the ball and stared hard at the runner who skipped back to third, unable to score because of the strong throw. Thank God Waitman had a canon for an arm, Garrett thought as he strode back to the hill.

Darn.

They were tied, and the next hitter was at the top of the batting order.

Hoping he wasn't being lifted from the game, he glanced over at Heather, who nodded to Dean to go out to the mound. A stalling tactic. Either she wasn't sure if she was pulling him or she was giving the bullpen more time to warm up.

Dean took off his mask and jogged in Garrett's direction.

"How's it going?" Sweat ran down the sides of his face and slicked his red hair. With his flushed face, he resembled an overripe tomato.

Garrett looked down at his cleats, then up at the sky, wishing he hadn't dug himself this hole. An organ played out notes and the crowd roared "Charge!" He wanted to yell with them, but he kept his emotions in that box he buried deep during games.

"Hanging in there."

"You finished?"

"Nah. Still got some in the tank. I'll pull this out."

"You dropped your arm on that last pitch, Wolf," Heather said, surprising both men as she joined them.

"It didn't feel that way."

"Trust me. It was slight, but your arm angle fell. Come straight over the top. Remember your hand to your head. Ninety degrees. Not eighty. Concentrate. It'll happen."

Tired of arguing and heartened that she wasn't pulling him, he nodded. "Got it, Skip. I have this last one." He figured he did, either way. He had to.

"I'm sure you do." The twinkle in her eye sucked the air out of him. Her encouragement filled him back up with confidence.

He squared off to the plate. At least he could take advantage of a full windup and gain some speed since the batter had made it to second and the runners couldn't steal.

The hitter tapped his spikes with his bat, tightened his gloves and stepped into the batter's box, his face impassive and relaxed.

Confident. It was clear the guy wasn't rattled. Concious of his arm angle, Garrett rocketed a pitch that caught the outside corner.

Strike one!

A few people got to their feet and began to cheer.

Garrett closed his mitt against Dean's throw and brought it up to his chest. He wound up, sweeping his hand close by his head as he delivered one on the inside corner at the knees.

Strike two!

Now the stadium was rocking. Catcalls, whistles and stomping feet echoed in the air. The Falcons' mascot raced around, flapping his wings.

The batter fidgeted and backed off the plate. He removed his helmet and wiped his forehead with his wristband. His face was tense when he stepped back into the box. Good. Now the guy was on his toes.

Garrett weighed his options. Since he'd thrown two fastballs already, the batter was probably expecting something off-speed—a curveball or changeup. But he still felt strong. He could deliver another heater and get it by him.

Dean signaled for a curveball, and Garrett shook his head no. Dean's fingers flashed for a changeup, and Garrett shook his head no again. Finally Dean showed three fingers, then swiped his index finger right.

Garrett nodded. Just what he wanted, a fastball to the inside of the plate. In a blur, the ball jetted over the plate and disappeared in Dean's glove. *Thwack!* The batter stood for a moment, looking into the empty air, then jogged to his dugout, head low. The stadium erupted in thunderous cheers.

"You froze him," hollered a boy's voice from a crowd of kids holding a banner lettered with his name. They were in the front row, right above the Falcons dugout, and wore bright blue shirts to show their support.

"Caught him staring," whooped another youngster. A few other kids fist bumped him while the rest stamped their feet as the speakers blared "We Will Rock You."

Garrett slid a glance in Heather's direction and caught her smug smile. As much as he hated to admit it, he had to hand it to her. She'd been on to something with the arm drop. If he pitched like that all season, he'd make it onto the radar for the Major Leagues. Crazy that she'd picked up on something when no one else had. Beginner's luck. Had to be.

The rest of the game passed quickly, with a

reliever saving his game after he left it during the eighth inning. When the crowd demanded a curtain call, he stepped out of the dugout, doffed his hat and waved before signing several balls the boys threw to him. Their shrieking excitement made him smile and linger until one caught his eye.

The redheaded boy with dark eyes was a ringer for the foster "brother" he'd lost. He ducked back into the dugout, his nose burning with every harsh breath that shuddered through him.

And he wished, like anything, for a drink. Scotch, gin, vodka…something to float that memory away.

He gritted his teeth as if someone held a bottle to his mouth. That'd been his old habit. His way of coping. He brought his fists down on his thighs, then buried his head in his hands until he had himself under control. The hole in his heart plastered over once more.

Returning to the locker room, he took a quick shower and pulled on his street clothes. He started when someone yelled, "All clear!"

Heather walked in, her snug dress slacks and silky top making her far too tempting for a guy who was trying to think of her as his boss.

"Congratulations, Falcons," she said as she

came farther inside the steam-filled space. She pulled a note card out of her pocket, the edges bent and creased, and cleared her throat. "You did a nice job out there. Good hustle, especially on that gap play that could have handed the other team three runs. If we give the same effort at every game, we're going to have a great season. Go Falcons!"

The team cheered, though he noticed their enthusiasm was lukewarm at best. It'd been a close game, and they'd won by only a single point. But that didn't account for their lackluster response. They still hadn't accepted Heather. While he understood their reaction, felt the same way, it burned him at the same time.

"Let's hear it for Skipper!" he shouted, eyeing his teammates so that their voices rose louder than before.

"To Skipper!"

"And Wolf," bellowed Dean, sending Garrett a wink.

"To Wolf!" echoed the team, and suddenly sports drinks were being shaken and sprayed around the locker room.

He ducked out and found himself beside Heather, who leaned against the outside wall, her chest rising and falling as if she'd been nervous. Funny. She always seemed confident. Now she looked as insecure as he felt at times. It touched something in him.

"Thanks for the tip out there," he said, his voice bringing her large eyes up sharply and quickly.

She studied him for a moment. "I'm glad it helped."

He made no move to leave, and neither did she. It felt as though they each had more to say, though what it was, he hadn't a clue.

"Heather." Her father rounded the end of the corridor, and Garrett stepped away, suddenly conscious of how close they stood.

"Hey, Dad," she said, her voice low, something in the tone making him linger.

"That was quite a ride," Mr. Gadway said, sounding slightly winded, his belly straining against the zipper of his blue Falcons warm-up jacket.

"Glad we could entertain," she responded, her hands twisting in front of her. Was she nervous around her old man? It didn't match up with his Daddy's-little-girl image of her.

"Would have preferred not having my ticker racing all game. Next time, get those boys moving from play one. You should be leading by a wider margin when you're playing a team like them. They're not even in division contention. Or they shouldn't be, unless you give up games to them like you almost did today."

"We pulled it off."

There was a note in her voice that caught at Garrett, something raw, lost, a cry for help that only he could hear.

"Thanks to this guy." A broad hand slapped Garrett's back. "Almost had her lost in the sixth, but you nailed it with that final strikeout. Keep pitching like that and you'll be looking at league MVP."

Garrett's smile faded when he noticed Heather's somber face and the hint of sadness she tucked tight inside the corners of her eyes. It bugged him. Why was her father handing him the credit?

"With all due respect, sir, Skipper gave me some pointers at practice. Plus, she kept me in when she could have lifted me. She deserves the praise." Despite his irritation at Heather, he had to be fair. Something about seeing her so flattened didn't sit well with him. He would have preferred her driving him nuts with her overconfidence, smug ignorance and irrational anger that flared at the strangest times. At least she glowed then. Now she looked like a snuffed out flame.

For some reason, her father harrumphed and shuffled his feet before turning to Heather. "I'll see you at home."

"Sounds good." She kissed her father's cheek, and the tender gesture tugged at Garrett. Despite getting ripped by her dad, she cared. Were they alike? Motherless, both holding tight to the people they had left. He'd felt close to someone once, until his own actions had severed that bond in the worst way imaginable.

Her father stomped away, and she turned to Garrett. Her glossy brown hair, free of its ponytail, swirled around her delicate face. Impressive that after such a dressing down, she looked as composed as ever. Heather had grit.

"Thank you," she said quietly, studying him for a long moment. "Now. If you'll excuse me?" She turned on her heel and strode away without waiting for an answer.

His eyes followed her as she disappeared down the corridor. He fought back that unexpected protective streak she brought out in him, wanting to run, catch up, grab one of her hands and comfort her. Strange, since she'd looked just fine. As if this was normal for her. Maybe it was. But still…he'd seen grown men blubber after getting a critique like the one Heather had received.

He forced his feet to stay put. Heather didn't need him. She'd shown she could handle things on her own. Preferred to, it seemed.

And although he'd always believed the same of himself, suddenly he wasn't sure he was as independent as he'd thought.

Not when it came to Heather.

CHAPTER FIVE

A WEEK LATER, Heather stood on the side of the two-lane rural route leading to Holly Springs and dripped. Not just her clothes. Not only her hair. Nope. Every bit of her was drenched including her nose, from which raindrops fell as fast as they collected. She needed to be wrung out and hung on a clothesline. But getting caught in a Carolina rainstorm made you feel as if you'd never be dry—or warm— again, despite the season.

She shoved back her tangle of hair and peered through the fat splatter of rain, shivering. Water drummed on the roof of her car as the tow truck driver hooked his chains to her rear bumper, his camouflage rain poncho pulled tight around his face. Good thing he'd come quickly. Even better, she'd had a fully charged cell phone to call for road service and postpone her meeting.

Guess her father knew best after all, as he'd been quick to point out when she'd phoned him. But he hadn't stopped there. Why waste a perfectly good opportunity to wax poetic on his favorite subject: Heather's screwups, the car edition.

He'd scolded her for driving too fast (she'd been below the speed limit), listening to the radio instead of watching the road (as if country music wasn't made for cruising) and not checking the tire pressure before setting out (wasn't that a biannual thing?!).

It didn't matter that none of these issues seemed responsible for the hydroplaning skid that'd sent her into the ditch —with a completely different car than the the one she'd left in California! He'd been on a roll and his message—she didn't care about vehicle safety— came through loud and clear. At least, after she'd made the usual agreeing noises, he'd eventually cranked down a notch. No sense arguing when his doctor had emphasized less stress. Yet lately she seemed to be causing him more of it. If she hadn't needed a ride home, she never would have bothered him in the first place.

She sighed and glanced at the steep, evergreen-covered sides of the road. The hills were hidden in mist, just snatches of green appearing and disappearing. Luckily, she wasn't hurt, and Dad had promised to send someone to pick her up. Across the road, a grinding noise sounded as her car's rear bumper lifted off the ground. Any minute now and they'd be gone, leaving her here alone unless her dad's errand boy arrived. Pronto.

And how was she supposed to meet with her postponed, ten o'clock appointment looking like this? Get her plan to restore Holly Springs' pride started? She ducked beneath a live oak, its wet leaves dark against a mottled, sulky sky. It gave some coverage, but not much. She plucked her sodden dress shirt from her stomach. What she'd give for an umbrella!

She would have grabbed one if she'd paid attention to the threatening clouds when she'd left earlier. But after making Dad breakfast and approving some travel arrangements for the Falcons' series next week, she'd barely glanced at her doughnut, let alone the weather.

Never a break. Or it felt like that after a long week of dealing with unreceptive players and two more game losses. She wasn't getting through to them, and if their record didn't improve, fast, the team would be out of contention for a division win before the month was out. Her quick inhale caught her off guard and juddered her whole body. She couldn't fail.

Around a bend splashed a red car. She squinted at it through the pelting rain, then backed up, too late to avoid the *sploosh* of water when it jerked to a stop.

"What? Hey!" she sputtered, wiping, if it was possible, even more water out of her eyes. If this was her dad's help, he could keep it. She would have stayed drier walking home.

The door opened, and a pair of long legs in cowboy boots and jeans appeared. The rest of Garrett followed, and in a second, he was standing in front of her, his irresistible grin matching the devilish twinkle in his eye. He looked as if he was enjoying her imitation of a drowned rat.

"Your chariot awaits." He gestured to his car, his voice holding more than a hint of laughter as his eyes ran over her. He held out a bright yellow object. "Umbrella?"

"It's a little late for that, don't you think?" She tugged at her clinging shirt, then let it go when she caught his eye. Her outfit could have passed for wet tissue paper, and a warm flush crept up her neck.

"I think I timed it just right." His lips twisted, sending her senses into overdrive. Why was it impossible to think of him as just a player? Being aware of him as a man—a very attractive one—had to stop. Her radar was off…waaaaaaay off…to consider him as anything more than a Falcon.

She broke their stare and glanced around him to see who else her father might have sent to pick her up. Surely Dad wouldn't expect her to drive with Garrett at the wheel? An addict struggling not to relapse? For all she knew, he might have fallen off the wagon already, though she hoped like anything that he hadn't. But the car was empty except for a few unidentifiable cans rolling around the passenger floor mat.

"Ready?" He looked up at the sheets of rain plastering his hair to his head. "This isn't getting any lighter."

"I'll wait." She crossed her arms and gave him her shark-eye stare.

His mouth firmed in a straight line before he asked, "Wait for what? There's no one else coming."

Her eyes darted skyward, her pulse racing. Tiny memories of her accident with her mother fell through her mind, blooming like flakes of flaming ash. Her eyes burned with the effort to keep her emotions in check. She was not a crier.

When she lowered her gaze, Garrett stepped

close, concern darkening his eyes to navy. His calloused thumb brushed her cheek, wiping away raindrops he must have mistaken for tears. "Hey. I know you're probably shaken up from the accident, but I'll get you home safe and sound."

He couldn't possibly know it wasn't this accident that had her in knots. A hoarse sound, halfway between a cough and a retch, escaped her. Her mother had been driving her home when they'd hit that tree. Sweat beaded on her forehead, mixing with the rainwater.

When she swayed in her heels, his arm slipped around her waist and pulled her close. Panic filled her, pushing the air out so that she struggled to breathe. She would not look weak in front of one of her players. Garrett most of all.

Garret steadied her. "I'm taking you to the hospital." His deep voice sounded far away, as if she heard him underwater. And maybe she did, since she felt as if she was drowning. She remained frozen in place, her mind traveling back to another road, another time.

When Garrett tugged her toward the car, instinct seized her. She jerked against him, needing to get away.

"Hey," he protested and held her tight. Secure. She panted, working for every breath. It'd been a long time since she'd had a panic attack or let herself think about her near-death experience. Why, of all people, was Garrett her witness?

But something about his solid warmth stole into her. The steadfast way he held her stabilized her rocking mind until her thoughts cleared. Her rigid body grew limp. He kept his arms around her long after she'd stopped struggling.

"You okay?" he asked, his voice gruffer than she'd ever heard it.

She nodded, humiliation banishing her from the land of the speaking.

"If I let you go, are you going to run?"

She shook her head, the rest of what she needed to say cowering at the base of her throat.

When he let go, a strange emptiness took hold. Did she want to be in his arms? It seemed she did. Another irrational thought to go with the rest zinging through her mind.

"Your dad is worried about you. Can I drive you home now?"

"No," she gasped out, the single word scraping the back of her throat raw. She forced herself to meet his eyes, her breath rushing between her teeth. As his manager, it was an order, even if it'd sounded like she was pleading.

He inhaled sharply and set his jaw, looking ready. But for what? If she didn't speak her piece, would he force her into his car anyway? Unease ricocheted through her. Her father was top dog, and if he'd told Garrett to bring her home, he'd obey. But she couldn't let him drive her. Not with memories sawing her heart in half.

"Not you," she insisted, wishing like anything that she could get some force into her voice.

His eyes narrowed. "And that's because—"

She gave him a long look until understanding dawned in his eyes. They darted from the disappearing tow truck back to her.

"Is this because of the accident with your mother?"

She nodded reluctantly and shoved words out of her mouth. "I won't trust an addict to drive me again. Recovering or not."

He shot her a look of pure, jagged incredulity. "You honestly think I would drive while intoxicated?"

The air heated up as they locked eyes; it pressed around them dense and scratchy as wool.

"No. I don't know," she snapped, though her voice had no bite. Certainly not the ring of authority she needed to get him to back off. "And why did my father send you of all people?"

Garrett ran a hand through his hair, frustrated. "Because Reed told him I was heading back from an AA meeting and could pick you up." He exhaled, heavily. "You don't trust addicts about anything, do you?"

She scrunched her eyes against the sudden pain that lanced through her. "No."

After a long moment, his shoulders lowered, and the anger drained from his face. "Guess that makes two of us," he surprised her by saying. "Why don't I call one of the other guys, and we'll sit in the car until he gets here?"

Relief flooded her. He understood. Wasn't pulling some macho act or trying to prove he would always be sober—something she could never, in her heart of hearts, bring herself to believe fully. She'd been let down too many times before.

"Thank you. But I…uh…actually would like to get out of here. Can I drive us?"

He studied here, his eyes quizzical, until he nodded and handed her the keys.

She slid behind the wheel, touched by his faith in her. He'd seen her at her worst, was picking her up from an accident she'd just caused, yet he still believed in her. Trusted her to drive them.

After he hopped into the passenger seat, he wrapped a blanket around her shoulders. The confining space closed around them, the beating rain making her feel as if they'd entered their own world. She stole a sideways glance at him as she started the engine.

It was a world she might not want to leave if she wasn't careful.

GARRETT'S FINGERS TAPPED lightly on his knee, his mind puzzling over what had just happened. He'd sensed Heather mistrusted him. Had known, on some level, that it was probably connected to her mother. But to have her put it so bluntly. To say she'd never ride in a car with him at the wheel. Trust him. It disregarded all of his hard work to get clean. Scattered it to the winds. Why her opinion mattered so much, however, bothered him more.

Heather didn't fit into any box. She was a

mystery he wanted to solve, even though he had no business being on the case.

After a mile had passed in tense silence, he asked the question burning through him.

"What happened back there?"

Her knuckles whitened against the wheel, and her mouth looked tight.

"I'd rather not talk about it."

"You basically implied I was a drunk driver. I deserve an explanation, don't you think?"

When she glanced at him, the wound in her expressive eyes flayed him. "It's not you, okay? I know you've worked hard to get sober."

"But you'll never trust I'll stay that way."

Her eyes squeezed shut for a second. When they reopened, they shimmered.

"I don't trust anyone. Growing up, it was always broken promises, secrets and lies."

His heart stalled with a twinge of pain. The silver spoon she'd been born with had tarnished fast. "That's rough," he said, inadequately.

Her chin jerked, and she stared straight ahead, her arms taut as she gripped the wheel. The sports car rounded each curve of the winding road a bit faster than it should have.

"She always vowed she'd stopped taking the pills." Heather's voice had less substance than dandelion fluff, and he leaned closer to hear it. "She claimed she didn't need to go back to rehab, but then I'd find bottles in her makeup bag, in the freezer, under the grandfather clock." Her neck cords stood out, and she swallowed hard before continuing. "Dad asked me to search the house for them every day. A twisted Easter egg hunt for pills."

The hurt in her voice was palpable, and it squeezed his chest. He pictured Heather as a little girl, crawling, hunting for proof she hoped she wouldn't find. Sympathy rose in him. Their childhoods were different, but they'd sustained the same damage. It connected them. Maybe that's why she was opening up. Still, he sensed she wouldn't ever fully let him in.

"I'm sorry. No kid should have to go through that."

"At least I had my dad." Her lashes fluttered down to her cheeks and, because of the tremble of her soft lip, he wondered if that'd always felt like a good thing.

Suddenly she turned to him, her eyes wide. "Oh. I'm sorry. That was thoughtless. Did you know your parents before foster care?"

"My mother," he muttered, needing to end this conversation before things got too deep.

The more they confided, the closer he felt to Heather.

He watched tall oaks and spreading maples flash by as Heather drove at what would be normal speed except for the weather. He peered at the speedometer and decided to lighten the mood.

"Ease up, Danica Patrick. We're not racing."

Her mouth curved in the way that made him ache to kiss the corners of her lips. She was getting to him. Big time. Being around her was like riding a carnival Tilt-A-Whirl. She had him spinning. One minute she was a tough spitfire he wished he'd never laid eyes on, and the next she was soft and open, making him want to hold her and never let go. Especially when he glimpsed the same vulnerability in her eyes that consumed and strangled him.

"And in case you lost your sense of direction," he continued, forcing his mind down a safer path, "we're heading the wrong way— this is toward Holly Springs, not home." He pulled off his wet hat and tossed it on the floor behind him.

"It's the right one for me." She hiked an eyebrow and sent him a sidelong glance that made him shift in his seat. It'd been a while since he'd been this close, and alone, with such a beautiful woman. Definitely not with one who kept him up at night, counting all the "what ifs" until he gave up and dreamed about her instead.

"I have a meeting in Holly Springs. After the accident, I called and postponed it. If I hurry, I'll make it on time."

When the car started to fog up, she turned on the fan, then rolled down her window to speed the defogging. The wind tossed strands of her citrus-scented hair, her long brown bangs falling forward and accentuating the curve of her chin and her thick eyelashes.

"And I have no say in this?" He tried keeping the amusement out of his voice and failed miserably. Since today's game was rained out, he had nothing better to do than spend an afternoon with a beautiful woman. One who drove him crazy and was completely off limits. Nope. No better way to spend his time at all.

She fiddled with the radio dial and stopped on a country channel, a Martina McBride tune making her fingers tap on the wheel. "Not from where I'm sitting."

"Maybe I shouldn't have given you those keys."

"I have you completely in my power," she teased him, the playful spark in her eyes making the air catch in his lungs and throat, producing a strangled sound.

"You okay?" she asked when he sputtered, looking cute as she cocked her head to the side to study him briefly. Seeing her confidence return felt good.

"Depends on what you plan to do with me." He played along and rolled down his window, letting the cool, wet air stream over him.

Down, boy.

Though he liked this banter they'd slipped into, a caution signal flashed in his mind's eye. He should be running for the hills. Not strapped in beside her, his eyes pulled like magnets to her shapely legs revealed by an above-the-knee skirt.

"After the meeting, if you're a good boy, I'll treat you to ice cream. How's that?" Laughter filled her voice, and he couldn't help but join her, the sound of their mingled amusement better than the country hit playing through his speakers.

"Deal." Her condescension was disarming. She didn't have a chance of denting his confidence, but it was fun to see her try.

"Deal." Her smile turned him inside out. He forced himself to look away, watching the old-fashioned facades of Holly Springs' main street come into view. Though the vintage lights gleamed like new, the pristine sidewalks contrasting with the colorful stores, the town had a desperate feel. For Sale signs hung in several windows, Closed signs in others.

He felt the familiar jab of fear whenever he drove in for an AA meeting. The small town was clearly fizzling. Ideally he'd move on before it shut down completely. His gaze strayed to Heather. He'd miss their daily squabbles, laughs and conversations when he left. There was no denying it. He tugged at his restrictive seat belt, a strange sense of loneliness washing through him.

Heather pulled into a small parking lot beside a large building at the end of the strip. Something about the nondescript, beige brick structure seemed familiar, yet he couldn't put his finger on it.

"This is it."

"I don't know if this is an important meeting, but you do realize you're all wet." He tried keeping his eyes off the small waist revealed by her clinging shirt.

Heather's eyes bulged. "Shoot. What do I do? I can't miss this."

He reached behind him and hauled out a raincoat. It'd be ten times too big for her, but at least it'd cover her to her knees and prevent any creeps from looking at her in those see-through clothes. His hands bunched. No one was checking out Heather. No one except him, apparently…

She took the coat and shrugged it on, buttoning it over her skirt and blouse. "How do I look?"

He met her anxious eyes. Adorable, he thought. "You'll do," he said instead. "Do you want me to come in or wait here?"

"Join me if you don't mind. It'll save me explaining all of this to you later."

"Huh?" He shook his head. She was speaking in riddles.

"Just come with me. I'm late." She pushed open the door without waiting for his answer, and he watched her slender form stride past the front of his car before he scrambled after her.

Inside the utilitarian building, he followed Heather through a small reception area that held sagging chairs and magazines with dusty covers. The walls were bare and painted a dull olive that matched the worn carpet. A tired-looking woman sat beside a crying child. Dark circles rimmed her eyes, her thin hair lying flat against her sunken cheeks. She casually flicked the kid on the arm with a jagged fingernail and went back to texting, the move making something heavy shift in his chest. It jogged a memory of his own childhood before his mother had lost custody of him. How old had he been? According to his file, five.

Sometimes he caught himself wondering about her... Where was she? And where was the father who didn't even care enough to have his name on Garrett's birth certificate? Who were the people who'd given him life, then given him up? The thought depressed him and, seeing himself, he looked away from the kid who now cried harder than ever.

Unwanted and disposable.

"Yes," he heard Heather say, "I called a while ago about being late for a meeting with your director, Mr. Lettles. I was told he'd be able to postpone the appointment."

A woman with red, fleshy lips picked up the phone without bothering to answer. Heather turned around while the woman spoke to someone on the other end of the line. A shrug was in Heather's eyes when they met his.

At the sound of the phone clicking back on its cradle, Heather turned.

"Mr. Lettles is available. He'll meet you in the conference room on the fifth floor."

"Thank you." Heather's smile was wasted

on the woman, who picked up a bagel and resumed eating.

As they crossed the room to the elevator, Garrett asked, "So who is Mr. Lettles?" He reached past her, their arms brushing. She jerked away like a skittish stray as he pushed the up button.

Heather opened her mouth, then closed it when a loud *ding* startled them. The elevator door whooshed open.

Inside, she pressed the number 4 and stepped back.

"We want five, don't we?" he asked. Her alluring scent clung to him as she moved closer and corrected her mistake.

"Thanks." She gave him a wavering smile. Was she nervous? An urge to take her hand seized him, and he stuffed his fingers in his pockets before he did something stupid. She was his manager, he reminded himself, no matter how much he wished otherwise.

"So who's Mr. Lettles?" he repeated. "Why are we here?"

"He's the director of—"

The door whisked open on the fourth floor, and they glimpsed a group of boys racing cars down the hall while others put together puzzles or built Lego constructions in an open space. A sinking sensation overtook him. None of them looked sick, and they appeared too old for this to be a preschool, especially on a Saturday.

No. He recognized that look on some of the boys' faces when they spied him and Heather in the elevator. He'd worn it himself until he'd given up hope of being adopted by visiting couples. Instead, he'd found a little brother in his roommate, Manny.

"This is a foster home." His chest expanded and deflated faster than it should have.

Heather glanced at him. "Yes. A group home for kids who haven't been able to make it in family settings. When you told me the other day you'd lived in one, I thought you'd want to be involved with my plans. I'm going to start a baseball camp for these kids, give them a sense of pride and self-worth. Help them the way baseball must have helped you. It'll be good for the children and for Holly Springs since we'll be inviting other foster group homes around the state to participate. They'll see our community as one that gives back. Great idea, right?"

"Wrong," he corrected her as the door closed and they rose another floor. She gave him a sharp look, but the door opened again before she could speak. He followed her off the elevator and down a hall to a glass-walled meeting area. Inside was a long conference table at which sat an older man wearing horn-rimmed glasses.

"Thank you so much for your patience, Mr. Lettles. I'm Heather Gadway, and this is one of my starting pitchers, Garrett Wolf."

An impossibly perfect set of dentures flashed as the man advanced and held out a hand. He shook Heather's hand, then reached for Garrett's.

Garrett briefly gripped the man's hand before shuffling back a step. Out of reach. He couldn't believe he was in a group home. Again. A place he'd vowed never to revisit. Memories, long suppressed, exploded in his mind.

He and Manny wrestling over the latest comic book. He and Manny sprinting after a soccer ball. He and Manny taking a hidden key and sneaking into the kitchen for extra fudge pops.

Grief was a knife to his throat. It kept him from speaking or moving as the director and Heather took their seats. Ambushed on every level. This was the demon he'd tried outrunning with alcohol. Now that he'd sobered up, he'd walked right into it anyway. Ironic.

Heather shot him a questioning look. "Garrett, please join us. We're going to discuss our plans to have the kids help renovate the Falcons' old park before turning it into the baseball camp. I'm hoping, with your encouragement, the players will volunteer some time to assist and coach the kids as well."

Manny would have loved a baseball camp. It was a world away from the gang-infested neighborhood where he'd grown up. He'd been an excitable kid. Had wanted them to cut their palms and shake when Garrett took him under his wing. Garrett had hoped to replace the sense of family the gang had given to Manny.

Garrett's heart plunged to the floor. A lot of good that'd done. His friend now lay in a cemetery outside Atlanta. And it was Garrett's fault.

"Can we count you in?" Heather's eyes were bright and expectant, her earlier pain gone. Yet his had returned with a vengeance.

"No," he forced out through his swelling throat.

Heather's eyes widened, and Mr. Lettles blinked in surprise. "I don't want to see any of those kids near that park," he added, meaning it.

"I'm afraid that's not an option," Heather remarked coolly, their earlier connection melting away. "They'll be around."

"If you'll excuse me," he ground out and turned on his heel, striding to the stairwell. He took the steps two at a time until he burst out into the parking lot.

He leaned against the building. Pounded the back of his head against its brick side, his body clamoring for a drink. Anything to make this moment disappear.

Only alcohol had chased away memories of Manny and the guilt he felt about his death. With foster kids crawling all over the ballpark, he'd be reliving it every day.

He should never have listened to an agent and left Manny for a Minor League team all those years ago. Could have taken an odd job and waited another year for his friend. But it'd been an opportunity to get away and feel important for the first time in his life, like he mattered, had a future. Plus, he'd planned to provide for himself and Manny. Give them both a home when his friend aged out of the system. They'd vowed keep in touch. Stay close—a promise Garrett had broken.

It shouldn't have been such a surprise when he'd phoned the group home around Manny's release date and discovered his friend had left without a message or forwarding address. How long since they'd spoken before that? Three months?

Whatever the time, they'd grown apart. Garrett's preoccupation with his new career meant their daily calls had become weekly, monthly and then so infrequent that he'd lost track altogether. If he'd kept his promise always to be there for Manny, his only friend wouldn't have lost faith. Would have joined Garrett instead of his old gang. If not for his thoughtlessness, Manny wouldn't have become another drive-by victim.

He stared down at his fists and unfurled them.

No amount of fame could wash the blood from his hands. It was a stain he carried for life. No way would he let it touch any other children.

CHAPTER SIX

HEATHER TROMPED OFF the Falcons tour bus in the drive leading to her house and the players' residences, never so happy to be home in her life.

It'd been a long five days away in Florida with only one win out of three games. She stretched her back and angled her stiff neck as the driver opened the outside compartment and started tossing their bags. Before she could grab hers, Hopson cut in front of her and snatched up his brown duffel. Now why couldn't he show that kind of hustle when running bases?

She crossed her arms and let a few more of the players retrieve their belongings, their silence tense and uncomfortable. Worry gnawed at her. Their unease around her seemed to have grown rather than lessened. She wasn't producing wins, and ultimately that was the bottom line for a manager. But if they wouldn't apply her corrections, how could she turn things around? It was a vicious circle. She had to win to make them trust her enough to follow her advice. But she couldn't win if they didn't take her suggestions…

Her shoulders drooped when she spotted her father standing in the drive with his arms crossed, his mouth pursed. They'd been in near constant contact since she'd left for the series. The two cell chargers and the extra prepaid phone she'd packed had worked overtime. She knew what he had to say. Had heard it already. And, by the look of him, she'd listen to it again over dinner.

Great.

"This yours?" came a gruff voice that sent prickles of awareness through her. Garrett.

She looked from the hand holding her black bag into vivid blue eyes that sent goose bumps down her arms. Since their visit to the foster home, they'd circled each other, avoiding interactions as carefully as two boxers in the opening of a prize fight.

"Thanks." Their hands brushed as she grabbed the handle, but when she tugged, Garrett held on.

Her eyes lifted again, her heart picking up speed. Was he going to repeat his comments about the baseball camp? The foster kids had been here all week fixing up the old field. With several group homes emailing her the names of children they wanted to enroll, this was a rolling ball she couldn't—and wouldn't—stop.

"You did your best this series," he muttered, his gaze swerving to her red-faced father. "Don't let anyone tell you otherwise."

His unexpected encouragement took her aback. She opened her mouth to answer, but he'd already spun on his heel, his long strides carrying him away from her.

Too far...came the unbidden thought.

She watched Garrett's broad shoulders disappear around the bend that led to the players' housing. Even though they hadn't spoken much, she'd been too aware of him throughout the trip. And she'd caught him staring plenty, as well. A strange bubble of togetherness had formed around them, and seeing him leave made her feel hollow.

She wished like anything that she didn't think about him so much. How could she be interested in a man who didn't want to help kids? Give back to the kind of institution that had cared for him growing up? She wished she understood his reaction. Had something happened to him in foster care? A past he wanted to forget?

"Welcome back, Falcons," her father boomed. Then he wrapped an arm around her shoulders and said, low, "Heather. A word?"

He nodded and smiled as the team called out greetings, their tone more enthusiastic than she'd heard it all week. They adored her dad. Looked up to him. She'd love to ask her father how he inspired that affection, but that'd only open the door to a blistering list of her failings that'd shake her confidence more.

Nope. She would figure this out on her own. There had to be a way to get through to the players. Maybe a team-wide project, like the baseball camp, would help. If they worked together in a different way, it'd strengthen their relationship and build trust. She hoped they wouldn't be as resistant to it as Garrett.

"Let's go. The pizza's getting cold," her father ordered, sending her marching after him up the small slope to their rambling, one-story ranch.

She stopped to give Scout an ear rub before following her father inside. Puppy stall-tactics had always been her go-to strategy when putting off one of her father's talks. Although, honestly, she deserved this one. Other than Garrett applying her corrections and pitching their only win, she hadn't disproven a single thing her father had predicted. Her jaw tightened. But she would show she had what it took to win over the team. She had to.

The smell of pepperoni and cheese filled the combined kitchen, eating area and informal living room with built-in shelves holding trophies from years past. This year she wanted there to be another one. Hers.

"Heather. It's nice to see you." Mr. Lettles rose from one of their leather sectionals, startling her as she bustled around the kitchen island, setting paper plates around an open pizza box. What was he doing here? Her father hadn't been enthusiastic when she'd shared her baseball camp plans after meeting with the director last week. In fact, he'd nearly poked enough holes in the idea to deflate it. But ultimately he'd given her his grudging approval.

Did the foster care director's presence mean Dad was now on board? Hope flickered inside her. Maybe this evening wouldn't go the way she'd imagined.

Mr. Lettles joined them, slipping his thin hand into hers and shaking it.

"It's good to see you, sir." Heather brought bottles of soda to the counter along with glasses. "How are the boys doing?"

He smiled, and his ultrabright teeth glittered

as he walked beside her to the kitchen area. "Wonderfully. Haven't seen them this fired up in a long time. Not since that local singer came through and played for them."

"Tamara Parks?" she asked as they sat on wicker stools at the granite-topped island, pulling themselves closer to the steaming pie.

"Great folk singer." Mr. Lettles nodded when her father pointed at the pepperoni pizza. "And a nice young lady."

Heather mouthed a thank-you to her father and accepted the slice he passed her. "I knew her in high school, though she was kind of a loner."

"She's terrific with the kids. Made a lot of them want to become musicians. We had to write a grant requesting funds for guitars after her last stop."

Heather's stomach grumbled as she bit into the warm, cheesy slice. It was the first thing she'd eaten all day.

"I hope we'll get some of them thinking about playing college-level sports as well," she replied after swallowing another large bite.

"No doubt about that!" Mr. Lettles smiled (or had he ever stopped?) and pointed his pizza crust at her father. "Your dad's been with the kids every day, directing the first phase of the camp, prepping the field and giving them some baseball tips when they finished."

She lowered her slice and stared at her father's sheepish expression. A lot had changed since she'd been away. He'd gone from resistant to helping out? He was not only on board but also practically driving the train.

"Thanks, Dad."

He poured them all sodas and spoke without looking up. "Just wanted to make sure this idea of yours worked out," he grumbled.

His words made her breathe easier. She'd been worried her idea might flop, despite the pep talks she'd given herself. But with her father involved, it couldn't fail. The Falcons needed to be known for more than their record. They should be role models, giving back to the community. In turn, she hoped the region would support them and start attending more games.

Air wheezed out of her father when he lowered himself to the stool beside her. "We should take a walk out there tonight. I'll show you what the kids accomplished. They did a heck of a job."

Heather smiled. There it was, the compliment that always seemed aimed in any other direction than hers. But still. This had been her idea. Any tribute he gave them was one for her. "I knew they would. Thank you, Mr. Lettles, for agreeing to this."

He reached for another slice and nodded. "Of course. It's great for the kids, and they're very excited to meet the players now that you're home. We're still starting on Monday?"

Concern rang through her as she nodded. She could barely get her team members to take a critique, let alone volunteer their time. What if they didn't agree to give the kids their attention? The boys had faced enough rejection in their lives. They didn't deserve it from athletes in their hometown. But her concern might be premature. She wasn't asking them to change their style of play. She'd be appealing to their goodwill. Ideally their frustration with her wouldn't get in the way. She bit hard into her crust and polished it off in two bites.

Tomorrow she'd call a team meeting and fill them in, officially, on the Falcons' new role and her expectations. She pictured Garrett and the kids' response to him when they'd attended a game earlier this season. Like it or not, he was a local hero. A role model. Was there any chance he'd changed his mind? She had to convince him—show him he could make a big difference.

Make him see how much she needed him…

"DAD. ARE YOU sure you don't want to come with me?"

Heather double-knotted her laces and glanced across the room at her father. He was sitting in his usual spot, a recliner they'd had as long as Heather could remember. Despite other updates through the years, the gray plush chair had faced their television forever. A lopsided heart in faded purple marker still graced its back. It was something her six-year-old mind had thought would pretty up the contraption. Why he hadn't gotten rid of it after she'd ruined it, she'd never know.

When the seat had started sagging, the seams fraying, Heather had tried persuading her father to buy something else. Failing, she'd ordered chairs—high-end models he sent back as quickly as they were delivered.

Nope. He liked what he liked. The chair was comfortable and it stayed, no matter how big an eyesore it was. After a long day, she could always find her dad there, his feet propped up on the tilted footrest, soda and peanuts by his side as he watched his favorite late-night talk shows, his rumble of a laugh reassuring because, unlike everything else in her life, it was always the same.

"Nah. Guess I'm feeling a bit tired tonight,

after all. But you go out and see what those kids did. You'll be impressed." The remote shuffled the television through a few channels before stopping on a news station with a fast-talking anchor woman.

She squatted beside him and kissed his leathery cheek. A life spent outdoors had made him tough, inside and out.

His mouth hooked upward a bit, and he grunted when she pulled away. "And wear a coat. Hill nights are colder than you remember after all that time in California. Managers never get sick. Got it?"

She smiled as she stood. Nope. Some things never changed. "Got it, Dad."

"And don't go hanging out there on your own too long. There's plenty of wild animals." He peered at her around the side of his chair, his close-set eyes studying her until she nodded.

"I hear you. I'll be back in an hour."

"We still need to talk about that series."

Her stomach soured. With Mr. Lettles's visit, she'd hoped she might have dodged this conversation. Especially since they'd had it on the phone twenty different ways already.

"I know," she said, keeping the disappointment out of her voice. Dad didn't tolerate weak. Or emotional.

She reached for the door and paused, waiting for a final question. He always had one.

"You got your phone?" he called over the sound of something exploding on screen.

A small laugh escaped her. "Locked and loaded."

"Huh?" He raised his voice and squinted at her again around the side of the chair. "Speak English. Is the darn thing charged or not?"

She held up the phone and waved it in the air, then pulled open the door. "All set, Dad. Really. I'll be back, okay?"

"Yeah, well—" he grumbled, then trailed off, twisting around to switch channels as Heather slipped out the door.

Phew.

Freedom.

Living with her father again was definitely taking some getting used to. She'd complained about his daily cell phone check-ins. But now that she was home, it was the Dave Gadway show, 24/7, at least until she felt he was strong enough for her to look for an apartment and move out. She strode down the steps, Scout at her heels. She'd forgotten how hard her father was to take in big doses.

But she wouldn't complain…much. He'd scared the heck out of her with his heart attack, and seeing him get stronger every day felt like a blessing she should never take for granted. Though she did sometimes. She'd admit it. No one was perfect. Especially not her, he'd be quick to remind her.

Was it too much to wish that, just once, he'd believe she was strong and capable? That she was an awesome daughter? The best he could have hoped for instead of a disappointment?

She looked up at the stars, knowing that'd be a pointless wish. Better to prove it to him by turning around her dismal win-loss record.

The baseball camp was another way to show him her worth. And she couldn't wait to see the new and improved field.

She picked up the pace, and the collie trotted along beside her as they skirted the new field. In the distance, lights shone down on the old park. Maybe her dad had kept them on for her. Either way, they helped guide her as she followed the familiar path.

She let herself in through the locker room entrance, smiling at the way the tiled space shone when she snapped on the lights. Her dad was right. The boys had used their elbow grease. She nearly tripped over her own feet as she made her way to the field, eager to see the rest.

The wind picked up and tossed her hair around her face, blinding her for a moment as she stepped onto the field. When the breeze died down and her vision cleared, she gasped. The blazing overhead lights illuminated neatly painted stands and railings and a clipped field. And the kids had painted colorful wooden banners advertising local businesses. Her call for help through the chamber of commerce had been answered. Holly Springs businesses had supported her as she'd known they would.

Her heart swelled for the boys, Holly Springs and the Falcons. Joy bubbled inside her, and she twirled, her arms so wide, Julie Andrews would have been proud.

Scout barked like mad and pawed at her until she fell on the grass, dizzy and laughing.

Yes!

This was exactly the boost she'd needed after her flop in Florida. Tomorrow was a new day. She hoped that showing the players this field, the hard work the kids had done, would motivate them as well.

"Are you okay?" asked an all-too-familiar voice. One that got her heart thumping.

She scrambled to her knees and peered up

through her mussed hair, unable to believe her eyes. Above her loomed Garrett, looking as tall and muscular as ever, a lopsided smile on his handsome face. He'd said he wanted nothing to do with her baseball camp. What was he doing here?

"Fine," she breathed. How much of her *The Sound of Music* imitation had he seen? What he must think of her. If she'd behaved like a real manager, she would have simply crossed her arms, eyed the field, nodded and spit out sunflower seed shells. But nooooooo. She'd had to recreate Maria's dance in front of the Alps and fantasize about bringing self-discipline and respect into the lives of motherless children.

Sheesh.

His strong hand enfolded hers as he helped her up, and warmth exploded up her arm. She forced herself to let go, although it was tough. Dimples dented his cheeks, the sparkle in his eyes making her wonder if he was silently laughing at her.

"What are you doing here?"

"Not looking for Julie Andrews, but thanks for the show." His white teeth flashed. "If only I'd had my phone to record it."

A bubble of laughter escaped her. "You wouldn't have dared."

"And ignore a perfectly good blackmail opportunity? You underestimate me."

The light in his eyes turned up her own temperature. Charisma at his level had to be taken in small doses—and definitely not as such close range.

She moved a safe distance away and shoved her wind-tossed hair out of her eyes. No. She would never underestimate him or his effect on her.

"Other than spying on me, why are you here?

His face sobered as he looked over the transformed space.

"I was planning on getting in a little throwing before bed. Forgot the kids were doing this."

Their arms brushed as they stood side by side, surveying the empty space. Scout circled them, occasionally stopping to bark out a demand to play. But she was too aware of the man beside her to do more than ruffle Scout's ears. Gone was the peaceful moment she'd planned. She was too on edge, her footing off, feeling as though she was about to cartwheel over a cliff she hadn't seen coming.

"They did a good job, didn't they?" she asked, her voice as steady as she could manage given her jitterbugging nerves.

An owl hooted from a nearby tree, soft light touching the field as the quarter moon rose. Shadows performed puppet shows along the walls as clouds drifted overhead, stars winking in and out like Christmas lights.

She waited for a reply and got none, her heart dropping to the grass between her sneakers. So his reaction at the foster home hadn't been a fluke. Some strange overreaction that he'd had time to rethink and regret. He definitely had nothing good to say about the baseball camp. But why? It still made no sense. She'd planned to get him to support her when she rolled out her plan for the team, but that seemed more unlikely with each silent moment that passed.

"So," she began softly, "what do you have against foster kids?"

His head fell back as he sucked in a deep breath. "Just keep them out of my way, okay?"

When he turned to leave, she raced around him and stepped in his path. No. The conversation was over when she said it was over. She was the manager. He was the player. End of story.

"What do you want from me, Heather?"

His full mouth drooped, his brows meeting over the bridge of his nose. He didn't appear angry so much as drained. She wished back the man who'd laughed at her moments ago. Her stomach spiraled downward. Was she being like her father? Pecking at him until he was too exhausted to fight?

"I just want to know what happened the other day at the group home. Why you don't want the kids around?"

"It's my business," he said evenly, though he made no move to leave.

"Since it has to do with the camp on my property, I'd say it's both of our business." Yep. She was definitely being as pushy as her dad, but she really wanted to know.

His nose flared, his mouth thinning into a straight line he held as firmly as his jaw.

"You don't let up, do you?"

She stepped closer, angling her head to meet his eyes. "No. I told you about my mother last week, so you owe me."

He shook his head, puzzled.

"Owe you what?"

"The truth. How a former foster kid could now hate them."

A muscle in his jaw twitched at the slap of

her words. Suddenly, he grabbed her hand and walked fast, nearly tripping her as she tried to keep up with his long legs.

"What are you doing?" she asked, breathlessly.

But he marched on faster.

When they reached the dugout he stopped and pointed to the bench.

"If you want the truth, you'll need a seat."

GARRETT BARELY REGISTERED the warped boards that had been replaced, the cobwebs scrubbed out of existence. His attention was snared by the strong, big-hearted woman sitting on a worn wooden bench, her expectant eyes on him. No one else knew what had happened between him and Manny. He'd vowed never to think about it, let alone talk about it, yet here he was, wanting to open up to Heather, needing to share this dark wound in him. Did a part of him believe she could heal it?

He rubbed the back of his neck and his eyes drifted upward as he struggled to speak. Where to begin?

"Garrett," Heather said, rising. "Forget it. I shouldn't butt into your business."

He cupped her shoulders and gently guided her back down, taking a seat beside her. Maybe this would be easier if he put the ball in her court.

"Ask me anything you want."

She looked at him for a long time before she asked, "What do you know about your parents?"

His chest loosened a bit. At least they hadn't gotten to Manny…yet. Still. This question was hard enough. And no one had ever cared enough to ask it before.

"I have a couple of memories of my mother I'd rather forget, and I don't know who my dad is." His throat burned and heat crawled up the sides of his face, making his temples throb.

"As in, he left you and your mom? Is that why you were in foster care?"

"No. His name's not on my birth certificate." He looked down, feeling the familiar shame smothering him. A heavy, dark cloak he could never take off. "Maybe she didn't know who fathered me. Either way, I'm sure he was a son-of-a—"

A soft hand fell on his thigh and squeezed, the caress quieting his ragged nerves and filling him with more pleasure than he could have imagined. He didn't deserve sweet gestures from nice girls. But he couldn't pull away any more easily than he could stop breathing—it felt that right.

"He missed out, then," she said in the sudden quiet.

He shot her a sharp look. "On what?"

"On knowing you."

And the way she said it. So certain. Calm. As if he was worth more than an autograph. Wasn't on top of the discard pile. He gave himself a mental shake. Still. Heather didn't know everything about him. Not by a long shot.

Truth time.

"I kept thinking my mother would come back for me," he said. "And when she didn't, I started scrubbing up nice whenever couples came to look us over. I was sure I'd have a home one day. A family. Even asked Santa for one the year I turned seven. That's how I learned the guys in the red suits didn't really live at the North Pole."

Her arms were crossed on her stomach, and her soft brown curls blew across her face.

"I'm so sorry. Were you jealous of the other kids who got adopted?"

He looked out at the moon, wondering where those kids were now. Eating dinner with in-laws, planning birthday parties for their own children? None of that had been in the cards for him. Never would be.

"Not really. I wished it'd been me, but I wouldn't take it away from them." He inhaled as deep a breath as his tight lungs allowed. "I had a brother. Not blood-related, but as close as one."

Her eyes lit up. "I didn't know that. Has he been at any of the games?"

The backs of his eyes burned and it took him a moment to answer.

"He can't."

"Why?"

"Because he's dead."

Suddenly, her arms wrapped around his chest, her cheek pressed to his thudding heart.

"I'm so sorry, Garrett," she said into his shirt.

When she made as if to move away, he pulled her closer, savoring her feel and how it warmed the chill inside him. It was wrong to hold her this way. She was his boss. He could look but not touch.

Correction. He shouldn't even look.

But in his defense, she'd touched him first. Everything inside him twisted with the need to keep her close, this woman who hid her scars almost as well as he did.

"We met when he got moved into my room the year I turned fourteen. He was a year younger."

"He was your roommate, but he felt like a brother to you."

"Exactly. He was all the family I had," he said fiercely. *Ever have had*, he added silently.

"What was his name?"

"Manuel. Manny. He taught me about superhero comic books. I showed him how to throw a fastball."

"What happened?" She pulled back but kept her arms around him, her eyes searching his face.

He shut his eyes, seeing the closed casket for the hundredth time, a picture of Manny in a backward-facing Braves cap on top. "He got shot in a drive-by when he aged out of the foster system and moved back to Atlanta."

"That's awful," she breathed. "I hope they caught the murderer."

He jerked out of the warm arms he didn't deserve, and stood.

"They haven't. But I'm just as much to blame."

The color drained from her face. "How?"

"I left him to play for the Minors. He asked me to wait. To stay with him one more year until he got out, but I didn't. Didn't stay in touch, either, and now he's dead. Killed by a rival gang."

His knees gave out and he sat again, dropping his head low. There it was. The truth. Every ugly inch of it. Now she'd have another reason to hate him besides his alcoholism. Of course, before Manny's death, he'd never had more than a beer or two. But after—it'd been the only way he'd been able to keep going, though he'd driven himself straight into the ground. *Might as well have joined his brother*, he'd thought on his worst days.

"But that's not your fault." Her fingers brushed through his hair, and he peered up at her, not seeing the condemnation he expected. "He didn't have to go back to his gang."

"I stopped being someone he could count on. Without me, it was the only family he had."

"It was still his choice," she said firmly, her eyes fastened on him.

"One I forced him to make." Why the hell wasn't she getting this? He needed her to understand, not argue. This wasn't some classroom debate in whatever private school she'd probably attended. It was his life. Manny's life. And death.

Her nose scrunched, and when she shook her

head, her hair fell across her cheeks. "You're wrong."

A roar filled his ears as every muscle tensed, the back of his neck bristling. He wasn't getting through to her. Probably never would. They weren't as alike as he'd thought. Not even close.

"Why are you so sure you're right about everything? Even things you know nothing about?"

She sucked in air, the shock in her eyes stabbing his heart. He didn't mean to hurt her, but she pushed every one of his buttons sometimes.

She shoved off the bench and marched out of the dugout.

"Heather!" he called, and she turned, nearly tripping on the shaggy dog at her heels. "I didn't mean that."

Her eyes leveled with his.

"You're better than you think, Garrett. I may not be able to convince you, but you need to believe in yourself. Why not help the boys who are working here at the field? Instead of pushing away the past, make up for it. Do it for Manny."

And with that, she slipped away, passing in

and out of moonbeams until she disappeared from view.

He gazed after her, wondering.

His baseball comeback was for himself and for Manny. Could the camp be another path to salvation?

One that would honor his friend...if the memories and guilt it raised didn't rip him to shreds.

He let his head drop into his hands. It was impossible. He wished he could take back what he'd said to Heather.

Take it all back.

But then, regret was his life's soundtrack. He'd just add this night to the list of moments he'd do over.

If only he could.

CHAPTER SEVEN

HEATHER AND MR. LETTLES strode into the
Falcons meeting room the next day, his smile
broad, hers forced but wider.

Fake it 'till you make it.

The mantra swam in her head, pushing
against the current of nerves running through
her.

She hoped the players would help out after
hearing about the baseball camp. Her gaze took
in the sea of men lounging in rows of fold-out
chairs in the windowless room. Fluorescent
lights illuminated expressions that ranged from
polite interest to barely concealed hostility. Not
exactly the receptive welcome she'd hoped for,
but coming off a losing series, she'd anticipated
some lingering bad feelings.

Maybe her expectations were a tad high.

But still, this had to work. She looked at
Garrett and he gave an almost imperceptible
headshake. No support there.

Not that she'd expected it after their dugout

confrontation. Still. She felt let down. Was it too much to hope that she'd gotten through to him? That he'd see the opportunity to turn his past into something positive? Working with the kids would help him as much as it'd benefit them.

Yet involving herself in his personal life wasn't her job. She was a baseball manager. Not a life coach. No matter that the ache in his voice, his painful past, rang a bell inside her. It reminded her of the sound echoing in the empty spaces her mother had left.

She and Garrett were alike. After his confession last night, something connected them, a ribbon of understanding that twisted and tied them together. They both needed to prove that their past did not define their present.

The men quieted when she stepped up to the podium, and Garrett's lids lifted. Their eyes locked for a heart-stopping moment, and the warmth of his embrace rushed back. She pinched the bridge of her nose. Last night, she'd crossed a major line. She was his boss, not his girlfriend.

She peered down at her note cards and focused. Seeing her speech thawed the anxiety freezing her vocal cords.

"Good morning, Falcons."

"Morning, Skip," several responded, Valdez's voice loudest of all. Others, however, stared at her without expression, their eyes already glazing over. She swallowed. If they accepted her fully as their manager, they'd be more receptive. Without their support, she had no idea how it'd go over. Regardless, she had to proceed.

"To give back to our community, Falcons leadership has decided to open a baseball camp using our old field and facilities. Foster children from around the state will be attending as a way to instill in them the pride and confidence that goes with gaining sports skills and competing. Although Mr. Lettles has been kind enough to reach out to local coaches and gain volunteers to work with the boys, we would be grateful if you would donate some of your free time to help out as well."

Several of the men ducked their heads and twisted sideways to look at one another. She couldn't read their expressions from that angle and wondered. Were they considering or rejecting her idea?

Mr. Lettles kept up his relentless smile and nodded encouragingly. At least she had one person on her side. She met Valdez's adoring look. Make that two. A few chairs made grating noises as the men turned back around.

"I need to know what you can offer and what times you're available to help. Please use the sign-up sheet on the table by the door. It will be hanging outside my office after this meeting as well."

She pulled sweating hands from her pockets and rocked up on the balls of her feet. "Part of being a professional team is giving back to your community. Volunteering would also be making a big difference in the lives of these kids, many of whom have experienced great hardship. Even tragedy."

She glanced at Garrett, whose features had sharpened.

"I appreciate any time you can offer." She turned to the beaming man beside her. "Mr. Lettles, is there anything you'd like to add?"

"The boys worked hard to fix up the field while you were in Florida," he crowed. "Some of the boys follow the team very closely and are big fans. We treated them to a game a couple of weeks ago, and they haven't stopped talking about it since. I believe you were pitching, Mr. Wolf."

Garrett's eyes widened, and his tense mouth dropped open slightly.

"The kids would be awed to meet you and the rest of the Falcons in person. All of you could be positive role models in their lives. Support like that is very important. Thank you for considering this."

Heather took in Garrett's pale face. What was he thinking? He'd been a role model to Manny until he'd left for the Minors. Was he beating himself up for leaving his little brother?

She stepped out from behind the podium. "The boys will be at the old stadium starting Monday, and I hope to see you stop by. As for tonight's game, let's give our home crowd something to cheer about."

"Got it, Skip!" hollered Valdez, who hustled over to the sign-up sheet. To her relief, a few players rose and followed him. Then a few more, and several more after that, until a line of men formed, stretching to the back of the room.

Wow.

Happiness filled her. They might be mistrusting her advice on the field. But off it, they held no grudge. These were the giving men she'd hoped for. It made her prouder than ever to manage them, even if they weren't fully accepting her.

Yet.

But they would. This was a start. Wins to-night and tomorrow would restore some good-will, and they'd enjoy working with the kids on Monday, their day off.

Garrett strode past the crowd and out the door without a backward glance.

Her stomach twisted. Everyone, possibly, but Garrett.

A COUPLE OF DAYS LATER, Garrett walked from the two-story dormitory building on a path that passed the old field. He was early for his pitching program but wanted to avoid the baseball camp kids. He hoped the time would guarantee they hadn't arrived yet and he'd get some extra throwing in. Since the Falcons had lost another game over the weekend, he needed to be in perfect form tomorrow when he took the mound.

But the smack of a bat hitting a ball followed by the hollering of kids made his stomach drop to his toes. No such luck.

He sped up, nearly jogging as he rounded the bend by the lowest part of the old field's wall. The bright morning sun shook off its cloud cover and lit up the day. The glare made him squint, nearly missing the ball that zipped over the wall.

Instinctively, he grabbed it. His palm stung and he shook it out, ready to hurl the ball back before anyone noticed.

He reached behind him for the throw, then pulled up short when a tall kid with red, spiky hair appeared, his head swinging from side to side, a frantic expression on his face. Manny, he thought for a moment, taken by the resemblance. While his friend had been dark-haired… Then he shook away the thought. This was the kid who'd yelled to him at a game a few weeks ago.

"Coach is gonna kill me if I lose another one," he heard the kid mutter, his eyes still on the ground.

Garrett looked around and noticed two more balls nearby. The kid was definitely going to earn his coach's ire if he let this many go. He flipped the ball around in his hand, debating. If he threw it now, the kid would see him. But if he disappeared, he'd be leaving the boy in the lurch.

Reluctantly he cleared his throat. "Hey. Over here."

The kid looked up, and his startled expression turned to wonder, his eyes growing wide.

"You—you—you're Garrett Wolf," he gasped, silver braces reflecting the light as his mouth dropped open.

Garrett forced a smile, wishing he was anywhere but here. "Guilty." And he meant that in too many ways to think about.

"Wow!" The boy scampered closer and leaned bony elbows on the wooden fence, large hands dangling over the side. "I want to throw as fast as you someday."

"Thank you." Garrett knew he should add something else. Ask the kid what position he played, maybe autograph a ball, but a need to get out of this conversation clipped his response short.

He scooped up the other two balls. Once he chucked them back, he'd shake off this conversation like a bad dream.

Manny had looked at him like that once. As though he was the greatest thing in the world—Manny's world. And maybe he had been since his little brother hadn't grown up with anyone who cared about him. Only what he could do for them.

Even a small kid could deliver drugs. A bigger kid, like Manny had been when they'd picked him up, carried guns. It was how he'd ended up in a group home.

As for Garrett, he'd been blamed for taking a foster family's car out for a joyride. The certainty that they'd never blame the real culprit, their son, had kept him mum. He'd been labeled too many times to fight against what others believed.

"So is it true?" the boy asked excitedly, his words tumbling over each other. "You were a foster kid like us?"

Garrett tossed him the first ball and admired how the kid caught it without seeming to look.

"Yes."

He had to keep this brief and get out of here. He lofted the next ball and watched the kid catch it with little effort. He had some natural ability.

"Holy crap." The kid's exclamation stopped Garrett's last throw. "And you made it."

"Anyone can make it," he forced himself to say. No sense crushing the kid. Besides, he glimpsed athletic promise in the boy that could be—should be—nurtured. Yet life didn't give kids like him a lot of chances. Garrett had been lucky when a talent scout had attended one of his high school games. Who knew where he'd be if that hadn't happened?

A defeated look crossed the boy's face, despite Garrett's encouragement. He'd been so excited just seconds ago, and now he looked glum. "Not everyone. I won't make it."

Garrett's breath stalled. "What do you mean?"

"I've already got a record," the boy answered, a small hitch in his voice. "Some people say I'm trouble." He hung his head, his thin neck appearing beneath a squared-off hairline.

"What idiot told you that?" Garrett snapped, his tone making the boy's head lift. Manny had said the same thing when they'd met. He'd warned that he'd make a bad roommate, but he'd been the best thing that'd ever happened to Garrett. Until his death became the worst.

"My old foster families. Me. Not Mr. Lettles, though." The boy made a sucking noise with his teeth. "I've done bad stuff, but I'm trying to be better now."

The desperate determination in the boy's voice touched Garrett.

He opened his mouth to say something but was cut off when a man wearing striped baseball shorts and a sleeveless shirt jogged up.

"There you are, Levi. They warned me that you pull these little disappearing acts."

His scowl turned to surprise and then pleasure when he spotted Garrett on the other side of the fence.

"Mr. Wolf. It's nice to meet you. I'm a big fan. I coach the local high school JV team and…"

"That's interesting," Garrett muttered, not interested at all. What he cared about was that Levi, a kid who already believed he was trouble, was being treated that way. No wonder he didn't think he'd make it.

"Yes, well—" the man trailed off, then looked back at Levi who seemed diminished somehow, despite his gawky height. "We'll stop pestering you. I'm sure you've got more important things to do with your time than bother with us."

Garrett glanced at his watch, an urge to do something he knew he'd regret seizing him. Pressure built and, unable to contain it, he blurted, "Actually, no. Thought I'd come inside to deliver this ball. Give Levi and the kids a few pitching tips if you have room in your schedule."

Levi's brown eyes lit up, and the man goggled at him, his mouth opening and closing until he figured out how to make it work.

"We'd be honored."

"The pleasure is mine," Garrett muttered,

striding around to the front locker room entrance, regretting every step.

How could there be pleasure when he anticipated only pain?

HEATHER COULDN'T BELIEVE her eyes when Garrett stepped onto the field, a ball already in his hand. A redheaded preteen—Levi, she recalled—raced up to him, his long arms gesturing wildly, his mouth moving even faster.

How did they know each other? More importantly, what had changed Garrett's mind? It'd felt great when Valdez had showed up and begun helping the kids with infielding. Even Waitman was over in the batter's box, positioning small hands around bats. But seeing Garrett flooded her with joy. This had to be hard on him, but he'd put the kids ahead of himself. That was impressive, selfless, strong, caring and every other good adjective her mind could wing his way.

When he caught her stare, he nodded and shrugged, a small smile tugging up the corners of his handsome mouth. Inside, she melted. There was a difference between a good-looking man and a good-looking, good-hearted man, and Garrett was the latter. Infinitely more attractive. Not that, as his manager, she should notice. Shouldn't even look. Especially given her fear that his addiction could return. But the fact that he was making an effort softened her defenses.

She hefted a cumbersome bag of balls and stepped up beside him.

"Garrett." She passed him the bag. "It's good to see you." She smiled, wishing his eyes didn't look so shadowed, his rigid muscles making him seem like a skittish thoroughbred.

"Skipper."

Interesting that he called her Heather when they were alone and Skipper in public. As if they had two relationships, one known only to themselves. Next time she'd correct him if he called her by her first name. After that intimate moment in the dugout, their boundaries needed more defining than ever.

"Thanks for coming out to help." She pointed to a few of the kids and beckoned. "I'll warm this group up, teach them some stretches and send them to you for pitching practice. Sound good?"

He nodded, his jaw set, his expression resolute. "Sure. I'll start with them." He gestured to the remaining five kids. "Then we'll swap."

"That'll work."

And it did. For the next hour, they traded

groups. The boys learned the rudiments of pitching, some better than others, all having a great time. Voices rang out in the large green space. Beaming, excited faces surrounded her.

Even her father was laughing in the outfield with one of the kids. He held his glove in front of his body, head high, demonstrating the best position to transfer the ball to his throwing hand. Heather felt a pang of concern at his profusely sweating face. She'd warned him this might be too much activity, but he'd waved away her protests. When had he ever listened to her? Besides, he looked like he was having the time of his life. He tossed another ball into a sky so blue it could have been a tropical ocean.

Heather smiled. This was how it should be. A team and family working together.

LATER THAT EVENING, with the last of the sun reaching through the trees, Heather pushed herself to run one more mile. She had six under her belt, and seven would leave her with that euphoric exhaustion that'd float her to sleep the moment her showered body hit the bed.

It was nice to have the night off. Even better not to dissect another game loss with her father. Tonight's dinner had been full of talk about the kids and how much they'd both enjoyed working with them. However, according to Dad, Heather should have started out with stance and body positioning rather than throwing. But the expected criticism lacked the usual bite. Her father had seemed too tired and happy to harp long. All in all, a good day.

If only her ever-present worry, her team, didn't dog each step. She'd hoped to leave it behind, just for a little while, but it kept pace as her feet crunched on pine needles. They'd won one game and lost another this weekend, making no headway on improving their record. If they kept losing at this rate, their chances of making the playoffs would be out of reach in a couple of weeks. So far the bleachers were still half-full, profits were lacking and the Falcons hadn't become a winning team.

Heather's promise to her father at the Gowettes' meeting felt emptier and emptier. All her life, she'd worked hard to keep every vow she'd made to her dad. Despair made her break stride, and she stumbled before righting herself. Things had to go flawlessly. She had to be perfect. Yet she was hitting a wall she couldn't climb, knock over or walk around.

At least practice had gone well today. A few of the guys who had volunteered at baseball camp had been receptive and applied her corrections. She hoped they'd do that in tomorrow's game. The Falcons needed to regain their momentum to have a winning season. If not, her father would go through with selling the team.

The thought twisted through her as she sidestepped a low-hanging bush and pushed through the pain searing her lungs. Without the Falcons, who would she be? Who would her father be? She couldn't picture him on a beach watching waves roll in. He'd be miserable, no matter what he'd talked himself into. Like her, he'd grown up with sports. She needed to make this work. That way, he could retire here, his approval at her success settling their uneasy relationship.

She turned down a right fork in the dirt trail and into a denser part of the pine forest. The trail was faint and crooked, but she'd run this way so many times, she knew it by heart. She kept a close eye on the ground in the fading light, watching for tree roots and anything else that'd trip her up. The mountain trees that grew between the evergreens rustled in a soft summer breeze. It carried the loamy smell of earth and growing things.

At the sound of someone jogging behind her,

she turned her head, nervous. As long as she could remember, only she had ventured this far out into the wilderness. The wind picked up, flipping leaves upside down and sideways as she peered behind her. From around a bend, Garrett emerged from the shadows, his seamless stride the gait of a practiced runner. Her heart rate picked up.

He was striking in fitted running shorts, with a T-shirt dangling from his waistband. Shadows pooled in the creases of his washboard abs. His broad, smooth chest tapered to a lean waist, making her swallow hard and nearly trip when her foot fell into a depression.

"Heather, hold up!" he called.

She threw another glance over her shoulder, unable to stop her appreciative smile at seeing him, panting, as he ran to catch up with her. He'd called her Heather now that they were alone...

Maybe it was the day, the weather, or the company, but she couldn't resist the playful urge to bait him.

"It's Skipper, not Heather," she called back as she speeded up. "Glad to see you working on your endurance. Keep practicing. One day, you might even pass me."

"Well, *Skipper*," he shouted, sounding

alarmingly closer, "you may have the stamina, but I have the speed."

His feet pounded harder and nearer. She flew, feeling her ponytail bounce with each stride. Birds squawked, startled out of bushes as she and Garrett barreled by at a blistering pace. Her lungs burned, but she wouldn't quit, had to show him that she was the best, the boss, the superior athlete. She'd been a distance runner all her life—this was a piece of cake.

If not for this handsome distraction, she'd never have missed the knobby tree root that caught the toe of her running shoe. Down she fell, flat on her face. Luckily, a thick bed of needles cushioned her, scraping off only a top, stinging layer of skin on her knee.

In a flash, Garrett was at her side. He must have been about to pass her, but instead he stopped and took her in his arms, his hands running up and down her sides as if feeling for bumps or bones at off angles.

She opened her mouth to tell him to stop, but being this close to him drove away her protest. If she'd been able to make an objection, it would have been a weak one at best.

"Heather. Are you okay?" His concerned eyes traveled over her, his hands moving up from her ankles, his fingers trailing along her calves.

She gasped for air. It was hard to catch her breath, especially with his finely shaped features and perfect body inches from hers. She loved his eyes, and her skin tingled at his touch. The wall that she usually kept between them crumbled, and she reached out to grab his muscular shoulders, steadying herself.

"I'll carry you home." He made as if to scoop her up, but she shook her head. Hard. Her father would have a fit if he saw them together this late. A sanctioned ride home in broad daylight was one thing. Nearly lying on the forest floor, the gathering darkness a warm blanket, was another animal altogether.

"It was just a root. Nothing major. No harm done." But looking up into his worried eyes made her feel as though a great deal of damage was about to be done. If she let it happen.

His arms tightened around her. "When you didn't speak, I thought you'd hit your head."

His anxious tone touched her. "Sometimes I have trouble talking in general."

He shifted slightly to the left until his back rested against a tree, still holding her. Despite willing herself to go, her head nestled against his chest. With so many highs and lows these past few days, it felt good to relax against him in this stolen moment. Thirty more seconds and she was out of here. But she'd soak it up until then.

"Why do you have speech issues? It's not that obvious."

"My mom," she found herself confessing. The struggles they'd shared made opening up to Garrett feel natural. Right. "Any sound set her off because of her migraines. Then, when her back pain made it hard to sleep, I couldn't make a noise in case I woke her. She was—" her lower lip quivered and she sucked it in before blurting, "—uncontrollable."

He smoothed back a lock of hair. "Sounds terrifying." His tender look made her ache.

"Yeah. It was," she said simply, not trusting her emotions not to betray her if she elaborated.

"No kid should go through that," Garrett murmured, and she shivered at the feel of his warm breath against her temple. She needed to break the subtle tension that wove around them, holding them tight. But she couldn't summon the resolve to leave. He was so warm, felt so right, yet this was wrong in every way. Maybe another thirty seconds?

"I liked working with the kids today," he

said into her ear, his mouth so close to her flesh that the fine hairs on the back of her neck rose. She relished the sweet brush of his knuckles against the side of her throat as he flipped her ponytail over her shoulder.

"I know how hard that must have been for you," she said, doing her best to appear cool on the outside. Inside she was a web of conflicting emotions.

"You're getting me to do a lot things I promised myself I wouldn't."

When she pulled back, he met her look with grave intensity. "Like what?"

Then came the silence. The long, long silence. Their eyes met until she dropped hers, her heart thumping faster. Red lights flashed. Stop! Leave! Retreat! But her tangled emotions wouldn't let her wriggle free.

His hand caressed the sensitive spot beneath her chin, and with a gentle pressure, Garrett raised her head until she stared into his deep blue eyes again.

"This."

Without waiting for permission, he brushed his lips gently over hers. Ohhh…a shiver went through her entire body. The gentle caress melted the last of her defenses into a gooey heap.

His fingers slid along her jawline, and the warmth of his touch radiated past her skin and into her bloodstream. Goosebumps rose on her arms and legs, and her ears rang with the staccato thrum of her heart. He slipped his hand from her jaw to cradle her head. His fingers pulled her ponytail loose and tunneled through the hair that fell around her shoulders.

He pulled back slightly, his eyes heavy-lidded. His lips hovered above hers, tantalizingly close. The blood pounded so wildly in her veins that she feared he'd sense the vibration. A magnetic pull took over the small distance between their lips. An energy she couldn't resist. So why was Garrett holding back? Her fingers were wrapped around the back of his neck, running through his hair.

And then it hit her. He was giving her a chance to return his kiss. To show him that she wanted him, and the truth was…more complicated than that. Cold reality doused her, and she leaned back.

She'd kissed Garrett. A player. And worse, a recovering alcoholic who might one day relapse. Someone she could, if she wasn't more vigilant, become addicted to herself. She couldn't let that happen.

Scrambling to her feet, she saw the wounded

look in his eyes before he covered it with a coat of indifference.

"That was wrong," she blathered, backing away. "I should never—we should never—We're not right for each other, I—"

He held up a hand as he got to his feet in his fluid way that was stunning to watch. "I get it. We'll pretend this never happened." His gaze roamed in every direction but hers.

It was obvious from the way he braced his body, his tense face, that he was taking this wrong. It wasn't as though she didn't want him. She just didn't trust him with her heart. It was too bruised to take another beating. Even if she wasn't his manager, his past alcoholism and his uncertain future sobriety were things she couldn't look past.

She opened her mouth to explain, but his mouth twisted, and he held up a hand.

"Really. It's fine," he said, the gravel in his voice denying his words. "Would you like me to take you home?"

She shook her head, wishing his eyes hadn't turned into mirrors, reflecting only what was outside, keeping her from seeing what he was thinking or feeling.

With a small salute, he turned. "See you, Skipper," he called over his shoulder as he took off farther down the path, leaving her slumped against the tree in the gathering gloom.

There it was. The respectful address she'd wanted from him on and off the field. Only now she knew that she no longer deserved it. Not after how she'd behaved.

The chaos in her mind cleared. She was under a lot of pressure, thinking with her body instead of her head. In other circumstances, she wouldn't have let Garrett get that intimate with her. He was a member of her team, nothing more.

Yes, they shared a unique connection. Maybe it was the hardships they'd both experienced? Either way, she was confusing lust with feelings, and that had to stop.

She was attracted to him, but the emotions going on…it was because she needed someone to turn to, and he was there. That was it. It wasn't like she had anyone else who listened to her. Who accepted her fears as Garrett did.

Strangely, her mother came to mind. She'd called again this morning. How many times would she have to hang up on her for Mom to give up? Get the message? She hadn't heard from her mother from her thirteenth birthday until she graduated high school. After that, it'd become a regular thing, a weekly, painful reminder of the parent she'd lost and could never count on again.

A part of her knew that this was why, at twenty-seven, she hadn't had a serious relationship. Another part of her understood that she probably never would. And she was fine with that. Or had been until she'd met Garrett. She hadn't thought before that she needed a man. Romance. Not after what it'd done to her father, her family.

Her hands brushed against the tree's bark as she rose, and her fingernails sank into its grooved, rough surface. Love was like that, she supposed. Not always the smooth road you expected. Not when you actually explored it. Went far from your comfort zone. In time, as she'd seen with her mother, it would lead to dead ends and uneven terrain with dangerous twists and turns. She would never let that be her future.

As much as she wished it could be different…and include Garrett.

CHAPTER EIGHT

HEATHER TOOK HER porch steps two at a time, eager to escape the tornado of emotions that blew her home. She imagined her dad, inside, watching a show. It'd be worth the lecture about running this late just to hear his voice. She needed it. Him. Whenever her world fell apart, he was the rock she clung to, the buoy she grasped in a stormy sea.

Behind her, thunder rolled through the trees, a wind gust twirling leaves in a mad dance. She fumbled for her keys as the sky threw its first salvo, a light drizzle that didn't fool her. A tempest was about to let go, and she needed to be indoors. Fast.

Scout scratched at the door and barked, the piercing noise echoing in the sticky-hot air that pressed all around her.

"Hey," she soothed him, running her fingers over his back as he paced before the door, the fur rising behind his neck. "It's okay, boy." For a large dog, he was a big chicken when it came to thunderstorms. Poor thing.

She inserted the key as Scout clawed at the glass, his nose snuffing loudly against the frame.

"Move back, Scout." She pushed him out of the way, but he squirmed between her calves and raced inside the minute she'd pulled open the door.

"Sheesh!" she exclaimed, ducking inside just as the sky opened up. "Glad I made it in before that started," she called.

She braced herself for her dad's inevitable comment. His hand dangled over the edge of his recliner, a sitcom talk show playing on the television. But he made no move to tell her she should have checked the weather before setting out, not run that late on her own, or at least brought her cell phone, which she guiltily glimpsed on the table beside him. He'd definitely give her heck for that.

Only the sound of a studio audience laughing and Scout's barking as he circled her father's chair answered her.

She took a hesitant step forward. "Dad?" Maybe he was sleeping. Normally she'd hear his snores from here, but why else would he lie so still, his hand so limp…? Her heart seized, and her throat strangled the breath out of her.

"Dad!" she called and rushed forward, her pulse pounding faster than her feet.

She skidded around the front of his chair and took in his open mouth, slumped posture and closed eyes and breathed a sigh of relief. He was sleeping. Deeply. Strange that he didn't notice Scout pawing at his legs, whining in a high-pitched way she'd never heard before.

Lighting slashed outside the large living room window and she jumped, heart in her throat. She rubbed Scout's head. "It's going to be all right buddy. It's all right."

And then she noticed it. Something so horrible her brain couldn't process it. She was wrong and Scout was right. Nothing was okay.

Her father wasn't breathing. His chest lay as still as the rest of him.

She sank to her knees and grabbed his limp fingers. "Dad! Wake up!"

Staring into his broad face, she willed his eyes to open and look at her.

"Daddy! Please! Wake up! Wake up! WAKE UP!" she pleaded, shaking his shoulder.

But his face remained rigid, a mask carved from hard wood. The ground seemed to roll beneath her, out of control.

She pressed her ear to his chest, listening, her own heart stopping as she waited for a sign that this wasn't happening. A nightmare she'd never dreamed would come true.

She fumbled at his wrist for his pulse. Feeling nothing, she put her cheek beside his mouth, desperate to detect his breath against her face. Her hand clutched his thigh while Scout tried leaping into his owner's lap and crashed backward.

Pain swept through her as she pulled away, her chest rising and falling too fast to take in air. Black spots appeared on the edge of her vision. Tears, the ones she never allowed herself to shed, fell as hard as the pelting rain outside.

She snatched up her cell phone, then threw it into the TV screen. The battery was dead.

"I'll be right back, Dad!" she called and dashed for the kitchen. He had to hear her. Would need her reassurance.

"9-1-1. What's your emergency?"

Heather opened her mouth and the words, the horrible, despicable, terrifying words refused to come out. Beside her, the fridge hummed grimly to itself.

"Hello. You've called 9-1-1. Is this an emergency?" the operator repeated.

If she stayed quiet, bad things wouldn't happen, her brain told her, a familiar voice from her childhood. A deep shudder made her grasp the granite island when her knees buckled.

"Are you there? Hello? This is 9-1-1. If this is an emergency, you need to respond."

"Yes," Heather choked out, the word cutting through her like glass.

"And what's the emergency ma'am?"

Heather gripped the phone, her mouth trembling, her eyes screwed shut.

"Ma'am, I need you to stay calm and talk to me."

"He's dead," she gasped, acid burning her throat.

"Who's dead?"

"My father. He's not breathing," she cried.

"Responders are on their way to the address coming up with your phone number. Thirty-one Macey Lane, Holly Springs. Is that correct?"

Heather nodded, then forced out a yes.

"EMS will be there in ten minutes. Have you begun CPR?"

"Not yet." Her voice was so low that she was startled when the operator answered her.

"If you know how to perform it, please begin resuscitation until help arrives. Can you do that for me?"

"Yes," she gasped, louder, then dropped the phone and raced back to her father. CPR. Why hadn't she thought of it first? She could do this. She could save him.

She pushed Scout out of the way and grabbed her dad around the waist and knees, struggling to slide him out of the recliner and onto the carpet. When his head banged against the side of the coffee table, she winced.

"Sorry!" she cried, soothing his temple, shriveling inside at the bluish tinge there and around his mouth. With the back of her hand, she swiped away her tears. She had to get a grip. Gadways didn't cry. Especially in emergencies. She forced her emotions behind the wall that let her function and began to work, methodically pressing on her father's chest.

One and two and three and...

She executed her training ritualistically, her body falling into a physical rhythm that blocked out reality. She didn't have to think or feel. Just perform.

She didn't realize how much her arms ached until a man and women burst through the unlocked front door, emergency gear in hand, and pulled her, protesting, from her father.

"Ma'am. Please let us do our job and step away."

Step away?! Heather's feet were rooted to the floor as one of the EMS professionals bustled around her father, checking his vitals.

"No pulse or respirations," the woman said. Her confirmation of his condition, delivered in a flat, toneless voice, leveled Heather.

The male responder brought out a portable defibrillator and connected it to her father.

"Stand back!" The man commanded. Heather stumbled backward as her father's bare chest jerked upward, then fell. She held her breath, hoping that his pulse would return.

But he remained motionless. The responders administered CPR again, and Heather held Scout's collar, keeping him from joining the fray.

After a moment, they applied the defibrillator again.

"All clear," yelled one, and they stepped back. Her father jerked again and flopped to the floor.

He was so pale, Heather thought, looking at the white skin that blended with his silver curls of chest hair. As a girl, she remembered resting her head on his chest as she sat on his lap. Would he ever hold her again?

"Pulse is back, but it's thready," murmured the male EMS. Heather's heart leaped. Yes!

Her father would make it. Beat this. He was a fighter. Air rushed from her, relief leaving her weak. Dad wasn't out of the woods, but they'd bring him through the rest of the way. He'd need more surgery, maybe a bypass on that blocked artery they were watching. But that would be the worst of it, and compared to what she'd imagined, it felt like winning the lottery.

"Ma'am. Can you grab your father's medicines? We're going to need you to ride in the ambulance and give us his medical history on the way."

She scooped up his bottles and grabbed his Falcons cap. He never went anywhere without it. Would ask for it when he came around. She forced a resisting Scout to stay inside the house, hurried after the twosome and her father and hopped inside the vehicle.

"Is he going to be okay?" she asked, just to be sure, as her father was loaded into the back with her, his body strapped to a gurney.

Without answering, they set to work, one inserting an IV lock and drip while the other continued CPR. The ambulance roared down the driveway, the private dirt road jarring them at high speed.

Heather scanned her father's face, waiting for an eye flutter, a grimace, anything to tell her that he was conscious. Aware. But maybe it was better if he wasn't?

An EKG was hooked up to his chest, and the electronic results flashed on the monitor overhead. One of the EMSs talked to the hospital through a radio, his hand cupped over his mouth, his eyes raised to the electronic signal. She waited for the line to spike upward, as it had before, but it stayed flat. Was it malfunctioning, or was Dad's heart not beating? Her own seized.

Another defibrillator round produced no change in the EKG readout, and the EMS worker turned his back and talked fast and low into the radio. At last he turned and, with a somber face, began disconnecting the leads.

"Shouldn't you be working on my dad?" Heather's voice rose, breaking off sharply at the end as she rose from a drop-down bench beside the gurney. She shook off the other EMS professional's hand on her arm.

"We've got the go-ahead from our signal doctor at the hospital to cease resuscitation efforts. Your father's no longer responding to treatment. Without oxygen or a heartbeat for several minutes, I'm afraid it's no longer sensible to continue."

Heather's head filled with a white-noise roar

that didn't let up. She didn't have a clue where she was or where she was heading as the sound kept coming at her from every direction. All she could do was be led back to the bench because if she didn't go somewhere, she'd want to just lie down and die herself.

"But he's not dead!"

Her voice was ripe and swollen, like some dark rotten thing ready to burst. She'd been on that gurney once, years ago, when they'd used the Jaws of Life to extricate her from the car crash. Now she understood how it must have killed her father as he'd ridden beside her, holding her hand—she vaguely remembered that and his reassuring tone as he'd spoken to her. Begging her to stay with him.

"Don't leave me," she exclaimed and grabbed his icy hand. She stared into his face, wishing he'd yell at her for something. Anything. She'd take a life of criticism over one minute without him.

The woman began scribbling on a clipboard containing forms.

"Please! Do something," Heather begged her. These were emergency professionals. Why weren't they acting like it?

"I'm sorry, ma'am. I'm afraid he's gone."

Heather doubled over, the announcement a

sucker punch to her chest. Thunder rolled over the ambulance as they zipped down the highway to the county hospital, a wind gust making it rock.

Heather stared at the ceiling, wanting to shriek with the siren, but it suddenly cut off, the vacuum of sound more ominous. She blinked hard, not wanting to cry in front of strangers, before giving in and letting her sobs fill the silence.

Then they rolled up to the semicircle entrance at the hospital, the doors yanked open and two men in matching white uniforms pulled the gurney, taking her father away from her.

Heather cried out. She wouldn't be separated from him. Not so soon.

But when she hopped off the ambulance, a calm-faced woman pulled her aside as her father disappeared through the swooshing glass doors.

"My dear. We'll need some information from you. Would you tell me who you are?"

Heather blinked at her.

Who she was? Without her father, she hadn't a clue.

HEATHER STUDIED HER father's temporary marker as the minister finished a brief, final message she'd hadn't heard. She shifted in her heels, her feet aching despite the Astro-turf carpet rolled out beneath a large tent. It was the only thing she'd felt in the past couple of days. Everything else had happened at a distance—to someone else—not her. None of this was true. Yet here she stood, before a hole she dared not look at, Reed and Smythe flanking her like protective uncles.

A bright sun in a cloudless sky mocked the occasion, the light air belying the heaviness in her heart. She brought her father's glove to her face, inhaling the familiar leathery scent she always associated with him.

She shivered, despite the warm day, feeling alone in the crowd of friends and Falcons.

Who was she? That was the thing about losing a parent. A part of you stopped being. She was no longer "daughter." Not to a parent who cared.

"Dave Gadway was a man of conviction and faith," the minister intoned. "A born leader admired and respected by all. He's earned his final reward."

Heather wrapped her arms around herself, sure that if she didn't, she'd fall apart. It'd taken everything she had to get through these past few days, to go along with what felt like a charade, like some kind of elaborate hoax.

Where would she like her father buried?

She'd named a cemetery close to home, feeling as though this was a trick question. Her father wasn't dead...until it'd hit her, at the most unexpected times, that yes—yes—he was.

What should his obituary say?

How could she sum up a huge life like her father's in a few paragraphs? It diminished him somehow. She'd slaved to get in every detail, desperate not to forget anything. Yet sometimes she did forget the most important thing.

Just this morning, she'd woken with a jolt, sure that she'd overslept and her dad would be at the kitchen island, ready to gripe about waiting on his egg-white omelet. Only, when she'd skidded into the empty space, no one but Scout had greeted her. The ache of it had made her sink to the floor beside her dog and weep.

"Several of you spoke at the funeral home. Given the heat, we have just a few moments left if there is anyone who would like to say something brief?" The minister shot her a look, and she met his eyes as steadily she could. What could she say that anyone would understand? That her father wasn't in that aluminum-gray casket poised above the hole? That at any moment he'd amble up the hill behind them, giving them heck for skipping practice? That even though she knew none of these things were true, a part of her needed to believe it or she'd crumble into tiny bits and blow away like dust? It was all surreal.

Reed patted her arm and strode forward.

For once his cheek didn't bulge from a wad of chewing tobacco, and he shifted in his dark suit, tugging at his tie.

"I knew Dave Gadway for over thirty years. We met when I joined the Falcons as a second baseman, and we became friends after he found out I like golf as much as I like ball. Through the years, Dave was always someone I could count on for advice. I knew he would back me up, and he made me proud to be a member of this franchise and his friend. He was a devoted father to Heather, and he loved her more than anything —even a league title."

That earned a few quiet laughs, the respectful kind that broke the tension. But his words wound Heather up tighter. She knew her dad had loved her, yet it wasn't something he'd said to her often. In fact, when she thought back to the last time he'd said it, her mind landed on the day she'd left for college. Ten years ago. Was it possible? And how long since she'd told him? A lump formed in her throat. She stuffed her clenched hands in her suit pockets to keep from lifting the casket's lid and whispering it to him one last time.

Now it was too late. He had to have understood that she loved him. But the comfort of knowing that she'd told him recently—that, she'd never have.

Her gaze strayed to Garrett, who stood across from her, the casket between them. He clasped his hands in front of his charcoal-gray suit, his eyes on her rather than Reed. They stared at each other, the quiet strength in his expression making her stand a little taller, hold her chin a bit higher.

"Thank you," she murmured to Reed when he returned.

Smythe ambled to the marker next, a hitch in his step, his cap twisting in his hands. "There was no better leader, better boss, better man than Dave Gadway. He made everyone he knew work harder and go that extra mile by his example. He was my idol and inspiration. When I tore my rotator cuff as a Falcons pitcher, I thought baseball was done for me until Dave offered me the coaching job. He never quit and didn't let anyone else quit, either. He demanded the best from everyone and nearly always got it. We can learn a lot from his example. I'll miss him."

Heather's eyes flitted to Garrett again, his gaze falling around her like a pair of strong arms. To her surprise, he broke their stare and strode to the front of the grave.

His smooth, low voice carried in the still air. "A little over a year ago, I would have been sitting in a bar after finishing my shift at the auto body shop, reminiscing about my former glory days playing in the Minor Leagues. One day, I ran into a guy I'd known in foster care. He'd just come back from Afghanistan and wanted to hear about my big baseball career, the one I'd left our group home for."

Heather's chest tightened when she saw a pulse throb in his temple, his jaw clench. This had to be hard for Garrett, who rarely opened up about anything. Why now? When his soulful eyes met hers, she had her answer. He was doing it for her, and the thought touched her deeply.

"I had to tell him that I'd been let go because of my alcoholism. That pissed him— sorry—that made him angry. He showed me his prosthetic arm and told me that he'd never waste any of his talents the way I was throwing away mine. After that, I knew I had to get my act together. I sobered up and got myself in shape, but wasn't sure it'd be enough until Mr. Gadway offered me a tryout."

Heather sorted through his words, fitting each together until they made a picture she recognized. She'd thought Smythe had recruited Garrett, had strong-armed her father into taking on an addict. Instead, her dad had been all for it...had even pushed to make it happen. Crazy.

Garrett cleared his throat and began again. "When I met him, I thought Mr. Gadway was the last guy in the world who'd give me another shot. He was blunt, told me I'd messed up big-time and asked if I planned on doing it again. When I told him I wouldn't, he took me at my word. It was the first time anyone ever had that much faith in me. It's what made Mr. Gadway the kind of man I aspired to be—still do—one who believed in himself and didn't need anyone else's approval."

Garrett's eyes bored into hers, and she made a strangled sound in the back of her throat. All she'd ever wanted to know was that her father believed in her, was proud.

Heather's stomach bottomed out. Why did her father have such confidence in someone with a track record like Garrett's and none in her? She'd always had to fight to gain her father's faith. Why? It was a question she should have asked before it was too late.

Her gaze flickered over to Garrett as he stood straight and tall beneath the tent, rows of well-wishers seated before him in folding chairs. Her father had trusted Garrett. Should she? After her childhood, it was hard to imagine, but being around him made it seem more possible every day.

Looking beyond the tent, Heather spied a slim, tall figure crest the hill. She blinked, trying to clear her vision, sure that the approaching woman couldn't possibly be who she seemed to be. But before she could be sure, an electric hum sounded. Heather whirled as her father's casket was lowered into the ground. Her heart beat in the roof of her mouth.

Her dad was going. Her father. Her rock. And he was disappearing into a dark place she couldn't follow.

She stood, frozen, watching the rounded dome drop. Hands squeezed her shoulders as family and friends passed by. She pressed her father's glove against her splintered heart. She stayed that way long after the last car door slammed, unwilling, unable, to leave him. To say goodbye. Even the funeral director's kind reminder that the service was over hadn't penetrated.

At last a hand tugged on her arm. She wiped away the tears blurring her vision, then blinked in shock.

"Hello, Heather," her mother said. "It's been too long."

CHAPTER NINE

"HEATHER! WAIT!"

Heather's heels clicked along Holly Springs' Main Street sidewalk a week later. She hurried from the lawyer's office, taking her as far, and as fast, as she could get from her mother.

She seethed. How could her father have let this happen? It was too incredible to believe.

"Please, Heather. We need to talk."

Her mom's freckled face appeared in the rear passenger window of the expensive sedan that was pacing her. A suited man drove, his expression impassive.

Heather shook her head and lengthened her stride, everything in her line of vision tinted red. Did her mother believe she had anything to say after that shocking news?

The car jerked to a halt, and Heather gaped when the door swung open. She was not going to talk to her mother. Not here. Not ever. Her mother's long legs appeared, and alarm seized her. She needed to get away. Now.

She bolted into the road. Screeching tires and the faintest brush of a bumper made her stumble and land on her backside, hard, her elbow scraping the pavement.

In seconds, a man knelt beside her, his familiar blue eyes so dark they were nearly black. His arm snaked behind her back, snatching her close.

"Heather. What were you doing? You could have been killed!"

Garrett sounded so like her father, her eyes stung. She wished she could speak, but the words tumbled in her head like laundry. Instead, she stared up at him, wincing at her stinging elbow. When a truck honked, Garrett waved, his impatient gesture ordering the pickup to go around.

"Oh my goodness. Are you okay?" she heard her mother exclaim, the hem of her green dress looming into view.

Heather closed her eyes. If only she could hit the rewind button on these past couple of minutes. Here she was, in the arms of the man she'd vowed never to touch again, dealing with a parent she'd hoped to forget. Even more difficult to take was the probate lawyer's news. That defied understanding.

"Garrett. Please get me out of here."

His eyes flicked up to her mother. She could see understanding dawning in his expression when he peered back at Heather. Except for the age difference, she and her mother could have been twins. But that was only on the outside. Inside, they were as different as could be.

"Sure." He helped her to her feet. "But you're not in any condition to drive."

She pulled a tissue from her purse and held it to her grazed elbow, avoiding her mother's pleading look. If she went with Garrett, he'd be behind the wheel. But if she left on her own, her mother would follow.

Garrett's handsome face hovered above her, concern sharpening his features, his mouth in a grim line. And just like that, she knew. Garrett. Her father had trusted him. Maybe she could too.

"Okay. You drive."

Garrett rested his chin above her head, his heart beating fast against her. "Okay," he breathed, his tone sounding relieved. With care, he gently guided her to her feet.

"Heather, please. Let me drive you home." Her mother extended her hand, a charm bracelet catching the afternoon light. "Then we can talk this out in private."

Heather stepped out of reach, her skin crawling. "Don't ever." Her mouth froze until she dragged the words from their hiding places. "Come to my house. Got it?"

Her mother paled and stepped back. "I never meant for any of this to happen."

"Thinking of others was never one of your strong suits," Heather said wearily and turned to Garrett. "Can we go now? Please."

"You got it." Garrett steered her to the passenger side of his car and opened the door. "Goodbye, ma'am," he said before sliding behind the wheel, his window open.

"Please call me Renee," Heather's mother urged as Garrett hit the gas and the car zoomed forward.

"Are you okay?" A redheaded boy poked his head between the front seats, his elfin features making him resemble Peter Pan. Neverland— a place without mothers, Heather recalled. If only she could fly there.

"I'm fine, Levi, thanks." She leaned against the leather headrest and pulled the tissue away from her arm. No bleeding. "Why didn't you go home earlier when camp ended?"

"Mr. Wolf got permission to treat me to ice cream. I struck out ten batters." His babble temporarily soothed the fire raging inside Heather.

She contemplated Garrett's neutral profile as he drove, wondering at this development. She'd been proud of his help with the kids. But rewarding one in particular for good work, giving personal attention, was taking things to another level. If she wasn't so irate over her father's will, she'd be excited. But right now, only two emotions consumed her.

Fury and betrayal.

She didn't have room to feel afraid of Garrett behind the wheel, his speed so slow that cars honked as they passed him. Her breath eased as his car stayed in its lane. No swerving. Nothing to frighten her. In fact, the extracareful way he drove made her wonder if he was trying to reassure her. If so, it worked.

To an extent.

Her pulse still thrummed and her fingernails dug into the door handle, her body rigid. Whenever Levi paused for breath, she nodded along politely while her mind worked in overdrive.

"Someday I'm going to be a professional ball player. Like Mr. Wolf," the boy gushed. "Not gonna be in foster care forever."

Heather followed his finger pointing and spotted the group home before Garrett swung into its parking lot.

"Will you be okay alone?" he asked her, his voice low and urgent. "I need to check Levi in."

Heather nodded but avoided his eyes. If he studied hers, he'd know she wasn't okay. Not by a long shot.

"Bye, Ms. Gadway!" Levi yelled before hopping out of the car. Heather waited for the door to slam, but instead she felt a thin hand touch her shoulder. She looked up, startled.

The boy's flushed, narrow face and wide eyes pushed close. "I'm—uh—sorry about your dad. I never had one, but if I did, I would have wanted him to be just like yours."

"Thanks, Levi."

Heather squeezed her eyes shut when the door clicked closed. Yes. Her dad had been great in many ways. But he'd never had faith in her, thought her capable. His decision to leave majority ownership of the team to his estranged wife was clear proof. In his eyes, Heather wasn't good enough. Although he'd let her work with the Falcons this season, he couldn't have believed she'd succeed. Her bid to make him proud had been a fruitless mission.

Always had been.

And why hadn't he confessed that he'd never

gone through with the divorce? It made no sense. She thunked her head against the glass. None of this did.

The beeping of a truck brought the ambulance's siren to mind. After a week, she still woke with it in her ears, the realization that her father was gone a stone in her chest. She'd appointed Smythe as temporary manager while she grieved, though how long that would be, she wasn't sure. Whenever she thought of returning, it felt like the fire that'd driven her had blown out. Now that her mother owned a majority share in the team, coming back seemed impossible.

Garrett's pine-scented aftershave filled the cab when he swung into his seat moments later. He angled his body her way and took her hand.

"What happened, Heather?"

Her heart expanded at the sound of her name on his lips. Today she wasn't Skipper. Not to him. And she wanted it that way. "Can we go somewhere?" She glanced out at the street, wondering if her mother's car lurked.

Garrett rubbed his thumb gently over her knuckles, sending a shimmer of sensation through her. "Anywhere. I have an AA meeting, but I can go to one tomorrow instead. And

I don't have to be at the stadium for a couple of hours."

She nodded, remembering. "You guys have a game tonight. I should know that."

"You've had enough to handle without thinking about us," Garrett grumbled, sending her an oblique look. Had he thought about her? She'd received his flowers along with many other bouquets but hadn't brought herself to open any of the accompanying cards.

He let go, started the engine and maneuvered the shift smoothly as he backed out of the spot. His hand settled on the blinker while they waited for traffic to clear. "Left or right?"

"Huh?" Her eyes traced the straight line of his nose, the cut angle of his jaw. She'd thought only of getting away. It hadn't mattered where.

"Where would you like to go?"

A special place came to mind. One that she'd love to see again. With Garrett.

"Ever been to Looking Glass Falls?"

His mouth curved upward. "Haven't seen much beyond a baseball field and a tour bus. Let's go."

After ten minutes of heeding her directions, followed by a twenty-minute off-road hike, they burst through a clump of pines onto a rocky outcrop.

Garrett's astonished expression was everything she'd hoped for. Water raced by, pouring over a wide stone lip to a clear pool below. Foam churned on the basin's surface, sprays of water cooling them off. Her restless spirit eased at the natural surroundings and the steadfast man beside her.

"I discovered it when I was in Girl Scouts," she said over the rushing stream that gurgled and splashed when it hit the rocks sixty feet below. "The old dugout used to be my thinking spot. But this was the only place my mother couldn't find me when I ran away."

Garrett's fingers laced with hers, and a bit of happiness nudged some of her grief away. He helped her down to the ledge, and they each took off their shoes to dangle their bare feet in the misty air.

"How often was that?" he probed after a silent moment.

She squinted at a large woodpecker across the narrow chasm, its *rat-tat-tat-tat* blending with the wind rustling through the trees. She inhaled fresh air and began. If she was going to confide in him, no sense in starting in the middle.

"As long as I can remember, my mother was always up and down. Sometimes she'd be great and would play with me for hours. Other times she'd stay in bed all day and yell for hot tea."

Garrett's eyes, as blue as the sky peeping through the canopy of leaves, searched hers. "How old were you?"

A lump formed in her throat. "Five is the earliest I remember."

His brows came together. "You were making hot tea at that age? Where was your father?"

"Working on team business. Mom did a better job of hiding her issues when he was around."

Garrett's hand found hers again. He turned her palm over, his finger tracing the lines that ran across it.

"You must have been lonely." His eyes darkened as he studied her. "We have that in common."

"I didn't know what was wrong with her then. Even though I brought her medicine, she got worse. When she went away to the hospital, I stayed up nights, crying and begging that she'd get better. Come home. I didn't understand where she really went until much later."

Garrett's hand tightened on hers. "Rehab."

She studied her swinging feet in the vapor-filled air.

"Yes. Except that it never worked. Not for

long. At first I'd think she was better. We'd bake and sew doll clothes. Dad didn't have much time for a little girl hanging around his baseball team, so for me, my world was her."

Her words came in fits and starts, sounding like an old radio tuned to a remote channel. Garrett brushed her hair from her face, and the gentleness of his touch made her want to weep.

"How many times did she go to rehab?"

"Not as many as she needed to. Three, I think." Heather leaned her cheek against his hand. "I tried keeping her clean. Being her best girl and doing everything so she wouldn't have any pain. By eight I could do the housework and cook, but I couldn't…"

A lump formed in her throat and blocked the rest of her sentence.

Garrett lifted her chin and stared deep into her eyes. "You couldn't keep her sober."

She shook her head, beyond words. The parent she'd loved most was gone, and the one who'd hurt her most had returned. Where was the justice in that?

"I got my hopes up so many times. Thought I had the power to control it. Her. But she hid the pills where I couldn't find them, learned to hide some of her symptoms too." Heather pulled a leaf off a scrub bush and ripped it into small pieces. Al-Anon had taught her not to blame herself for her mother's actions. Still. It was tough not to feel that she could have done more. Helped.

"When I got in the car on the day of the accident, she was only a week out of rehab. I was so happy she was home. Should have been paying closer attention. But I wanted her to be better so badly. I missed the signs."

The crushing disappointment fell through her, taking what was left of her heart with it. All her life she'd wanted her mother to love her more than drugs. Her father to be proud of her. She'd failed on both counts.

Garrett slid closer and gathered her in his arms. After everything, the small voice of protest at his touch was easily silenced. Yes, he was her subordinate. Yes, he was a recovering addict. But he was the only one who got past her defenses. Helped her open up. And she needed someone to talk to. Was it selfish, just for this moment, to give in to her feelings? She'd reassemble the wall between them later. She rested her head against his chest.

"Until the funeral you hadn't seen her since the car accident?" His voice vibrated against her ear when he spoke.

"No. She left before I woke up in the hospital. It was my thirteenth birthday. Guess that was her present to me." She tried to make a joke of it, but her attempt at a laugh sounded more like a sob. Instantly, Garrett slid a hand beneath her knees and pulled her calves across his legs, snuggling her.

"In her state, it was the best thing she could have done."

Stung, Heather pulled back. "Leave her daughter for pills? That was the best thing?" she snapped.

His thumb brushed down the side of her cheek, his expression insistent. "Better than putting you in harm's way again. I wouldn't have stood for that. Not if I was your dad. Not if I loved you."

The intent look in his eye, the low rumble of his voice as he said the word *loved*, made the butterflies swarming in her stomach take flight.

Oh.

"I would have stayed for my child," Heather answered, her anger at him dissipating. "I wouldn't have waited until years later to start calling. Where was she when I was in high school? A teenager? I needed her."

"She should have been there." Something inside her melted at his earnest expression. "But from where I'm standing, you turned out perfect."

Her breath caught at his sincere tone. "My father didn't think so."

Garrett's eyebrows lifted. "He made you his manager. He thought highly of you."

Heather's lips twisted. "He planned to sell the team. I had only until the end of the season to turn things around and make a profit. Now that's not going to happen."

He angled his head, puzzled. "You straightened out my arm. No one else has done that before. As for the other guys, they're coming around. Besides, now that you own the team, you can decide what to do with it."

She dropped her head. "I don't."

Garrett ducked down to meet her eye, but she turned away, close to breaking down. It'd been a heck of a day.

"Don't what?"

"He left fifty-one percent of the team to my mother." Her anguished confession startled a warbler from its perch. She watched it disappear across the falls, wishing she could vanish, too.

"Why would he do that? You're his daughter." Garrett's voice hardened, his indignation bolstering her.

"Because he never thought I was good enough. Do you know what he said when I won the National Collegiate Player of the Year award?"

"I'm thinking it wasn't congratulations."

"He said, 'You'll never get that twice in a row.'" Her stomach lurched, resentment and longing for him mixing inside.

"But he was wrong. You won two," Garrett responded, surprising her. He'd remembered her father's long-ago speech. Hadn't forgotten that about her.

A ray of pleasure pierced her dark mood. "Right. I know Dad loved me. So why would he leave Mom majority ownership? It makes no sense."

Garrett settled her head on his shoulder and rested his cheek on top. "Maybe she won't be as bad as you think."

"Yeah, sure. She was dangerous before. Now she can make every bad decision she wants, drive this team into the ground and walk away for her next fix."

"You don't think there's a chance she's cleaned up for good?"

"Ha! I know her too well."

"People can change. It's not impossible."

Heather flushed, remembering how she'd

warned him that she could never trust him or any addict. Had pushed him away when he'd kissed her. So why, then, was she telling him things she hadn't even shared with her father?

"How many times did you go to rehab?" she asked.

"Once."

"How long were you an alcoholic before that?"

"Five years. I was twenty-one when Manny got shot."

Heather stiffened in his arms, realization spiking through her. He'd turned to alcohol because of Manny.

"You drank so you wouldn't think about it."

"Basically." She felt his head nod against hers. "And, after a while, because I had to."

"And now you're never tempted." She tried keeping the skepticism out of her voice and failed.

"I'd be lying if I said I wasn't. But I'm committed." He lifted his head, tipped up her chin and looked her directly in the eye. "I can only promise one day at a time. But I'll keep that vow. Continue renewing it. I want more out of life than a bottle."

Heather reached up and touched the sides of his face, unable to stop her impulsive action.

It was sending him mixed messages, the same ones she felt.

"What else do you want?" The question came from a part of her she didn't recognize. Asking a man like Garrett a flirtatious question was playing with fire.

Garrett groaned, longing sharpening his features. "You."

Without waiting for her response, his lips captured hers. She knew she should push him away, but instead her head fell back, her pulse leaping in her throat. The pressure was exquisite as he nibbled and explored. Soft. Warm. Gentle. His lips moved slowly, gradually exerting more pressure.

This felt incredible. Better than the last time. She had to stop this, but need seized her, shoving aside her good intentions.

Her body hummed and a fuzzy sensation filled her head, making it hard to focus on anything but the feel of him, the evergreen scent of the forest and his aftershave heightening her senses.

His hands gripped her waist as she swayed against him, holding her as his mouth sampled her lower lip, then put pressure on the top. Nerves sent small shock waves through her chest, and her hand rose to stroke the back of his neck, making him tremble against her.

Suddenly his kiss intensified, growing fierce and demanding. His lips moved fast against hers, their tongues tangling, causing warmth to explode in her body, melting every piece of her.

She moaned and Garrett's arms tightened, bringing her closer still. Her lips maneuvered against his in response, loving his sweet taste. Garrett shuddered, curling his fist into her hair with a groan. She loved how her touch affected him, how it affected her.

At last his lips let her go, and he looked down at her tenderly, pleasure in his eyes, his chest rising and falling hard.

"I wasn't getting involved with anyone. Planned to focus only on baseball," he said when his breath came easier. "But I can't stay away from you. You follow me, even in my sleep. Your eyes." He kissed each lid. "Your smile." He pressed his lips to each corner. "These freckles." His warm mouth brushed her cheeks.

Her chest expanded, taking in his beautiful words. This incredible moment. And then it hit her, reality a cold shower.

She opened her eyes and scooted away. "Garrett. I don't know."

His eyes moved out over the falls, tracking the sprays of water as they hit the jutting rocks and tumbled to earth. "You don't trust me."

Her mouth opened and closed. He was right. While he touched a chord inside that'd never sounded for anyone else, she still couldn't put her heart in harm's way again. And she knew without a doubt that if Garrett let her down, he'd devastate her as much as her mother had. Even more. She'd loved and lost too many times to try again, especially with her father gone so recently.

"I'm sorry," she said inadequately as he stood and helped her to her feet.

His blank expression gave little away. She wondered if, deep down, a part of him was relieved they weren't taking things further. He'd said he hadn't wanted distractions. And now she wouldn't be one.

"I can't make you believe in me, Heather." His voice was steady and strong. "I need someone who'll give me a chance to earn her trust."

She crossed her arms and looked down at the falls, speaking from her heart. "You could be sober a hundred years and I'd still be waiting for the one day you slipped."

Air escaped him. "I've never had a drink as long as you've known me. Put you in danger."

"It doesn't matter. I'm sorry."

"Me too," he said as they wandered back to the path. "But better to be up front now. So... this is for the best."

She wasn't sure if it was pride talking, or she'd convinced him that they were wrong for each other. Either way, incongruously, she felt let down. Had she wanted him to push it harder? Make her change her mind? If he had, she'd only have distanced herself more. No. He'd made the right call.

Only it felt completely and absolutely wrong.

HEATHER STOOD IN the doorway and watched Garrett back out of her driveway. An ache filled her now that he'd gone. It took everything she had to turn around and enter the lonely house, the only possession—along with partial team ownership—that had been left to her.

"...so Heather, if you get this message, please call me. My number is—"

Heather clicked off the answering machine message, noting the blinking number 5. She'd bet every one of those messages was from her mother, the last person she'd ever want to speak to.

Garrett, on the other hand...

She dropped onto one of the kitchen stools and pressed her flushed forehead against the cool granite. Why was she always chasing after what she couldn't get? Or shouldn't.

If only her father was here. Her feet carried her down the hall toward his room. She hadn't dared to enter it all week. Why torture herself by going inside? But a need to be near him in some form pushed her to turn the knob and step forward, her heart in her throat.

The room was pristine. His bed was smooth, his belongings stored or carted away for donation. Her wonderful female neighbors had twisted through it like a tornado after the funeral. She sent them a silent thank-you. Organizing it herself would have been too painful.

Still, her head swam, and her breath rasped. Being here felt as if she'd stepped into suspended animation. She expected her father's loud voice in the doorway, asking her what the heck she was snooping for.

She slid her hand over the blue quilt, but that wasn't enough to comfort her. She curled up on top of the mattress and buried her face in his pillow, inhaling the subtle musk of his cologne and some other intangible essence that was him. Tears burned her eyes. How strange that his scent stayed after he had moved on.

His clock radio was off, and for some reason she rolled over and plugged it back in. The red digital numbers flashed at her. Stupid. Stupid. Stupid.

But she didn't want time to be over for Dad. For their relationship. Her lungs burned. Now he'd never know how well the baseball camp kids were doing—the one thing he might have been proud about. At least for their sakes.

When she reached across to set the clock, an unfamiliar scrapbook caught her eye. Its brown top appeared through the crack of an open drawer, and curiosity took hold. She rarely remembered her father snapping pictures.

When she pulled it out and opened the first page, she gasped. It was a sonogram picture with his neat handwriting next to it proclaiming "Healthy. Large for age."

Her eyes welled, touched that he'd kept this grainy photo. Why would he do that?

The next page was a birth form that listed her information—her length, weight and so on. And right beside it, he'd written "10 out of 10 Apgar score!" A small smile lifted her lips. He'd always been obsessed with stats.

She flipped to the next page and saw a picture of an infant—her—lifting her head, staring directly into her smiling father's eyes, his cheeks puffed out, his complexion rosy. The words "Lifted head a week before expected" appeared next to the photo, making heat suffuse her face, turning it pink,too, she imagined. She'd shown some strength, even as a baby. Had her father been proud of her? It seemed so.

Her unsteady hands turned page after page of every accomplishment, meticulously preserved and commented on, from a tooth taped to a page with the words "Fearless girl yanked this out with a string" to a spelling bee award she'd won in fifth grade, to her first license, the one she'd thought she'd lost, with the words "Passed on her first try," to her acceptance letter to Morro Bay University with a full softball scholarship, and clippings from newspapers cataloging all of her achievements through the years.

It was like looking at a short film of her life, one that showed only the highlights, the good parts, the things to be proud of. Tears misted her eyes. Had he been proud of her all these years?

She thumbed through the pages again,

unable to believe that this could be true. It seemed, incredibly, that he had thought highly of her. Despite his constant criticism, her father had been proud of her. A hundred-pound weight seemed to fall from her chest, lightness filling her instead.

She'd worked so hard for his approval, yet she'd had it all along. Now that she knew he had believed in her, she realized that she hadn't needed it. Her success hadn't depended on his thumbs-up. She'd accomplished things on her own and would keep doing so…starting with rejoining the team at this afternoon's practice. It'd be hard to see Garrett again after their latest kiss, but they were both professionals. She needed to fulfill the promise she'd made during the team sale meeting. Not to her father, but to herself.

She wouldn't quit on the Falcons.

No matter who was the majority owner.

CHAPTER TEN

GARRETT PROWLED AROUND the locker room later that day, twenty minutes early for the impromptu players-only meeting he'd called. Although these gatherings let the team vent without management around, he couldn't get Heather out of his mind. It didn't matter if she was near or far. He always felt her.

He stopped and leaned against a metal pole. Seeing her back at practice today—the first time since her father's passing—had shocked him. He'd been all thumbs, his thoughts on their afternoon at the falls. Holding her, their kiss, was unforgettable. But she'd closed the door on a relationship. And a part of him should feel relieved.

Only he wasn't.

In the quiet, a leaking shower dripped. Clothes were strewn atop wooden benches, heaped on the floor, or half in and out of open stalls. A carton of bubblegum spilled from a gym bag upended in the corner. Baseball bats were propped against walls, name placards above each locker. The smell of sweat and muscle ointment mingled in the air. It was cooler in here than the eighty-five-degree day, dim and peaceful.

Yet his restless mind wouldn't settle.

Why had he kissed Heather again? He knew better. Wanted to focus solely on baseball and sobriety. Falling for Heather wasn't in the plan.

He turned and pressed his forehead against the cool metal, wishing he could shake her hold on him. She'd been right to push him away. Both times. It was stupid to think she'd return his feelings. They'd both survived tough childhoods. That didn't mean she'd overlook his past. And he shouldn't either. He'd let himself love another person once, and the loss had driven him to drink.

It shook him that his first impulse after dropping off Heather had been his drive to the local liquor store to buy bottles of whiskey. He'd wanted to float her rejection away on malt. Forget her and his anxiety about pitching later tonight. Luckily a call to his sponsor helped. Not wanting to bring attention to himself, he'd put the bag in his trunk and planned on getting rid of it later in an isolated spot. Though a part of him, a dark place he thought he'd shut away, wondered if that'd been an excuse. That he'd kept the liquor as a safety net. A bailout if things fell apart.

Something shriveled inside him. He wouldn't go back there. Yet he'd taken a step in that direction. The wrong way. Those bottles had to go before he relapsed, especially after Heather had surprised him and shown up to practice.

It took guts for her to attend so soon after losing her dad. Though they hadn't spoken, their eyes had met plenty. She inspired him. Had given him the idea to call this pregame meeting.

The sound of the second hand ticking on the wall clock jarred him back to the present. His muscles tensed. Ten more minutes and the guys would file in. He had to put aside his emotions for the good of the team. Say what needed to be said, no matter how Heather had turned him inside out.

He'd had plenty of warning to avoid her. If he needed an even stronger warning, today's trip to the liquor store was it. From now on, she was Skipper only. Forget that she was silk in his arms, the taste of her like wild honeysuckle, her citrus scent driving him insane. Forget that she was the only one who'd made him open up since Manny. That she listened. Understood. Their bond needed to be cut.

When he paced to the front of the benches, he dropped his head into his hands. He'd done the two things the foster system had taught him never to do: felt too much and imagined a different life. Ideas and feelings like that would only lead him astray. Wreck him.

His past promised no future that included a family. Or love. He was a ball player, end of story. That was all he'd ever be good at. He'd tried to be more once, for Manny, and he'd screwed that up. He didn't have a clue how to enter the world of relationships. Better not to try. It just didn't work for guys like him.

The door from the tunnel banged open and Waitman tromped in, followed by the rest of the team.

"Since when do we have meetings right before a game?" the left fielder grumped, his face still red from practice, his hair curling beneath his blue Falcons cap.

"You got a problem with it, we'll talk about it later," Garrett answered evenly. "Alone."

Waitman shrugged and hurried to sit. "Hey. No skin off my back."

"Can't believe Skipper was at practice

today," babbled Valdez as he and some of the younger players crowded by.

"Yeah. She's as tough as her old man," answered another in an awed tone.

"Thought for sure she'd quit and go back to California with Mr. Gadway gone," put in Rob, their center fielder, as he pushed through the group and shoved in next to Waitman.

"She won't give up on us," Valdez said. His crush so obvious it would have been comical if it hadn't irritated the crap out of Garrett. Not that he had a right to be jealous. But no one thought of Heather that way. Not even him. Not anymore.

"Ready for tonight?" Hopson asked as he ambled by.

"Are you?" Garrett drawled, meeting the third baseman's eye. He was exactly the kind of player Garrett planned to reach at the meeting. Now that he'd gotten his priorities straight—namely, no Heather—he was doubling down on his career. He'd been winning more since correcting his arm angle, but his teammates' poor fielding had let him down a few times. They'd allowed runs that shouldn't have happened, hits that weren't meant to be.

Hopson dropped his eyes, then nudged the back of Valdez's striped jersey. "Give me some of those." He held out a hand, and the shortstop poured sunflower seeds into his palm.

Garrett swore under his breath as he looked at the jabbering crew. Their lack of urgency bugged him. The season was at the halfway mark, and their win-loss record was dismal. Seventeen and thirty. If they didn't turn things around now, they'd lose a shot at the playoffs. Didn't they care about that?

"Anyone up for Tailgates after the game?" bellowed Rob, their center fielder.

Garrett held in his angry exclamation. They needed to focus on the game, not their after-hours destination. They played the best team in the league tonight. That called for concentration.

He needed better play from these guys to improve his stats. To impress the scouts and join the Majors, his numbers had to improve. And leaving the farm team meant getting away from Heather, a bonus given how she affected him.

The team needed to accept her. He was done with the lack of effort and commitment under her management. Time to make things right. She was a good leader, and these guys should trust her. Otherwise, they'd end up with a losing season and bad bottom lines of their own.

He held up a hand until the room quieted.

"As most of you know," he began, "I'm not one who believes in all those 'Kumbaya' feelings."

"Someone pass him a tambourine," wisecracked Hopson, whose smile fell when he met Garrett's hard look. The rest knew better than to laugh.

Garrett took a gulp of his sports drink and set it back on the floor. "But there is something we all realize here," he continued. "Without pointing fingers, we know we can do better. Today, everyone saw just how dedicated Ms. Gadway is to helping this team succeed. She put us ahead of her grief by coming to practice and promising not to give up on us."

Valdez leaned forward in his seat and steepled his fingers beneath his pointed chin, nodding.

"We should all look in the mirror and make sure we're giving the best effort we can." Garrett stared around the room, daring anyone to contradict him. No one did.

"Like some of you, I was reluctant to take her advice. However, you can see what it's done for my pitching. Given our record, we can't afford to let our personal feelings interfere with our performance. She has been a coach in the past. She's been around baseball, and particularly this team, all her life."

Several of his teammates nodded while others leaned in, listening. He had them. He could feel it. Heather's unexpected appearance at practice had already softened them up. He was just making the final push.

"Skipper has an innate ability to spot flaws and mechanics. No one before her noticed that I dropped my arm when I got tired. She's talented and driven. Follow her lead, do what she's asked of you during the game, and see where it takes us. We may never be a great team, but we owe it to ourselves, our manager and the late Mr. Gadway to work hard. You never know, we may surprise ourselves."

Valdez lifted his fist. "For Skipper!"

"For Mr. Gadway!" Waitman hollered.

"For the Falcons!" Garrett called and was gratified when the rest of the guys answered.

Hopson clapped his hands together and leaped to his feet. "Let's win this thing!"

"Yeah!" roared the group, and, for once, instead of jogging, they sprinted out of the locker room and onto the field.

Garrett raced with them, smiling. Win or lose, he'd already scored a victory.

IT WAS THE top of the ninth and the crowd stomped its feet, roared and danced along with Freddy the Falcon, the team mascot. The fur-clad figure balanced on top of a railing, clapping its wings and pointing in time to "We Will Rock You." In the distance, men bearing boxes of beverages and food climbed up rows of seats.

"Popcorn. Popcorn here!" they called.

"Cold soda. Get your cold soda!"

"Peanuts. Peanuts. Peanuts!"

Garrett jogged onto the field, his hand sweating inside his glove. The spectators were fired up, and they had a right to be. He was three outs away from shutting out the best team in the league. It was the fresh start the Falcons needed, the vote of confidence from the fans energizing the players. They took their places and zipped the ball to one another, the white sphere arcing against the darkening sky, the air so still it seemed the wind held its breath.

Garrett took the mound and snapped his glove around the ball when Hopson winged it.

"Play ball!" someone shouted from the stands, and Garrett bit back a smile, tucking his emotions somewhere he couldn't feel. He had a job to do. A game to win. He was trying to hold the number one team in the league, the

Panthers, scoreless. It was one-nothing and he meant to keep it that way. The Panthers were the best hitting club in the Minors, and it'd be a big deal for the Falcons to beat them without letting one run by.

Garrett put his glove on his hip and watched as the first batter took warm-up swings in the on-deck circle. Martinez, the fastest guy on the team and a left-handed hitter, Garrett mused. Someone to keep off the bases at all costs.

After a couple more practice swings, Martinez stepped up to the plate and raised his bat. Dean's fingers signaled a fastball away and Garrett wound up, releasing his first pitch.

Martinez turned at the last second, lowering his bat to push the ball down the third baseline.

A bunt.

Hopson charged along with Garrett, who lunged for the ball. He turned and wheeled toward first, firing the ball as hard as he could. Martinez's feet were a blur as he overran first, just beating the throw.

Not a good start. Especially when Garrett noted the next player on deck was a solid base hitter rumored to be heading to the Majors soon. It was going to be a tough out. He dug his toe into the dirt. Any other game, he would have pitched around him. Given up the walk. But this was do or die.

His first pitch flew just outside.

The umpire hollered, "Ball one!"

The crowd quieted slightly.

Garrett set and delivered again, keeping his frustration off his face when the ball dropped low.

"Ball two!"

He stepped forward and caught Dean's throw along with the encouraging nod from his friend.

With his glove raised to his chest, he fired off another that appeared to catch the corner of the dish. Strike!

But the umpire's arm stayed by his side.

"Ball three!"

Garrett's jaw clenched. Bad call. This far down in the count, he had no choice but to groove one down the middle. A good hitter like the Panthers' number one batter would be waiting for a pitch like this. If he homered, the Falcons would lose the shutout and possibly the game.

"You can do it, Wolf," came Levi's unmistakable voice, his howl disturbing Garrett's concentration.

The ball slipped slightly from his fingertips as he released it, and it rose high.

"Ball four! Take your base."

The hitter tossed the bat and jogged to first. The fans moaned, and Freddy the Falcon lowered his head and tucked it beneath his wing, covering his eyes. Garrett wished he hadn't seen that, either.

Out of the corner of his eye, he caught Heather's slim form climbing the dugout steps. He hoped he wasn't being yanked. Not this close. He'd had shutouts before during the early part of his career, but none he needed this badly.

Dean reached him first. When he pulled off his mask, his red hair spiked straight to the sky.

"Are you okay?" His close-set eyes searched Garrett's.

Garrett nodded but waited to answer as Heather appeared.

"Do you have anything left, Wolf?"

He ignored the jerk of his heart when he met her dark green eyes.

"Yeah. I can finish this."

She studied him for a long moment and he kept himself still, thinking about the game, his pitch, this inning, anything but how good it'd felt to hold her earlier.

At last, she nodded. "All right. Don't forget. Keep that arm up."

"Got it."

Her even teeth appeared in a smile that stopped his breath. "Finish them off, Wolf."

And with that, she and Dean ran back to their places, and he stepped to the back of the mound and grabbed the resin bag. He dried off his hands and replaced his glove as the next hitter came to the plate.

He came with heat on the first pitch.

Smack!

A one-hop smash down the third baseline. Miraculously, Hopson dove, snaring it, then scrambling to the third base bag to beat the Panthers' fastest runner.

Incredible. Elation filled Garrett. That was real hustle. Just the kind of play the team needed.

One out and men on first and second.

The crowd went wild, screaming, and the music rose, a rowdy country tune that had everyone stomping.

Garrett tuned it out and angled his body sideways. He let loose on the next batter, aiming for the outside of the plate. But he missed his target, and the ball slid over the middle.

A thunderous crack sounded, and it seemed

all in the stadium, including Garrett, held their breath. The ball sailed high over the Rob's head, a possible home run. Garrett bit his tongue as he watched his wall-shy teammate chase the long fly ball.

The player sprinted toward the wall, looking over his shoulder, his glove held high. Something was different this time. As the fielder stepped on the warning track, instead of pulling up on the gravel, he made two more strides to the wall and leaped. Reaching over the top, he snatched the would-be home run, bringing it back into the park for the second out.

Garrett pumped his fist, even though the runners had tagged up and moved to second and third base. Now there were two runners in scoring position. And the best power hitter in the league sauntered up to the plate and slammed his bat on it.

Meanwhile, Freddy the Falcon waved his wings for everyone to rise, and the crowd eagerly obeyed. It seemed as though all were on their feet, many howling the new call they deemed "The Wolf," according to the waving signs.

One group held up a large sheet that read Wolf Pack, and Garrett turned his head before he smiled. He wouldn't give anything else away right now, not with a known home run hitter facing him and two men on base. He couldn't afford even a single.

He needed this out.

Valdez chucked him the ball, and Garrett held it close to his pounding heart. The Panthers' first baseman squinted at him, and Garrett stared impassively back, ice-cold. His teammates had done their job. Now it was his turn. He had this guy.

Dean signaled, and Garrett delivered a curveball that caught the guy staring as it floated in. He'd been looking for a fastball to drive.

The umpire's right arm shot out, one finger pointing. "Steeeerike one!"

Dean put down three fingers and swiped his index finger to the left.

Garrett raised his leg and threw a scorcher that was fouled back into the net.

The umpire's right arm flashed. "Steeeerike two!"

The roar of the crowd filled Garrett's ears, the blistering noise a wall of sound flooding the stadium. Freddy the Falcon flapped his wings and raced up and down the aisles, looking ready to take flight.

A bugle sounded and the crowd hollered, "Charge!"

The excitement was palpable, though Garrett wouldn't let himself be affected by it. He was the pitcher. In control of the game and himself. One more out. He would do it.

Dean held his glove off the plate for a target, flashing a fastball signal.

Garrett nodded. Dean was right. The hitter had already gone for a fastball and was probably hungry for another. With no balls and two strikes, it was time to make this guy chase a bad pitch. He'd throw an unhittable ball to make the player swing and miss.

But the experienced basher let Garrett's outside pitch go, not fooled.

"Ball one!" called the umpire, and the crowd's noise receded like an ebbing tide.

But just as quickly, the racket started up again, the organ pounding out *dun-dun-dun-dun, dun-dun-dun-dun...*

"Cold beer here!" hollered a vendor, and Garrett marveled how narrowly he'd avoided having a drink this afternoon. Now here he stood, close to earning the Falcons their first shutout of the season. It stung that he hadn't fooled the batter into swinging at a bad pitch. Still, he was confident. He'd come so far, professionally and personally, that he knew he'd never go back. Would Heather ever believe it?

Garrett shook off Dean's signal for a curveball. Time for a changeup pitch. It'd look just like a fastball and might trick the overly aggressive batter into another swing.

He gripped the ball further back in his hand, wrapping his fingers around it to slow down the speed. After leaning in, he lifted his left leg and strode forward, releasing the pitch. Just before the ball crossed the plate, the cocky first baseman swung hard and missed.

"Steeeerike three!"

The crowd shrieked and wailed, and fireworks lit up the sky.

Game over.

Garrett pumped his fist in the air again. Dean rushed the mound, as did the rest of the team. Dean pounded Garrett on the back, and the others gave him high fives.

"Way to go!" Valdez yelled, knocking his knuckles with Garrett's.

"Great pitching, Wolf! Great job," Waitman said, smiling.

"Way to get us out of that jam," Hopson added.

"You guys really bailed me out with those

catches," Garrett said, grabbing both Hopson and Rob in headlocks.

"Yeah. Those were some highlight reel plays," Valdez enthused.

The fireworks continued while the crowd oohed and aahed. Garrett glanced up at a large blue spray, then lowered his eyes as Heather joined them.

"I agree." Her soft voice tiptoed inside him, filling him with warmth. "Excellent pitching, Wolf. Great effort all around."

"We couldn't have done it without your help, Skipper," said Rob, his smile wider than Garrett had ever seen it.

Heather laughed gently. "It was all you, boys. Now clean up and celebrate!"

The group sprinted off the field, jabbering, but Garrett lingered, watching the play of lights reflecting in her beautiful eyes.

"I'm glad you came to practice. The guys played harder because they saw you weren't giving up on them."

Their gazes locked, and his chest squeezed. He couldn't have her. This brave, kind, gorgeous woman who touched his heart in a way no one else, not even Manny, ever had.

"I'd never give up on any Falcon." Her tone suggested she meant more than she said, but he didn't—wouldn't dare—read into her words. Maybe her feelings were as mixed up as his. If so, all the more reason to avoid each other.

"'Night, Skipper," he forced himself to say before leaving the field, wishing like anything that he could celebrate with her.

HEATHER WATCHED GARRETT DISAPPEAR, the ache in her heart growing with every step that carried him farther from her. She'd been right to push him away earlier. If only she hadn't given into her feelings to begin with. She was sending him all the wrong messages, and it wasn't like her to be so indecisive.

Her sneaker slipped a bit on the grass as she headed for the tunnel, wishing she could cheer alongside the guys. But if Garrett was there, she couldn't handle it. Better to keep things separate and professional. Her judgment was bound to be muddled, her reactions impulsive and her heart vulnerable after losing the most important person in her life: her father. Maybe part of the reason she'd kissed Garrett was her need to be close to someone who cared. And the tender way Garrett had helped her after she'd learned about her father's will, how he'd whisked her away, no questions asked, touched her deeply. She sensed that he was there for her, that a bond had grown between them that might be too strong to break.

"Heather!" called a voice that made her shudder and stop.

Explosions of color continued to light up the sky, whistles and pops sounding overhead.

"Since when do we have fireworks?" Heather asked. Her mother, seated at the end of the now-empty front row above the dugout, looked up.

Her mom's smile was bright. "It's fireworks night. I'm planning a number of themed promotional events for the club to draw a bigger crowd. I looked over the books this afternoon, and we need to bring our fans back."

Heather flushed hot. Like she needed her mother, of all people, to tell her this. It took every ounce of her control to bite her tongue instead of giving a blistering response.

"Then you'll know we don't have the money for this."

Her mother stood and leaned over the railing, forcing Heather to take a step back. "You have to spend money to make money. It's an investment, and the fans love it. We had higher attendance tonight than at any other game this season."

Heather grappled to take all this in. Her

mother had been able to focus on their accounting? Was organizing marketing events to fill seats—exactly what Heather wanted… It all felt surreal.

Her mind landed on the only possibility she could conceive. "Is someone helping you?"

Her mother stood straighter and smoothed a hand over her elegant dress slacks and silky top. "I earned a marketing degree before I met your father. For the last seven years, I've been using it to manage public relations for a Manhattan finance company."

"But you're—you're," Heather gasped, the words stumbling over one another and blocking the rest.

"Sober." Her mother raised an eyebrow. "That's what I've been trying to tell you, but you haven't returned my calls."

Heather backed up another step. No. Another lie. It had to be. She wouldn't be fooled, no matter how much she longed for family to fill her father's void. Suddenly it was all too much.

"Why do you care?" The words came from a place beyond conscious thought or will.

Her mother's manicured hands reached over the rail, and Heather lurched back again.

A sad look crossed her mom's face as she lowered her arms.

"Honey, you'll need to sit down with me sometime if you want to know that."

"The only thing we'll ever talk about is the team. And only then when we must. I promised Dad I'd turn this team around, and I won't have you derail it with reckless spending we can't afford."

Her mother shook her head. "You may not think so, Heather. But I'm on your side. Besides, we have an investor."

"Who?"

Her mother's mouth curved up at the corners. "Me."

CHAPTER ELEVEN

A MONTH LATER, Heather followed her equipment manager onto the Falcons bus, exhausted and happy. Players lounged in seats, some jabbering about their triumphant series against the Tallahassee Wasps, others putting in earbuds and leaning their heads against the windows, eyes shut. After a contentious but ultimately victorious three games, the team deserved this rest. These recent wins put their win-loss record at fifty-seven and forty-three, in playoff contention.

A shiver of excitement ran through her. One more win and they'd clinch a spot. It amazed her how much the team had turned around, starting with Garrett's shutout. It'd been a tough four weeks spent grieving her father, dealing with her mother and battling her feelings for Garrett, but she'd managed to focus, and her team had too. She caught her smile in the window as the bus pulled away from the Wasps' stadium, a full moon heavy and low in the midnight sky. Heather couldn't wait to rest and admire the view once she found a seat.

The bus swayed beneath her as she held on to the backs of the seats, looking for an open spot. Valdez glanced up from his phone and flashed a smile, looking like he'd squeeze her onto his lap if he could. Yikes. She hurried to the back and pulled up short at the last available space. Beside Garrett.

Her heart sank. They'd managed to avoid being completely alone, for the most part, until now. The snoozing players in the opposite seat only added to the unwanted sense of privacy.

"Mind if I sit?"

Garrett glanced up from a sports magazine. Studied her before nodding. "Sure."

His blond head lowered again. He turned a page while she settled in. She crossed, then uncrossed her legs, reclined the seat, then straightened it (horizontal was much too intimate a pose), pulled a blanket from her bag, then stuffed it away when it—again— looked too suggestive. In other words, she couldn't have felt less settled.

Garrett's eyes slid her way, and one side of his mouth ticked up.

"Everything okay over there?"

She lost her grip on her bottled water. Before it tumbled into her lap, he neatly caught it.

"Fine. Peachy. Couldn't be better," she chattered nervously, his proximity short-circuiting her brain, apparently. "Why do you ask?"

He raised an eyebrow, then passed her the bottle.

"Thanks." She took a long swallow, wishing she could splash it on her flushed face instead.

"You're welcome." He flipped another magazine page. At his sharp inhalation, she peered at the text.

Minor League Players to Watch proclaimed the headline. She scanned the article and stopped on a picture of Garrett caught midthrow, his powerful legs and arms flexed, his handsome face fierce. Her breath caught. Strange how she'd seen him pitch countless games, but a freeze-frame did something funny to her heart.

A brief bio including his impressive stats appeared beneath his snapshot. They'd dramatically improved when the team had upped its level of play after their win against the Panthers.

"Congratulations. Guess you'll be called up soon." She feigned excitement, though the thought of him leaving made her heart swoop low. They rarely spoke, but seeing him on the field every day comforted her. Made life less lonely—a feeling she battled and lost with her father gone.

He nodded, his gaze still on the page. "That's the plan."

"Has your agent had any news lately?"

He closed the magazine and turned. "The Buccaneers are sending scouts next week."

Her blood froze. Scouts? Once they saw Garrett in action, game over. He'd be gone, and she'd be left behind. But was he ready for the big leagues? It was more pressure. Would he drink again? Although she'd watched him closely this season, there'd been no sign. Yet addicts hid it well. Look at her mother.

Since returning to Holly Springs, her mom had set up office in a space downtown, organizing promotional events that had grown their attendance, slowly but surely. Her efforts, combined with the good press for their baseball camp and their successful last half of the season, had increased ticket sales and, according to Mel, a local diner owner, attracted more business for the town.

It felt good to know things were on track. If only her mother wasn't part of that equation. Though she had to admit, so far, there were no signs of her old behavior. Maybe her mother was telling the truth. She was sober.

Heather cleared her throat. "I guess that means you've achieved your goals. Or nearly."

Garrett scrutinized her for a long minute. "I haven't gotten everything I want."

Her eyes dropped and her heart drummed. Did he mean her? She'd thought, after keeping his distance this month, he no longer cared. That he'd meant it when he said he needed someone who believed in him. A person she could never be. But the intent look in his eye made her pulse speed.

She forced a casual tone and shrugged. "No one does."

He scrubbed a hand over the stubble on his jaw, the shadow giving him a dangerous look. "The Falcons are doing well. You should be proud of that. Your dad would be."

Her hand rose to her heart, touched. "I hope so. Did I ever tell you about the scrapbook I found by his bed? It had everything I ever accomplished—even a baby tooth I pulled out with a string."

Garrett's lips twisted into a lopsided smile. "I'd like to see it sometime."

Why? she wanted to ask, but was afraid of the answer. They'd come to a professional place in their relationship, and she needed to keep it there. So did he—especially if he was heading up to the Majors soon. He had to focus on baseball and sobriety, as he'd said, not on complicated women with trust issues. No matter how much she wished it could be different.

The bus hit a bump that sent a spray of water over both of them.

He tugged the bottle away from her. "You're a menace," he teased, a smile in his voice.

"Public enemy number one," she agreed, her own grin matching his as their eyes met. Suddenly it was impossible to look away. Air stalled in her lungs and pressed hard on her chest. Her skin heated as she lost herself in his blue eyes.

At last, Garrett looked away and out the window. The city lights had disappeared as they coasted up a remote highway, the thrumming of wheels on pavement the only sound. The dark quiet pressed around them, making her acutely aware of the brush of his shoulder and thigh.

"Are you tired?" he asked without turning. "We don't need to talk."

Better they didn't, she thought, but said instead, "No. I mean, not unless you want to go to sleep." She curled up sideways and rested her face against the seat.

He leaned back, his eyes lifted to the ceiling. "Still too keyed up from the game, I guess."

"You did a great job, Garrett. Your pitching has been top-notch."

He turned so that his cheek lay on the headrest, his forehead an inch from hers. Her pulse skittered. A slight move and their lips would touch. Not that they could kiss on a bus full of players, even if more than half were asleep and they were in the last row.

"Thanks." His voice lowered to a husky whisper that did something funny to her heart. "Your advice made the difference."

"And all your hard work," she insisted. "Smythe says you haven't missed a day of the pitching program. He wishes he could sleep in sometimes with his bad hip and all, but you're always there waiting for him."

He searched her eyes. "When I make a promise, I keep it."

If only she knew that was true. He'd vowed to work hard at never drinking again. She'd give anything to believe him, to trust her feelings and follow her heart.

She couldn't deny it. She'd fallen for Garrett. Maybe it was his troubled past that reminded her of her own. Or his drive to make up for it with his present. It could be the warm way he looked at her, like he understood an unknowable part of her and cared. Whatever it was, she felt closer to him than anyone in her life. Yet circumstances couldn't keep them farther apart.

"How are things going?" Garrett surprised her by asking. A change of topic. Good idea.

"The team is good. The baseball camp is doing well. Fans are finally coming back. Even Holly Springs is getting some commerce. Overall, great."

He considered her, his eyes delving into hers. "I meant personally."

"Oh."

"Are things working out with your mom?"

She squeezed her eyes shut, wishing the conversation had taken a different direction.

"If by working out, you mean she does her stuff and I do mine, then yes." She opened her eyes to peer at him. "I guess."

His brows rose. "So you haven't tried to talk things out?"

"Why would we?"

A burst of air escaped him, and his chest rose and fell. "I would have given anything for a parent. Seems right to work things out with the one you have left."

His words swarmed around her, biting.

"She can't replace my father."

Garrett inclined his forehead so that they touched, his skin warm.

"No one can take his place. But your mother's trying to help you. She got the pros down here for an alumni signing night, lets veterans in for free on weekend games, holds after-hours concerts...overall, the actions of someone who wants this as much as you do. Considering that, our improved record and the baseball camp, you two make a good team. Like it or not."

She didn't like it, though deep down she knew it was true.

"We're better off apart. As long as I hear from her only through emails and phone calls, I can handle it." She moved back a bit, his proximity making her stomach jump and flutter.

"You're going to have to hash it out one day."

"Not if I can help it."

"So that's your strategy? Cut out anyone who might hurt you?" His voice rose slightly. She glanced around at the still snoozing players before turning back.

"It's the way I learned to survive."

"How about living?"

Her eyes stung. When was the last time she'd done anything for the simple enjoyment of it? For as long as she could remember, everything had had a purpose. To keep her mom healthy, to impress her father, to save the Falcons... When had she just existed in the moment? Heat crept up her neck as she recalled Garrett's kiss at Looking Glass Falls. That had been pure, thoughtless pleasure.

Something they couldn't repeat.

"What about you?" She pulled back slightly, her tone accusing. "What do you do for fun?"

He ran a knuckle over his upper lip, his expression pained. "Fun's not an option for me."

"Why not?" Heather pressed. "You should get out. Make the most of this second chance."

His quiet words pierced her. "What's the point when you have no one to share it with?"

You could share it with me.

Just as quickly as the thought came to her, she brushed it away. If his words were intended to make a point, they hit the mark. She pulled out her blanket and scooted to the edged of her seat. Withdrew. "I think I am tired." She was beyond caring if the move looked suggestive; she needed space.

Disappointment flashed in Garrett's eyes. He didn't dwell on her comment, however. Instead, he tucked the cloth higher around her shoulders.

"We both are."

"ONE CINNAMON DANISH and a double double." A smiling woman with a long gray braid passed Heather her breakfast order. "Have a nice day."

"Thanks, Mrs. Mapes." Heather dropped her change into the tip jar and turned, bumping into a slight woman behind her.

"So sorry," Heather exclaimed, tightening her grip on her cup of coffee. "I didn't know anyone was—" Her words trailed off when she met her mother's wide eyes. "Oh."

"It's nice to see you, Heather. In fact, I was planning on mailing some paperwork for you to sign, but this will save me the trouble." Her mother pointed to an envelope under her arm. "Will you wait a moment?"

"May I help you?" Mrs. Mapes, the owner of Cupa Java, looked expectantly from Heather to her mother, no doubt noting their resemblance and recalling their dramatic history— past and present. Heather held in a sigh. The proprietor lived to gossip. Was practically the town crier and more informed than the local newspaper. If Heather left in anger, the news would spread fast. It was bad enough she'd reacted so strongly after the lawyer's meeting. She wouldn't give the public anything else to speculate about. Especially when it came to the Falcons.

"I'll be over here." Heather pointed to a small, marble-topped round table beside the door, then sat. The nearby exit comforted her.

After Heather added a third cream to her coffee and scalded her tongue with an impatient taste test, her mother joined her.

"Nice to see you, Renee!"

Heather's mom returned the owner's wave and sat across the table, her eyes crossing.

"Apparently Mayor Watson is out of the office for heel spur surgery, and Peggy Carlton's husband visited the fertility clinic in Raleigh this week." Her mom twisted her slipping hair back into a bun and sighed. "Really? Do we need to know these things before we've eaten?"

Heather held in a laugh. Her mom was right. Breakfast at Cupa Java came with a side order of rumors and scandal. Still. She wasn't here for a Hallmark moment with her parent. No bonding was about to happen. Just scribbling her name on whatever paper her mother had and beating it out of here.

"You said you had something for me to sign?" She fought to keep the resentment out of her voice, especially now that Mrs. Mapes approached. With no other customers, the owner pulled out a broom and swept it slowly around the spotless floor beside their table.

Could she be more obvious?

Heather avoided her mother's laughing eyes and bit into her Danish. The sticky, sweet glaze melted on her tongue, and she chased it with her coffee. Not in a million years would she have believed she'd be breakfasting with her mother. Apparently it wasn't having an effect on her appetite. She had the pastry down to half when her mother produced the paperwork.

"I need your signature to approve these purchases."

Her mother ran down a very practical list of equipment and other acquisitions that were long overdue for replacement.

"Did Reed and Smythe take a look at this?" Heather asked, her eyes running over the inventoried items and prices. How could her mother have identified all of these needs on her own?

"Of course. We've been holding those

weekly meetings. It'd be wonderful if you'd stop in."

"I'll stick to emails, thanks," Heather said dryly, pitching her voice low. The proprietor, blast her, now carefully wiped the sparkling tabletops beside them. What Heather would give to really say what she thought…

Her mother sucked in her lower lip and nodded, her features composed. "Of course."

Heather scrawled her name on a few pages, then stopped on the last.

"You're booking a party planner to celebrate the Falcons getting into the playoffs?"

Her mother lowered her coffee and nodded. "We're going to clinch a spot."

"Mom!" Heather leaned forward when her rising voice brought Mrs. Mapes's head around. "You can't know that."

"I can bet on my daughter. Have faith. You and the Falcons have had an incredible month. You'll pull this off."

Heather stared at her mother, incredulous. Her pupils looked normal-size, her eyes shining but not glassy. When she spoke, her words were crisp, not slurred. It didn't seem like she was using pills… Could this inflated certainty be genuine? After years of harping from her father, it was hard to take in.

"And what if we don't?" Heather's eyes smarted when she thought of how hard they'd all worked to turn the team around.

"Then we'll have an end-of-the-season party. You'll deserve it. What do you say?"

"We still need to conserve costs," Heather grumbled, liking the idea but unwilling to give. She sensed that if she did, she might slip right back into becoming that trusting girl who did whatever her mother told her, including getting into the car that fateful day.

Her mother waved a hand. "This is my money. You just need to approve its allocation. Please sign, Heather."

The industrious barista gave up all pretense and simply stared at them, a dishrag dangling from her hand.

Trapped. To say no sent the message that she and her mother weren't working as a team. Signing would encourage her mother to plan more of these get-togethers. Lose-lose. But when it came to her mom, Heather never won.

She scrawled her name across the line and stood. "Enjoy the rest of your day," she said as graciously as she could, conscious of their avid audience.

Her mom's hand alighted on hers before she could escape. Despite everything, Heather's heart skipped a beat. It'd been a long time since she'd felt her mother's touch. "You too. Have a good one, sweetheart."

Heather forced her feet out the door, wondering why they dragged with each step.

Did a part of her want to stay?

Impossible.

Yet she couldn't explain her smile…or the way her hand tingled long after her mother let go.

"SQUARE YOUR HIPS to the plate," Garrett urged the next day as Levi stood on the mound, his glove to his chest. "Push hard off the rubber."

"There's too much to remember," Levi protested, dropping his arm and rubbing it.

"If you do it often enough, your muscles will remember so your brain can do the thinking."

Levi laughed. "Hah! Muscles having memory. Good one, Mr. Wolf."

"It's true." Garrett pulled a ball from his pocket and tossed it to Levi without warning. The boy caught it and looked up at him in surprise. His freckles seemed to have multiplied under the midday sun.

"See." Garrett smiled. "You didn't have to think to catch that, did you? Your muscles knew what to do. It's instinctive."

Levi nodded. "You're right."

"So let's keep practicing. Eventually this is going to feel as natural as riding a bike."

"I never rode a bike."

Now it was Garrett's turn to stare in disbelief.

"Never?"

"None of the foster families let me near them once they read my record about running away. At the group home, we only have the backyard. Never had a chance to learn."

Garrett's jaw clenched. He hadn't meant to get close to Levi. Wished like anything he hadn't, but something about this kid, his tough life and need for someone to believe in him made him impossible to ignore.

"That ends now. Get your stuff."

Levi looked around the empty ball field. Like usual, he'd gotten special permission to stay longer and work on specific skills with Garrett.

"Am I in trouble?" he asked in a small voice.

For some reason, that irritated Garrett more. He knew what it felt like to have people assume the worst.

"No, kiddo. We're riding bikes."

Levi's eyes widened. He bounced on his toes, excited. "Really?"

"Yes, really. Now hurry up before I change my mind."

Garrett strode out of the stadium, Levi hot on his heels.

"Where are we getting the bikes?"

"The team has some in the training room," he replied once he'd crossed into the cool, shadow-filled tunnel. Since Levi was tall for his age, he could handle an adult-size bike.

Levi tugged on Garrett's shirt. "Where are we riding?"

"The skate park." He ushered his charge into the locker room.

"The big one in Holly Springs?" Levi pranced ahead of Garrett, his face bright with excitement.

"Yes."

"But that's just for skateboards."

Garrett shrugged as he pulled open the training room door. "They have a bike path there."

Levi stopped short as Garrett lifted the bikes off their hooks.

"What if I fall and look stupid?"

"I'll laugh at you."

A snort escaped Levi. They each wheeled a bike outside and down to Garrett's car. He reached for his keys and came up empty.

"What's wrong?" Levi's anxious eyes took in Garrett's frown.

Garrett forced a smile. He wouldn't let anything stop their outing. "Left my keys in the locker room. But I always keep a spare set here." He reached for the magnetic box beneath his car and pulled out another set.

"See?" He dangled the keys. "All set." After opening the trunk and shoving the bikes in as far possible, he tied the top to the bumper with string, securing it. He glimpsed a familiar brown bag, the whiskey he'd yet to throw out. What was he waiting for? He knew he played with fire, keeping it in there, not telling his sponsor, AA group members, Heather…but whenever he went to get rid of it, something stopped him. A low hum of warning that urged him to wait until he was sure that this incredible direction his life had taken wouldn't swerve off course. He had no intention of drinking, but somehow he couldn't pour the bottles out, either.

A snuffling sounded behind him and he turned, catching Levi wiping his eyes.

"Hey, bud. What's going on? Change your mind? Would you rather go home?"

He watched as the boy's shoulders rose, his body tightening all over.

"You don't have to do this," Levi said, his voice defiant.

"Do what?"

"Be nice to me just because I'm a foster kid."

His words slid between Garrett's ribs, slicing him.

"I'm not." He stepped close and put a hand on Levi's bony shoulder. "You're a great kid. Who wouldn't want to hang out with you?"

"No one would." Levi kicked a piece of gravel. "Not superstars like you."

"This one does." Garrett angled his head, trying to catch Levi's eye. "Besides, I'm counting on you falling to make me laugh."

Levi guffawed and lifted his face, his expression relaxing. "Thank you, Mr. Wolf."

"It's Garrett."

The boy threw his thin arms around Garrett's middle. "Garrett," Levi murmured, holding on tight.

Garrett's heart jumped. He squeezed Levi back, remembering his last hug with Manny, then opened the passenger door before scooting around the car to slide into the driver's seat. He started the engine and headed into town, his eyes on the road, his mind inward.

Was he taking a risk, letting himself get this close to another troubled kid? Maybe. But Levi eased his pain over Manny. He could shower the boy with the attention he wished he'd given his foster brother. The wound would never heal, but it was more bearable.

He wanted to be a part of Levi's life. Planned to stay in touch when he moved to the Majors. Levi wouldn't think Garrett had given up on him. The more time he spent with the boy, the more he believed that he could have a real human relationship. One that didn't end in tragedy.

Could that be possible with Heather, as well?

A sign flashed by. Holly Springs, 10 Miles.

Amazing how much he'd come to care for this sleepy town and the incredible woman determined to save it and the Falcons. How could he convince her to trust that he wouldn't fall off the wagon? She'd said she'd always wait for the day he slipped. He shook his head.

It was impossible.

Especially given the bottles lurking in his trunk. She'd never understand that.

If only his brain could convince his heart to stop wanting her so much. He looked forward to being around her each day. Needed to, if he was honest. If he went to the Majors, he'd rarely see her. The thought rattled around the lonely space inside him.

He nodded along, his mind still full of Heather, as Levi chattered excitedly beside him.

Once he would have considered sobriety impossible, but he'd conquered that. A second chance at a professional baseball career had seemed even more out of reach. Yet here he was, getting scouted by his home team, the Falcons one win away from clinching a spot in the playoffs, his bronze AA coin still untarnished, despite his close call.

If he could manage all of that, why doubt that he could have something even more important? Heather. Every conversation they had, small or big, touched him deeply. Laid him bare. She'd come to mean a lot to him. He couldn't imagine his future without her. His fingers tightened on the wheel as he steered them into the skate park.

Somehow he had to get through to her. After tomorrow's game, he'd find a way. He'd grab her before she left and never let her go. Maybe then the part of him that held on to those bottles would let go, too.

"We're here!" Levi bounced up and down in his seat, throwing open the door before Garrett put his car in Park.

"Hold on, speedy."

But Levi was already undoing the string and dragging his bike out of the trunk, metal screeching on metal.

Garrett gently nudged the boy aside and grabbed the wheels, hauling them out. When he looked up, Levi was gone. He swore under his breath. He should have known better than to take his eye off a kid with a reputation for disappearing. With his gaze roaming the park, he slammed the trunk closed.

"Over here!" shouted Levi. He stood with his fingers hooked in a chain-link fence, watching kids on skateboards zipping up and down half-pipes and performing aerial tricks.

"No running away like that again," Garrett growled. Levi looked up, chastened.

"Sorry. Promise not to do it again. But this is so cool. I wish I had a skateboard."

Garrett smiled down at him, already planning the custom board he'd buy Levi. "Maybe Santa will be good to you this year."

The preteen shrugged. "I'm always on the naughty list. Everything I get is practical—like socks."

Garrett pressed his lips together to hold in his angry exclamation. That wouldn't happen to Levi again. Garrett would guarantee it.

He pointed to a large concrete circle between a clump of maples that swayed in the stiff breeze. "Let's start there."

Levi flushed as red as his hair when they reached it. "I don't think I can do this."

"Of course you can't. You've never done it before." He leaned his bike against a tree and rolled the other to Levi.

Levi's shoulders lowered. "Are you really going to laugh at me if I fall?"

"That's *if* you fall, and I promise—though I'm not going to lie, it'll be hard."

Levi snickered, threw a leg over the bike and sat. He reached for the handlebars, then looked up at Garrett.

"What do I do?"

"Put your feet on the pedals. Pump your legs to make the tires go forward. Squeeze the metal bar on the handles to brake."

"Okay." But Levi remained motionless, his knuckles white against the black handles.

"I'll push you off."

Levi nodded. "Don't let go until I say so."

"Got it. Ready?"

"Ready."

Garrett rolled the bike forward as Levi pressed on the pedals, his knees rising and falling. The bike wobbled as they crossed the circle to enter one of the paths.

"Can I let go?" Garrett hollered, racing alongside the bike.

Levi shook his hair out of his face. "Not yet."

They rolled farther down the path. "Ready yet?" called Garrett.

"No." The brakes squealed, bringing the bike to a jarring halt.

"What's wrong?" Garrett squinted down at Levi. The boy's chest seemed to have shrunk into itself, his chin low.

"How do you know when you're ready to do something?"

Garrett raked a hand through his hair. Good question. One he had no solid answer for.

"You just have to have faith. Hope for the best."

Levi squinted up at him. "That's what you do?"

Not as much as he should. Not when it came to Heather. But he was going to change that. "As much as I can."

Levi squared his shoulders. "Okay. Let's go."

Garrett pushed off again. They raced down the pavement, the back of the bike in his grip.

After a minute, Levi yelled, "Ready!"

Garrett's hands dropped to his sides. He

watched with pride as a furiously pedaling Levi wobbled down the bike path.

Levi was riding his first bike. But in the next instant, the boy was down in a tangle of gears and limbs.

Garrett raced to the scene and pulled up short at Levi's laugh. The kid's delighted face shone up at him, his silvery smile glinting in the light.

"Did you see that? I did it! I rode a bike!"

Relieved, Garrett helped Levi to his feet and set him back on the bike.

"Good job, Levi." He pushed the boy off again, watching with a grin as the kid rode away fast, a success.

And all it took was some blind faith.

Time to have some with Heather.

HEATHER TAPPED HER pencil on the conference table, eager for this meeting to start. Mandatory meeting, she corrected herself. Now that her mother was majority owner, she called the shots—and this conference was one of them. Just the two of them. Dread filled her. Would her mother put on a phony sober act? Or worse, would she slur her words? Babble nonsensically? If so, Heather would walk right out. She'd been okay at the coffee shop, but her mother's behavior was as unpredictable as the weather.

The door opened and her mother walked in, the aroma of her expensive perfume preceding her. "You're looking lovely, Heather."

"Thank you." Heather folded her hands in the lap of her dress, careful not to talk more than she had to. As a child, she'd never known which words would set off her mom. Especially when they were alone. At least in Cupa Java, Mrs. Mapes's presence had made her feel safe.

Mom pulled out a fabric-backed chair and slid into it, opposite Heather. Gold hoops swung from her ears, a diamond tennis bracelet on her wrist. She'd certainly done well at the finance company she'd worked for, thought Heather.

Though she hadn't asked, Heather wondered if some of her mother's investment came from her wealthy family. As the sole heir of her deceased parents' fortune, she would have money to burn. But why spend it on the Falcons?

"The parent team owners contacted me," her mother began. "The Gowettes."

Despite Heather's resolve to stay silent, she broke in. "Tell them we're not selling. We're one game away from making it to the playoffs.

Our stadium is nearly selling out every night. There's no need to hand it to them." Heather's pulse zipped through her, adrenaline making her knees jitter beneath the table.

"I agree," her mother surprised her by saying, a small smile appearing on her carefully made-up face. Heather looked away, Mom's former snarl juxtaposing, in her memory, with the now friendly expression.

Heather twisted her sweaty hands in her lap. It was beyond uncomfortable being this close, physically. Deep down, it terrified the part of her that recalled every out-of-control moment from her childhood. At any second, her mother could rip off her nice mask, revealing her old hurtful self.

"They want to send up a Double-A third baseman, Tony Formetti."

"But the trainers told me they'll clear Hopson to play any day. His ankle's nearly healed." Heather hated taking orders from the parent team, especially when it involved her players.

"I explained that as well, but they feel Hopson's on his last season. Since they're not renewing him, they want Formetti to get some playing time in now."

Heather sucked in a hard breath and coughed. Her mother hurried to the credenza, returning with bottled water and pushing it across the table at her.

"Hopson's come a long way this season. He's made some great plays, showed more hustle..." Heather's hands shook slightly as she lifted the bottle and drank. Poor Hopson. All that effort and now this. The decision was business, but that didn't make it easier.

"My hands are tied." Her mom's sculpted brows came together, a line forming between them. "I'm sorry. I wanted to let you know first. Ask what you'd like to do with George for the rest of the season."

Bitterness rose in Heather's throat, eroding what she'd intended to say. How could her mother look so composed? So unaffected? But then again, she'd never had any real investment in the players or this team. Not, Heather qualified, until recently. Her reasons for getting involved still defied understanding. Many of her mother's actions always had.

"I want to play Hopson," Heather said firmly. "Tomorrow, if he's cleared."

Her mother splayed manicured hands in front of her. "Even though the playoffs are on the line?"

"Especially because of that," Heather insisted, certain. "If this is George's last year, then he deserves the glory. He's earned the spot, not some unknown player from a Double-A team. We'll win with Hopson if he's healthy. I have faith."

A slow smile spread across her mother's face. "And I trust your judgment."

Heather sank against the back of her seat. Just like that, her mother had confidence in her. No criticism. No second-guessing. Just blind faith like in the coffee shop. It was such a strange, heady sensation.

A soft hand fell on hers. "Sweetheart, I know I haven't been the best parent to you. Not by a stretch. But please know that I never stopped loving or believing in you."

Suddenly the words, long held back, tumbled out of Heather before she could prevent them.

"Then why didn't you quit taking pills? Why were drugs more important than me?" She ducked her head, her features contorting as she strove to control herself. This was a business meeting. She hadn't planned on it dissolving into a family intervention.

Her mother hurried around the table and sat beside Heather, wrapping an arm around her. "I was sick. Plain and simple. There wasn't anything you or Daddy could do. In fact, in lots of ways, you saved my life."

"You nearly cost me mine."

Her mother's sudden quiet made Heather look up. The color had drained from her face, leaving only bright pink blush and matching lipstick behind.

"There's no excuse for what I did that day," her mom said, her voice a notch above a whisper. "Getting behind the wheel while under the influence, letting you in the car with me—it's the most disgusting thing a person can do."

Heather nodded. Turned toward her mom. Finally, an apology along with what sounded like genuine remorse. Surely her mother couldn't be this good at faking her sincerity?

"That's why I left when the hospital discharged me," her mother confessed after blowing her nose.

Shock rolled through Heather like a thunderclap. "I thought you didn't want us anymore."

Her mother took in a shuddering breath. "Oh, honey, I wanted you so much. But I wanted you safe more. The only way to guarantee that was to stay away until I got sober. Your father and I agreed."

"Dad knew about this?" Heather gripped the

edge of the table, sure she'd slide to the floor if she didn't.

"Yes. Once the drugs cleared from my system, we had a long talk to decide what was best for you. We still loved each other, but we knew we were better off apart."

"That's why he left half the team to you," Heather breathed. "He loved you."

"No." Mom shook her head. A wisp of brown hair fell from her bun and curled beneath her chin. "He cared so much about both of us that he hoped it'd get us together."

"Is that what he told you?" Heather tossed back another drink of water, heated and off balance.

"He mentioned it a lot. The last time was right after his heart attack. But I always said no. The entire team should belong to you, Heather. When it's safely in the black, I'm signing my share of it over."

Heather's mouth dropped open. At last she was getting her team. But a tug of unease dampened her excitement. This wasn't what her father wanted. Had he hoped to save not only his team but also his family by reuniting his wife and daughter? Shouldn't Heather care about that, too?

"How often did you two speak?"

Her mother's cell phone buzzed. Without looking away from Heather, she clicked it off. "Mostly on your birthdays and holidays. Those were the toughest times for me. He always gave me updates, told me all of the amazing things you were doing. He was so proud of you."

"I wish he'd told me." Despite her efforts, Heather's sentence ended in a watery gulp.

"Oh, honey. That wasn't his way." Heather resisted her mother's attempt to hug her.

"But his father was like that," her mom continued, twisting two rings on her left index finger. With a start, Heather recognized her mom's wedding set. "He parented you the way he was brought up. Good or bad, it's the best he knew how. He cared so much about raising you right. Called me sometimes about that."

Understanding took root inside Heather and sprouted.

"I'm ashamed to say," her mom continued, "that at first, I wasn't always sober enough to advise him. I guess he parented you the only way he knew how, by showing you what you'd done wrong so you wouldn't do it again. He wanted to make up for you not having a mother. Hoped he'd help you be your best, despite having only him, but I suppose he went overboard. It came out of love, even if it was wrong."

Heather's chest expanded, making room for the knowledge flowering inside. Her father wasn't perfect, but he had done what he could to be the best parent for her. She peered at her mother's earnest face. Was it possible another loving parent sat beside her?

Suddenly she knew what she had to do.

In a swift move, she swept her mother into her arms, holding her close until her mom's rigid body collapsed against her.

"I love you, Heather," her mom whispered in her ear.

"I know," Heather replied, meaning it.

Sometimes you had to trust others not to let you down rather than pushing them away.

And, she finally realized, perhaps that included Garrett.

CHAPTER TWELVE

GARRETT FINISHED UP with a reporter, then headed off the field to the locker rooms. He was ready to celebrate tonight's all-important win—preferably with Heather.

"Psssssst! Mr. Wolf. I mean, Garrett!" someone stage-whispered.

He looked up at the bleachers beside the tunnel, surprised to see Levi alone. His thin body swam inside Garrett's present: an over-size blue-and-white Falcons jersey.

"Hey, Levi. Where's your group?"

"Waiting for me at the bus, but Mr. Lettles is still here. He's in the bathroom." Levi jerked his thumb over his shoulder. "Great game."

"Thanks. It was a big one."

"This means the Falcons are in the play-offs, right?"

Garrett nodded. He was filled with pride that he'd won this clincher. "We have more games to go," he said, his mind on the scouts coming in a few days. "But win or lose, we're heading to the playoffs."

Levi held out his knuckles. They fist bumped. "The Falcons are going to be league champions! Here." He reached into his pocket and pulled out a glittery gold-and-green four-leaf clover sticker. "I had to spend two dollars to win this, but I wanted to give it to you. For good luck."

Touched, Garrett took the sticker. Levi was a good kid, no matter the bad rap he'd gotten in the past. If Garrett moved up to the Majors, he'd make sure they stayed close. As for now, however, he needed to leave and catch Heather. Tonight, he'd convince her to count on him, on and off the field.

"Thanks, Levi. We'll do our best. How long has Mr. Lettles been gone?"

Levi looked over his shoulder, then shrugged. "I don't know. Maybe I should head back to the bus. They could have left without me."

"I doubt that, but I wouldn't hold them up. If Mr. Lettles looks for you here, I'll let him know."

Despite Garrett's urging, Levi remained. "Or you could drive me back. Maybe we could stop for ice cream…"

Garrett's heart sank. He hated saying no to the kid. Especially when he looked that hopeful. But he had to get to Heather. With the season slipping away and a good chance that he'd be called up to the Majors soon, he wouldn't waste another minute.

"How about ice cream tomorrow?"

To Garrett's surprise, Levi shook his head. His freckles stood out under the stadium's bright lights. "Can't tomorrow. It has to be now."

Garrett's eyes narrowed. "Why? What's happening tomorrow?"

"Can we just go for ice cream?" Levi's voice rose, wheedling. "I'll tell you then."

"I'm sorry, Levi. I can't tonight. Let's go biking the day after tomorrow. We'll stop for treats afterwards."

Levi looked down. Shuffled his feet. Quiet, for once.

Garrett moved closer to the railing. "Are you okay?"

"It'll be too late then," Levi muttered.

Concern filled Garrett. "What will be too late?"

Levi shook his head. He raced up the aisle, taking the cement steps two at a time.

Worried, Garrett pulled out his cell phone

and dialed Mr. Lettles. A message announced the voice mail box was full. He swore under his breath.

"Mr. Wolf." A man in a tailored suit, his hair gelled, stepped forward. Garrett turned. "I'm Andrew Layhee from WHCN TV. Would you have time for a quick interview?"

Garrett looked from the top of the stadium seats to the camera. Doing press was part of his job, and turning down an interview with Raleigh's biggest news channel would label him as the rude, uncooperative player he used to be. With scouts scrutinizing him, he couldn't afford a misstep. Mr. Lettles remained on the upper level. A bus waited out in front. Levi would be safe.

Still, guilt swamped him for not taking Levi out. They'd done it plenty of times before. But tonight he had other plans. He'd make it up to the kid. Fix whatever was bugging him then. At war with himself, Garrett extended a hand. "Sure. I can only give you a few minutes, though."

"That's fine." Andrew adjusted his tie. After holding up his microphone, he faced the camera with a broad smile.

"I'm here with Garrett Wolf, standout pitcher for the Falcons. The team just made the playoffs with a dramatic turnaround, winning forty of their last fifty games, thanks in large part to your work. What was the key to your comeback?"

Garrett's mind flashed to Heather, her lovely face as she pointed out his arm slot issue, her determination in winning over the rest of the team. "Well, we knew the talent was here. It was just a matter of it all coming together. Our new manager gets a lot of credit for that."

"About your manager. She's the first female manager in the Minor Leagues. How is that different for you?"

For a moment he imagined Heather in his arms. Her body soft and pliant against him. Her lips tasting of honeysuckle. Spending time with Heather was special. She'd opened him up. Changed his outlook. He couldn't wait to find her so he could tell her. He brushed his gritty hands on his shirt, stalling. Finally, he looked up into the camera.

"We're all professionals, and the main thing is that Ms. Gadway knows baseball and is respected for that. It makes no difference whether she's male or female. We don't see that on the field."

Andrew grinned like a cartoon character. His head bobbed.

"You're a bit of a Cinderella story yourself. Out of baseball for three years and now a serious Major League prospect. How do you explain that?"

Again, the incredible woman who'd made that possible captured his imagination. He couldn't wait to speak his heart to her.

"I have new priorities in my life. My number one goal is staying sober. I always knew I had the ability to make it to the Majors, but my drinking got in the way. I also had some mechanical issues which, thankfully, our manager noticed and helped me to correct. I'm thankful alcohol is out of my life and Heather Gadway is in it."

Andrew shot him a puzzled look, then quickly recovered his professional polish. "And what are your expectations for yourself and for the team going forward?"

That's where things got murky. He knew what he wanted for the team. When he imagined leaving Heather for the Majors, his thoughts stalled. It was his lifelong dream, the way he'd ensure Manny had not died in vain. But what if his dream was changing?

Garrett forced a charming smile, adding a laugh to sound less serious than he felt. "A championship for our team and a Major

League position for me would be a good start." His smile slipped. He was ready for this interview to be over.

The sharp-eyed reporter gave his cameraman a subtle nod, then held out a hand to Garrett. "Good luck, Garrett, and thank you." He turned back to the camera. "This is Andrew Layhee with WHCN."

Garrett raced down the tunnel. "It's been a pleasure—" he heard the broadcaster say behind him.

"Same," he called over his shoulder with a wave.

Though the pleasure he had in mind had to do with a certain green-eyed beauty.

CHAMPAGNE CORKS POPPED in the Falcons locker room. The teammates sprayed one another with liquid. Their cheers echoed in the space as trainers, coaches, players and local reporters jostled for elbow room. Heather watched from a corner, taking it all in. Where was Garrett? Tonight's win guaranteed them a spot in the playoffs. The farthest the Falcons had gone in over ten years. Pride for her players filled her. They'd worked hard, and their efforts had paid off. They deserved this frenzied celebration.

Hopson jumped onto a bench. His ankle

healed, he did some kind of jig. "Woo-hoooooooooo!" he called, dumping an entire bottle of champagne over Waitman's head.

Waitman, who'd scored the final homer that'd won the game, shook off the fluid. He grabbed Hopson around the knees, lifting him in the air and twirling him. "We did it!"

"OW-OOOOOOOOOOOOOOOOH," the Falcons howled when Garrett strode through the door. Heather couldn't tear her eyes away from the gorgeous man. He'd struck out thirteen players. Had given up only one run. An incredible performance. His move to the Majors would be a big loss for the Falcons…and for her. But she intended to do something about that. Soon.

She watched as he pulled off his cap, damp blond hair falling across his forehead. His blue eyes swerved her way, catching her staring. Their eyes locked until someone grabbed his arm. Dean pulled him away. Perhaps he didn't want Garrett around all the champagne? Funny how that hadn't occurred to her… It proved that she was ready to trust him, just as she now had faith in her mom.

As Garrett disappeared in the crowd, a cheer broke out in the back of the room, led by Valdez.

"Let's hear it for Skipper!" he called from atop another bench. He leaned forward, a hand cupping his ear.

"To Skipper!" roared the other young players crowded around him.

"Who?" Valdez hollered again.

"To Skipper!"

Whistles and whoops followed, making Heather glow like a lightning bug. A slim arm slipped around her waist. She started, still adjusting to her mother's affection.

"Congratulations, sweetie. I knew you could do it. Deep down, your father knew, too."

"Having the extra fans in the stands helped, Mom." She held herself still, resisting the urge to pull back. Her dad wanted them to work this out. Now, she did, as well. "It really motivated the players. We couldn't have had that great second half of the season without the momentum you built."

Her mother's hands slid down and grasped hers. Her mom leaned back and smiled at Heather. "Honey, showing up to practice just a week after losing Dad, that showed the players how much you wanted to win. It proved it to me, also. Let's call it a team effort."

"Whatever happens in the playoffs, I already feel like I won. I love you, Mom."

Her mom grew tearful. "I don't deserve that."

Heather touched her mother's cheek. "You've worked hard to get to where you are now. So, yes, you do."

A blinding flash interrupted their hug. They blinked up at a man wielding a large camera.

"Jim Bosch with the *Raleigh Telegraph*." He flashed a smile and held out a hand as his assistant took more shots. "I'd like a few comments on tonight's win if you have a moment." He shook Heather's hand, then her mother's.

Before Heather could respond, her PR-conscious mother nodded. "Of course. Shall we step outside where it's quieter?"

The photographer snapped additional pictures of the exuberant team, then followed them into the tunnel. Above them, the whisking of brooms sounded, workers busy cleaning up the stadium. The only other noise was the occasional crash followed by raucous laughter inside the locker room.

"I'd like to begin by giving you my condolences for the loss of your father, Dave Gadway."

The familiar ache at hearing her father's name scoured Heather's heart, but it was duller than it'd been in weeks. She could breathe through it.

"Thank you."

"I understand you were hired as his general manager when he failed to offer a fair contract to your predecessor. Was that a planned move?"

Heather gasped. "My father would never force someone out of a job."

"Not even to make way for his daughter?" The reporter's friendly smile didn't reach his sharp eyes.

"We were in financial trouble, so I was taken on without salary. It was the only way to keep the team afloat," she blurted, too incensed to think before she spoke.

The reporter rocked back on his heels. His cheeks puffed out as if he'd just eaten a canary. His pencil flashed across his notepad.

Heather's mother stepped forward, forcing the reporter back. "My daughter has attended nearly every practice, advised and motivated this team to their winning position. Paycheck or not, she is the first female manager, and doing a better job than many other managers in the league who wish they'd made the playoffs." Her mother straightened her spine and raised her chin. "Besides, the team is now firmly in the black and, although she is also co-owner, she will be offered a contract. I'd hoped to surprise her with the news tonight rather than reveal it this way, but that's your answer."

Instead of looking cowed, the reporter's expression grew pinched. It gave his narrow face a feral appearance as he looked up from his notepad. "Yes. I understand you are Mr. Gadway's wife, Renee Gadway, or is it ex-wife? We haven't heard much from you since your nasty car accident. Can you explain your whereabouts during the past fourteen years and how you came to own the majority share of the Falcons?"

Heather felt her mother stiffen beside her. She leaped into action.

"My mother had to travel for her job, but she was in regular contact with the family. Her dedication has been constant. As for her ownership of the Falcons, my father always had an eye for talent. He knew the right person for the job. My mother."

Heather wrapped an arm around her trembling mother to draw her close. "Any other questions?"

The reporter backed away, shaking his head. "I think we have everything we need." He signaled to his assistant to follow him back inside the locker room again.

"We'll have to rethink some of the press credentials we hand out," Heather said.

Heather's mother snorted at her quip. Her eyes were wide as she gazed at Heather. "You didn't have to cover up for me."

"Mom. You *were* traveling. And your job was to get better so that you could come home and I…" Heather choked up, emotion pressing her words against the back of her throat. "I am so glad that you did. Dad was right to make you an owner. I hope you stay on for as long as you want. I'm happy working with you and managing the team."

Her mother pulled her close. Heather buried her head in her mom's neck, inhaling her familiar perfume, her heart full.

"Honey, I'm thrilled. How about fifty-fifty ownership? Right down the middle."

Air expanded Heather's lungs. Finally, she'd achieved her goals. She'd helped her hometown, saved the Falcons, and proved to her family and herself that she could lead them.

Now for her next goal: Garrett. Her life was full. But as he'd pointed out on the bus, none of that mattered if she didn't have someone to share it with.

Before she saw him again, though, there was one final place she had to visit. A part of her childhood she needed to let go before she could embrace a future with Garrett.

After everything they'd been through, would he still want her?

"Skipper? Has anyone seen her?" A showered Garrett pushed through his partying teammates, his sneakers squishing on the damp, sticky floor.

Hopson's eyes were red-rimmed. Bleary. "Don't know. She was over there." He pointed to an empty corner.

Garrett made his way farther into the crowd, searching. He bumped into Valdez. "Have you seen Skipper?"

"She went off with some reporter. Didn't even come back. Was hoping for a hug."

Garrett clapped him on the back, hard. "Keep dreaming, because it isn't going to happen."

Valdez opened his mouth, then shut it at Garrett's look. "Anyway, she went that way." He pointed to the exit door, then backed into Waitman. The move spilled the veteran's drink on his jersey. Waitman whirled, arm up. Garrett ducked out.

Drinking and crowds were a bad mix. What started off as fun often ended in a brawl. Once he would have enjoyed working off excess energy by scrapping. Now, he needed to find Heather.

Outside, he nearly ran into her mother as she finished talking to Andrew Layhee.

When the reporter sauntered away, the new owner turned to face him.

"Great work tonight, Garrett."

"Thanks, Mrs. Gadway." He ran a hand through his damp hair. "Have you seen Heather? I mean, Skipper?"

Her eyes, so similar to Heather's, bored into his. "You like my daughter, don't you?"

His restless movement stilled. "What do you mean?"

She led him out to the empty parking lot where they wouldn't be overheard.

"No need to deny it. I've seen the way you look at each other when you think no one notices."

"I'm not sure—"

"How you feel?" Mrs. Gadway cut him off, waving a hand in the warm night air. "I doubt that. You seem like a man who knows his mind. Let's face it, my daughter's a good catch."

He stuffed his hands in his pockets, more uncomfortable by the minute. She was right, but these were things he wanted to confess to Heather, not her mother.

"She's an incredible woman," he said as neutrally as possible.

"Yes, which is why I need to get this off my chest." Mrs. Gadway crossed her arms. "I'm talking to you as a mother, not your team owner." Her deep-set eyes met his. "Obviously you know my history." Her voice lowered but remained strong. "We've listened to each other speak at AA meetings—although we haven't spoken to each other."

He kept his face impassive and nodded. It'd been uncomfortable the first time she'd joined his group a month ago. They'd kept a respectful distance from each other, a pretense of being strangers—which they were, more or less.

Mrs. Gadway's head dipped slightly. "Then you know why we need to talk before things go any further."

He nodded. He supposed he did. "Yes, ma'am."

"Heather seems strong, but she's had a hard life." Mrs. Gadway twisted her lips in a grimace. "She doesn't deserve more hurt."

He opened his mouth, but she held up a hand, silencing his protest.

"It's obvious you're committed to recovering. You're at more meetings than I would have expected with your schedule."

When she paused for breath, he jumped in. "It means a lot to me. As does Heather. I would take myself out of the equation before ever causing her pain."

Her eyes narrowed. "Promises like that are hard to keep for people like us."

Garrett nodded. "True. But she's worth it. I care more about her than anything else, including alcohol."

"Even baseball?" Her quick question cut to the heart of the matter, one he still grappled with since advancing his career meant leaving Heather. "If you had to choose, who's the winner?"

"I suppose I'd work it out so that we both won. But that's still hypothetical. What I know is that a life without Heather is no life at all. Not for me."

Mrs. Gadway's eyes glistened.

"May I ask you something?"

She nodded.

"Where's Heather?"

Mrs. Gadway caught him in a swift hug,

then let go. "Take care of my girl," she whispered gruffly. "She said something about going to her thinking spot…"

Garrett remembered Looking Glass Falls but rejected the possibility. Too far.

If she hadn't gone there…then it hit him…

The dugout.

HEATHER LAY ON the worn bench of the old field's dugout, looking up at the ceiling, surrounded by gloom. The dugout was freshly painted now. The warped boards replaced. The cobwebs wiped away. But it still felt familiar. Comforting.

After a tumultuous few months, she needed this quiet moment. Her heart was in a tailspin. She was falling fast for Garrett. Would she land softly? Or crash and burn?

Her gut told her that she could trust Garrett. That it was time to believe instead of question. Yet she hesitated to take the final step. Lay her splintered heart bare. If she didn't, however, she'd be as stuck in her past as this renovated dugout.

Her fingers slid under the bench, feeling the grooves she'd once dug with her fingernails. How many hours had she spent here, wondering why she wasn't good enough? Why her mother preferred pills to her? Why her father saw only her faults?

But now she knew the truth. Her world looked as different as this dugout. Garrett was a recovering addict. A label he'd carry for the rest of his life. But he was also someone she could depend on. He'd vowed to work hard never to drink again. She needed to trust him. Knowing that she'd been loved had begun to heal her childhood wounds. She was strong enough to embrace a future with Garrett now. To believe that, like her mother, he cared enough to stay clean. Wouldn't lie to her.

She bolted to her feet, ready to knock on Garrett's dormitory door. Tell him so. But he appeared out of the darkness, a flashlight bobbing by his side.

"What are you doing here?" she gasped, both pleased and surprised.

He stepped inside, the light illuminating his gold hair and tanned skin. "Looking for you." The deep grit in his voice made her tremble, despite the balmy evening.

"I was going to find you."

He drew closer still. His strong hands wrapped around hers. "And what were you coming to say? 'Atta boy'?" His full lips quirked at the corners, his dimples appearing.

The smile transformed him from handsome and edgy to all-American cute. Her insides jittered when she met his eyes.

His fingers laced with hers, and she breathed in his clean, outdoorsy smell. It was hard to think with him this close.

"Let's sit," he said, leading her back to the bench.

They settled close, their bodies touching from calf to shoulder.

"So what were you going to tell me?" he asked when the silence stretched to its breaking point.

"Atta boy," she murmured.

His deep chuckle sounded. "Do I get a reward?" He tipped her face to his. The passion in his eyes swept her breath away.

"Garrett—" she pulled back. "We need to talk."

"That's never a good start to a conversation."

"This time it might be. I hope."

Their eyes met. "I hope so too."

"You first," they said at the same time. Their laughter trailed off into silence again.

In the dim beyond the dugout, a lone bird trilled, then hushed, a flap of wings whispering in the night. The stars twinkled, diamond pushpins in black velvet. The sliver of moon carved out a white C in the sky. All was calm. Tranquil. Everything but her.

"I spoke to your mother," Garrett surprised her by saying.

She glanced up at him, wishing his eyes weren't in shadow, the flashlight no longer reaching them. "What did she say?"

"That she noticed the way we look at each other."

Heat overran Heather's face. "Is it that obvious?"

"Maybe to a mother. But I don't think the guys know. Definitely not Valdez. He'd probably call me out for a duel."

She laughed. He had a point. "What else did she say?"

Garrett brought her palm to his mouth for a shivery kiss. "That you've been hurt enough. She's worried another addict will put you through more pain."

"Oh, Garrett. I'm sorry. I—"

He placed a finger against her lips, hushing her.

"It's nothing you haven't said. I've been questioning myself, too. I wasn't sure if I'd drink again under the pressure of performing for the team and having the foster kids around. But it forced me to deal with old issues. Thank you for that." He pressed her palm against the scratch of his jaw stubble.

"You're welcome," she breathed. Anticipation shook through her. Was he about to open up? Share his feelings about how they could be together?

"There's only one answer," he continued, ducking his head to give the center of her palm a light kiss. His fingers trembled slightly against hers.

"Faith," her heart spoke for her, knowing deep down that it was all they needed.

His eyes flashed to hers. "You mean everything to me," he said, his voice hoarse. "More than alcohol ever could. I don't want my old life. Being numb. Not feeling pain or anything else. I'd miss out on all of the incredible things—like the way I feel about you. In your arms, the world makes sense."

Her heart stuttered. She twined her hand in his, loving his calloused flesh against her tender skin. This blissful moment seemed too incredible to be real. "You care about me."

He pulled her close and spoke softly into her ear. "'You are whatever a moon has always meant and whatever a sun will always sing.'"

She angled her face upward, wonder filling her. "That's my favorite poet."

"E.E. Cummings." Garrett rested his chin beside her temple. "I read when I was bored. When I got through the children's books, I moved on to poetry." He wrapped one of her wavy locks around his finger. "That one suits you."

So beautiful, she thought. Would she have ever guessed that this hotshot, recovering alcoholic pitcher would one day recite poetry to her? It was a dream.

"'I think I made you up inside my head,'" she quoted from one of her favorite poems, meaning every word.

"Sylvia Plath." Garrett gathered her hands in his and looked down at her steadily, his eyes tender. "We're not imagining this, though. I said I needed someone who believed in me. But I have faith for both of us. Give me a chance. I'll make you happy every day for the rest of your life."

Her heart glowed bright. It was exactly what she needed to hear. However, this wasn't all about her.

"I do believe you." Even through his T-shirt, she soaked up his warmth and energy. "That people can change. That they won't let me down. You never will."

"Not in a million years." The words were reverent enough to be a prayer.

She rested her head on his shoulder. Despite being pushed away, he still cared. Hadn't given up. Had fought for her. He was everything she'd never wanted, but now, couldn't live without.

"Do you trust me, Heather?" At the slight shake in his voice, she looked up. She glimpsed the foster boy asking Santa for parents.

"With my whole heart."

His eyes blazed down at her with an intensity she'd never seen before.

He dipped his head, his lips a kiss away from hers. She swayed against him, flooded with feelings. She could feel her pulse at every pressure point. A wave of warmth rolled through her, and she tugged at her collar. His fresh, outdoorsy scent enveloped her, and her heart tripped over itself.

Garrett ran his hand through her hair, and every cell in her body vibrated with the gentle pull.

"Heather."

"Yes." It was hard to breathe.

"Kiss me."

Garrett didn't wait for an answer. Instead his lips met hers, and his arms slipped around her body. Within seconds, their mouths parted against each other. She lost herself, loving the way her body molded with his, how Garrett gripped her hair while he traced the ridges of her spine.

Shock waves and earthquakes. Both happened at the same time as their mouths coaxed and teased. She couldn't get enough of him. The nearer she drew, the more she wanted to crawl inside this delicious world of warmth.

Garrett hooked an arm around her waist, and their breaths sounded in unison. Her fingers curled into the muscles of his arms.

As much as she loved this, however, it was time to slow things down. The relationship was all so new.

"Too much?" he asked, pulling away when her lips stilled against his.

"Not enough. That's the problem."

His devilish smile, full of male ego, made her swat him. He sat up straighter and held her tight against his side.

"Better?"

"Let's just say it's for the best."

He rubbed the sensitive spot near the curve of her neck. "We have all the time in the world. I'm not going anywhere."

Wonder filled her, a light that chased away

the last of her shadows. She pressed a soft kiss to his jaw. "We can always count on us," she sighed and snuggled closer. "I'll never doubt that again."

CHAPTER THIRTEEN

GARRETT PUNCHED OFF his alarm clock and rolled onto his back, arms crossed behind his head. The past few days had blown his mind. Heather filled his thoughts nonstop. His heart, too. Every chance possible, he pulled her aside, kissing and holding her like he had after last night's jog. Their conversations stretched long into the warm summer nights. Everything they had in common——baseball card collecting, caring about the camp and its kids, their mutual love of the sport—brought them closer. It was hard sticking to their decision to keep the relationship a secret until the season ended. Until they knew for sure that he was moving to the Majors. Hiding his feelings around the other guys was tough.

Watching her without wanting to touch her… to hold her? Not happening. Meeting her eyes without giving himself away? Impossible. He groaned, wishing he could see her now, though they'd be together later at practice. No matter how much time they spent together, it was never enough.

Amazing how all that he'd thought he'd never have—a loving relationship, a promising career—had come together. And the last woman he'd thought he'd ever care for was also the person who'd helped him achieve his dreams.

Everything was falling into place. He shoved off his covers. Sitting on the edge of the bed, he listened to the light rain tapping on his window.

Was he ready for all of these changes? Yesterday, Heather told him the scouts who'd watched him pitch Wednesday wanted him for the Majors. Neither he nor Heather had spoken up about what it meant to them. How they'd handle the separation.

What if he lost Heather because of distance? He'd spend a long season away with the Buccaneers, commuting when he could to Holly Springs. And she couldn't join him on the road. She had a career of her own. He respected that. Wouldn't ask her to sacrifice for him.

He strode to the bathroom and turned on the shower. While waiting for the old plumbing to warm up, he caught his reflection in the mirror. Strange that he looked the same. Inside, he was a new man. Heather's doing. Somehow they'd stay together. Make it work.

Now he just had to get rid of those bottles. It was time. Overdue.

Beneath the lackluster water spray, he lathered up and shaved. He'd learn the details of his move today, which—going by Major League time—could mean he'd fly out tonight.

His stomach twisted sharply as he shoved back the dripping curtain. Saying goodbye to Heather would be hard. Even if it wasn't permanent. But what choice did he have? He'd made this comeback bid for himself and Manny.

Yet Heather complicated things. He wrapped a towel around his waist and used another to dry off his hair, his mind far away. She said she trusted him. Would her doubts return when they lived apart?

If so, he couldn't bear it. Growing up in the foster system was like living under a microscope. Every action examined. Questioned. Labeled. Guilty until proven innocent. That hadn't been the case for all the kids in the group home, but it'd been his experience.

However, Heather no longer saw him as an addict on the brink of a relapse. A wild-card player who'd lose as often as he won. It'd taken her a long time, but she now counted on him. That belief meant a lot. Especially because it was difficult for her. He wouldn't lose such a precious gift. Before heading into the stadium, he'd swing by his car and toss those bottles as far as he could throw them.

He pulled on his practice uniform and headed for the kitchen. He hoped Levi was feeling better. Some bug had kept him from camp this week, and he missed the kid. Garrett still didn't know what had bothered him the night the Falcons had clinched the playoffs. They still needed to clear that up. Plus, if he left soon, he had to reassure Levi he'd come back. That he was only a phone call away. He wouldn't repeat his mistakes with Manny.

If he had to, he'd swing by the foster home on his way to the airport…he pictured Heather accompanying him, but his mind veered away from how they'd part. Would there be kisses or tears?

The phone rang as he poured water into the coffeemaker. Heather's name on his cell's screen got his pulse speeding. This was early. Did she have news about his move or just want to talk? He tapped the speaker button on. Scooped the pungent granules into the machine's top.

"Hello?"

Immediately a gurgling sounded, drowning out whatever Heather said.

He crossed the housing unit's efficiency kitchen to get better reception. At the table by a small window, he sat and looked out at the old field. Small puddles of rain gathered in depressions. Streams snaked down the baselines. It'd be a long, wet day. Possibly his last in Holly Springs.

"Heather?" he tried again.

"Yes." Despite the distance from the sputtering machine, he strained to hear her low voice. He brought the phone to his ear.

"Morning, beautiful. Didn't expect to hear from you so soon." He recalled how long they'd lingered last night and smiled. When had he kissed her good-night? Two? Three o'clock in the morning?

Practice wasn't for another couple of hours. No need for her to be up. As for him, he planned on throwing early. Being in top form before debuting in the big leagues. His pitching was under control, but he had to be sure. Besides, nerves left him with plenty of excess energy to burn.

"Yes. Well…" Her distant voice trailed off,

and a humming sensation vibrated beneath his skin. Something wasn't right.

"Is everything okay?"

When the coffee stream slowed to a drip, he prowled to the cabinets, phone in hand.

"Can you come to the office?" He heard more than the usual fatigue in her voice. Yes, they'd been up late last night, but her tone sounded more serious than that. Did she have the final information on his move? Strangely, instead of mixed emotions, his heart tripped in his chest and fell, heavy and hard.

He poured the coffee and leaned against the counter.

"Did the Buccaneers call?"

"Yes. But there's something else."

He gulped the scalding black brew. "What did they say? Am I leaving today?"

"Just come quickly. Please."

A soft buzzing sound ended the call. He stared at his cup before placing it in the sink. She'd said she was excited about his Major League move. Yet he wondered if, deep down, she was upset. He was. Her terse responses, however, sounded more ominous than parting jitters.

His mind ran over possibilities as he shoved his feet into his sneakers and yanked on his cap. Did her mood have something to do with Levi? Had the boy gotten worse? Worry sawed through him. Or had something happened with Heather's mother? A relapse? Heather had come far. She trusted her mother. And him. Having that faith challenged would devastate her.

He zipped up his rain shell, grabbed his bag and ducked outside. A fine mist fell from purple-bottomed clouds. He slammed the door shut. At a dead run, his feet pounded down the muddy path that led to the main office.

Whatever it was, he'd be there for her. If the Majors needed him tonight, they'd just have to wait.

HEATHER STOOD AT the window facing the distant, fog-covered Appalachians, her mind even farther away. When a deep shiver lanced through her, she released a shaky breath and zipped up her sweatshirt. She glanced over at Mr. Lettles. In a chair opposite her desk, he crossed and uncrossed his legs, his face pinched into disapproving lines. How could his story be true? A sickening nausea clawed through her bloodstream.

"Mr. Wolf should be here any minute." She forced herself to return to her seat, though every instinct told her to run. Hide. Leave this all-too-familiar situation. The crisis echoed through the twisted corridors of her childhood memories. Her fingers massaged the painful pulse that'd penetrated her temples. "And please know how sorry I am about Levi. This kind of thing should never happen." *Ever*, she added silently.

Mr. Lettles nodded, his expression grave.

Stay calm, Heather reminded herself. Garrett had to have an explanation. "We would not have anticipated this and don't condone it." She focused on the steady movement of her breathing. In…and out. In…and out. A rhythm that should settle her. Only it didn't.

A knock sounded on the door, and Garrett's face appeared in the opening. For a moment, everything fell away but the man who meant so much. Someone who, possibly, had betrayed her on the worst level.

"Come in," she barely whispered, then repeated it. Louder.

Garrett strode into the room but pulled up short when he glimpsed Mr. Lettles. Emotions crossed his face. She read each one. Surprise, confusion, worry…but no guilt. Interesting, considering the facts.

"Please have a seat, Mr. Wolf."

His blue eyes darted to hers and a muscle jumped in his jaw at her formal address. In the office chair, his long body looked impossibly large.

The air-conditioning whooshed and the rain drummed on the roof as she struggled to speak.

"What's this about? Is Levi okay?" Garrett turned toward Mr. Lettles.

"No," Mr. Lettles snapped, his voice sharper than she'd ever heard it. "He's not."

Garrett bolted from his chair. "Is he in the hospital? I've been calling the foster home this week, but they said he had some kind of stomach bug. Didn't want visitors..."

Heather signaled Garrett to sit again. "Levi slipped in the shower last night and broke his arm."

Garrett paled, his knuckles purple against the chair's arms. "Will he need surgery? Is it his throwing arm, his left arm?" His voice rose in obvious concern, adding to her confusion.

He genuinely seemed to care. Then again, addicts could lie their way through anything. Her heartbeat stuttered to a halt. Could this be one of those times? She trusted Garrett, thought they were past him keeping secrets but these facts made it hard to hold on to her slipping resolve.

"Luckily it was a clean break of the right radius. No surgery required." Mr. Lettles gave her a significant look. As in *Hurry up and get on with it. Question Garrett.*

Still. She hesitated.

It was like pricking herself with a needle. She could barely bring herself to do it. Her eyes lingered on a desktop picture of her father with the team that'd won the last league championship. He would have handled this situation directly. Not let sentiment get in the way.

She pulled back to that place inside that buffered her from pain. After reconciling with her mom and opening up to Garrett, she'd never thought she'd need it again— but there it was, waiting, as though it knew she'd be back. Soon.

"Is Levi asking for me? I can shoot over there now before practice and—"

"That won't be necessary," she broke in. "Any contact between you and Levi is prohibited until we've conducted an investigation into this."

From the floor, she produced a bag with a local liquor store label and two empty bottles of whiskey.

Garrett's face tensed, the flash of guilt in his eyes making her stomach bottom out.

"Do these belong to you?"

His nostrils flared and his eyes darkened. "Yes."

Heather's hand splayed across her chest. "Can you explain how Levi might have gotten hold of them?"

He shook his head, looking shell-shocked. "They were in my trunk."

Her airways no longer worked. Small lights fluttered in the periphery of her vision. Hadn't Garrett sobered up? If he had, then why purchase liquor? At the very least, he should have told her—an omission was as good as a deception. Could he have duped her so completely? Hidden it from her? She thought back to her years with her mother. She'd fallen for this act many times. Possibly had been fooled again.

She would have given herself a kick, but she was already down.

"Levi fell in the shower because he was drunk," Mr. Lettles interjected, his hands clenched on his lap. "He said he got the alcohol from you."

"That's not true." Garrett's insistence sounded sincere, and despite everything, Heather found herself believing him. He might have lied to her and himself about his sobriety, but he genuinely cared about Levi. She doubted he'd put a child in danger. But by the sound of Mr. Lettles disapproving cluck, he blamed Garrett.

"Would you explain why it was in his possession?" Heather asked.

Garrett tried to meet her eye, his expression conveying a message she could read easily. He was innocent. He wouldn't endanger a child. And although she sensed that much was true, that another explanation for Levi's behavior existed, the fact that he'd had the liquor at all made him guilty of breaking her trust. It was all too familiar. Her life in reruns.

"I can't explain it," he insisted. "Maybe he snuck into my trunk to get it? I'm not sure. Whatever happened, I wouldn't give a child alcohol. Heather, believe me."

Heather's stomach lurched, and a high-pitched buzzing washed away his voice. She twisted her hands in her lap, her fingernails scraping over her flesh until she was as raw on the outside as she felt on the inside. She felt flayed, but not by his supposed culpability over Levi. He'd already admitted to, possessing a substance he'd sworn never to abuse again.

Mr. Lettles looked at her, then spoke rapidly.

"Facts speak louder than words," Mr. Lettles spat. "Levi was either under your supervision or ours at all times. He had no access to your vehicle while on our watch."

Garrett stiffened. "What about last week's game? He stopped me as I left the field. Said you were up in the bathroom and would walk him to the bus. Did he meet you?"

Mr. Lettles shook his head slowly. "He came to the bus late. In fact, he was punished for holding us up, but he said he was talking to you. You could have given the alcohol to him then. His backpack is big enough to hide bottles."

"No. I was on the field at the time." Garrett threw himself out of his chair and paced. "This isn't a discussion. It's an indictment." He stopped and faced them, his jaw set. "A formality. No matter what I say—" his eyes swerved to hers, the pain in them making her wince "—I'm guilty."

Mr. Lettles spread his hands. "I have faith in my charges. When you trust in someone, they almost always meet your expectations. Levi has never lied to me. And given your past record, I'd say this all seems consistent."

Mr. Lettles pulled out a handkerchief and mopped his brow. "The ramifications of this are severe. It could impact our license and funding to operate. Furthermore, it gets added to Levi's permanent record. And possibly yours." He jabbed a finger at Garrett. "I hope you understand what you've done here."

Garrett stopped at the edge of the desk. He picked up a glass paperweight and turned it over in his hands. "So because of my past, I'm automatically guilty. Correct?"

Heather cleared her throat. Garrett had a point, but his version of events didn't automatically disprove Levi's. At least, not in Mr. Lettles's eyes. They would need to talk to Levi again and share Garrett's recollection. Maybe it would prompt the boy to come clean. It'd be the only way to convince Mr. Lettles. And she needed to smooth the older man's ruffled feathers. Fast.

"Since you've admitted the alcohol is yours, and Levi said he got it from you, I'd appreciate an apology to Mr. Lettles."

Garrett's face reddened. "Gladly. If I'd done anything to Levi."

Mr. Lettles stood and draped a raincoat over his arm. "I didn't expect an apology, though it would have been nice. The trustees and I will review this case. We'll determine whether or not to continue our association with the Falcons."

"Mr. Lettles." Heather followed him to the door, desperate to convince him. "The Falcons have worked hard to build community relations. Please don't deprive the boys until we've conducted a full investigation. Having alcohol around a minor was reckless, but perhaps questioning Levi again…"

She ignored Garrett's harsh intake of air, needing to focus on the situation. Not him. If she thought about what it meant to their relationship, she'd fall apart. No. She'd think about it later. Discuss it when they were alone. For now, she'd stay safely behind her wall, letting emotions bash against it without causing damage.

She had to keep her connection with this group home and, by extension, the rest of the homes with children attending camp. If word got out, the scandal would undo her work to bring pride back to Holly Springs and to the Falcons. Fans would lose their loyalty when they heard rumors—founded or not—of players giving alcohol to minors.

Mr. Lettles paused in the doorway. "Heather. I know you mean well, but I have to consider the well-being of the boys. This was a nice experiment, but I'm afraid it may be over. Good day."

And with that, he walked out, leaving her staring into the empty hall, feeling just as hollow.

She whirled, closing the door behind her.

"How could you?" she whispered, wishing like anything for a voice that didn't betray her.

Garrett strode toward her, and she backed up, not wanting him close, her skin crawling. When his eyes searched hers, he froze, his expression wounded.

"So that's it? You believe Mr. Lettles?" His voice was thick. Hoarse. "Think that I'd endanger Levi? Wouldn't care about his safety?"

From his expression, she guessed he was thinking of Manny. Why didn't he see what really upset her? "Of course I don't think that. You cared about Levi. I only wish you'd felt the same way about me." Her voice trembled like an autumn leaf, crisp and dead at the edges.

In two steps, he was closer still, her icy hands in his. "I do care about you, Heather. More than I can say."

"Then how could you have bought alcohol? Kept it in your trunk? Have you been drinking this whole time?" The words tore out of her, pushed by a wave of betrayal.

He rubbed his temples, shielding his eyes. "Heather, I messed up. But I had no intention of drinking that alcohol."

"You bought it. What was your intention, then?" She squeezed her eyes shut. Deception. Would it always be a part of her life? If she stayed with Garrett, it would. The thought pierced her, an arrow through her aching chest.

"I bought it the day after we kissed at the falls. When you said you'd never trust me, I drove to a liquor store. Stupid. Weak. But I didn't drink it."

She snatched her hands away and wrapped her arms around her stomach as she swayed. Visions of her mother's former out-of-control behavior swam in and out of focus, making her shiver. She begged her feet to move, but instead they became stone, embedded in the ground.

Her mind raced to the afternoon they'd spent at Looking Glass Falls. How she'd opened up to him. The way he'd comforted her. Reassured her. Made her dare to wonder if she could trust him.

What a cosmic joke. Outside, the rain transformed into a deluge. Sheets of it flooded the gray, murky world.

"You pitched that night."

He nodded, his forehead creased. "A shutout, Heather. Think. Could a drunk do that?"

Suspicion sharpened her voice. "Maybe you saved it for later. To celebrate."

His head snapped back as if slapped.

"I understand why it's hard for you to believe me, Heather, but you need to. I need you to."

She stared at him. Her mind replaying the betrayal, unable to see past it.

He picked up a picture of her and her father from the desk, studied it, then set it down. "I can't convince you, can I? Once an alcoholic, always one."

"I learned that in Al-Anon meetings. It's not something you can control. We were kidding ourselves to think you could." Her breath came out faster, and she couldn't draw in enough air to compensate for the loss. "You told me once you couldn't make any guarantees. I should have listened."

"Heather, I promised you I'd work hard to stay sober and I meant it. A part of me wasn't sure I could do it. Maybe I'll never be certain. But after spending time with Levi, you…I'm different. Stronger. Don't you see that?"

She wanted to. Or her heart did. It whispered for her to trust him. But the voice was too faint, unconvinced.

He shoved a hand through his tangle of hair. "If I'd been drinking all this time, could I have performed as well as I have?"

The world spun, and all the thoughts in her head jumbled together. She rubbed her throbbing temple again. None of this made sense.

"Maybe you waited until after and between games," she thought out loud.

"No. Those bottles are the only ones I've bought in over a year. I called my sponsor from the liquor store parking lot that day. We talked, and I never drank it."

"But you kept it."

"Yes. And I should have gotten rid of it sooner." He tipped his head back and spoke to the ceiling. "I was reckless to have held on to it for reasons I don't even understand. But being with you this week, seeing everything the future held for both of us, made me realize I didn't need it anymore. I planned on getting rid of the bottles today."

Were these explanations just excuses? There was no way to know. "You should have thrown them out immediately."

His gaze lowered and held hers. "You're right. I should have done that. Instead, I rushed to practice and called a players-only meeting. When the team listened to me and hustled for the shutout win, I didn't think I needed the bottles anymore. But I couldn't get rid of them, either—knowing they were there gave me a strange sense of security, even though opening one would have destroyed everything I care about. Heather, I'm human. I made a mistake. One I deeply regret."

Her spirits dipped lower. "You called a players-only meeting to tell them to hustle? That's my job." She wheeled around, hiding her face. "I thought we won because they finally accepted me as their manager. Applied my corrections. Worked hard for me. Not you."

Garrett drew closer, chagrined. "You were so brave to come to practice after losing your father. I wanted them to win for you. Thought lighting an extra fire under them wouldn't hurt."

Heather shambled to her desk and sank into her chair when her knees gave way. "You didn't think I could do it on my own. You decided I wasn't good enough."

He followed her and leaned a hip against the edge. "No. I just wanted to help."

"Because you thought I needed it."

He looked at her. Mute. It was all the answer she required. Old insecurities rushed back. Garrett hadn't thought her capable or good enough. His actions were ripping the scabs off her healing childhood wounds.

"You should have told me."

He rubbed his beard stubble. "I wanted you to believe—"

"That I'd succeeded on my own," she broke in. "A lie."

"But it's the truth. You came to practice that day. You inspired them. Not me."

"Then why hold the meeting?"

Again he fell silent and shook his head. Despair flooded her. They were at a stalemate. She'd never fully believe he'd stop drinking and lying. He'd never think she was capable, able to succeed without his help. She pointed a shaking finger at the door.

"Please go."

He placed his large hands on her desk. Leaned in. "Heather, please. I had your best interests at heart. I would never hurt you."

"But you deceived me." Her voice was so low she barely heard it. "You didn't tell me how close you'd come to drinking again, and you went behind my back because you thought I couldn't handle my job."

He shook his head, his expression pleading. "It looks bad, but it came from a good place."

"Good never comes from bad."

"And that's what I am to you? Bad? The dishonest addict?"

"I'm sorry, Garrett. Unless you prove me wrong, I can't see you any other way."

When he straightened, he met her eyes. "I will prove you wrong. I'm everything I said I was. A committed man who loves you. Who'll stay and fight. For us."

He loved her? Her heart sank. Why did he have to tell her now? Now that she had too many questions and not enough faith.

"No. You won't. You're flying to Pittsburgh tonight. The Buccaneers want you for tomorrow's game. But know that if we confirm Levi's story, the ripple effect may impact your Major League play and require us to file charges against you."

He closed his eyes briefly, and when he opened them, they were sadder than she'd ever seen them. Despite everything, she would have thought he'd be a little happy to achieve his Major League goal, even if it was threatened.

"I see. Then it's goodbye. For now." The door clicked shut behind him.

Heather dropped her head into her hands. She'd never believed she could open up to someone. Have a normal relationship given her past. But after learning that her father had been proud of her, that her mother was capable of changing, she'd felt ready to try.

Fool.

Garrett was the last person she should have trusted. If she'd followed her instincts instead of her heart, she would have steered clear. He'd deceived her on so many levels. Buying alcohol, drinking it (or keeping it around in case he wanted to) and going behind her back to do her job for her.

Like her dad, he didn't think she could manage the team on her own. It stung. No. It burned. She should be glad about Garrett's call-up to the big leagues. She wouldn't have to see him every day, be reminded of his betrayal. With him, she would always be on guard, waiting for the hammer to fall. It'd been stupid to try. Yet he'd made her happier this week than she'd ever been in her life. Why did it have to turn out this way?

A sob tore from her throat, followed by another. She looked at the team picture, a tear rolling down her cheek, another tracing a line to her chin. Gadways didn't cry.

Though this Gadway did, it seemed. For Garrett.

GARRETT TRUDGED BACK to the dorms, heart heavy. Scout appeared from where he'd lurked outside the offices, running laps around his legs. The drizzling rain matched Garrett's mood. His boyhood dream was coming true. Tonight, he was heading for the Majors. But he couldn't care less. Thoughts of Heather consumed him.

Why would she jump to conclusions so quickly? It reminded him of his childhood. Being blamed for crimes he didn't commit because he was the "troubled kid." The outsider. Before Heather and Levi, only Manny had helped him feel like he mattered. Lately he'd begun to think he'd made a fresh start.

Idiot.

He paused to pet Scout and looked out at the old field. Working with Levi gave him hope. He'd thought he could make a difference. Not mess up as he had with Manny.

Why would Levi have taken the alcohol? The night they'd secured a playoff spot came back to him. He remembered Levi's disappointment when he'd turned the boy down for ice cream. Had he grabbed the spare keys from under Garrett's car, popped the trunk and taken the alcohol? He might have spied the bottles on their bike trip when he'd reached far into the trunk. Garrett should have guessed the boy might have noticed, no matter how deep they were lodged. Being in a hurry or eager to teach Levi were not excuses.

And what had motivated Levi? He'd been upset about something that night. Had wanted to talk about it. Until Heather's investigation was complete, Garrett wouldn't know. Still. It made no sense that Levi would blame Garrett.

He leaned on the fence, remembering the day they'd met. Levi was a good kid. Maybe he'd lied so he wouldn't be accused of stealing. It was self-preservation, not ill will. A child's action he totally understood.

He took off his cap when the rain stopped, brushing the water from its brim. Why hadn't he gotten rid of those bottles sooner? He should have trusted more in his strength. Had faith in how much AA had helped him. Recognized how far he'd come and that he wouldn't need alcohol. Even when times got tough.

Shoving away from the fence, he trudged back to his housing unit. He pulled up short at the sight of his teammates lounging on his concrete stoop. A homemade sign draped across his door read Welcome to the Show!

When Dean caught sight of Garrett, he let loose a howl that got Scout barking. The rest of the crew chimed in, owwwww-ooooooh's filling the midmorning air. Garrett tried to smile, but his face was as numb as his heart. He simply stood, taking it in.

"You look like you're actually sorry to go," boomed Waitman, striding forward and clapping Garrett on the back.

"He's going to miss me, that's for sure." Hopson put him in a headlock and rubbed his knuckles over Garrett's head.

Dean shoved the other guys aside and gave Garrett a one-armed bro hug. "Knew you could do it, buddy. Heard about it from Smythe."

Their pitching coach waved from his spot on one of the steps. "I'd get up, but my hip is bothering me again. This time next year, boys, I'll be in dry Arizona. No more arthritis flare-ups."

"You're retiring?" Valdez looked the older man up and down as if only now noticing his lined face and white hair.

"This is Garrett's time. No more talking about this old geezer." Smythe raised a sports drink, and Dean handed Garrett one as well. "To our comeback kid. You made it off the farm, Wolf, but remember, you'll always be a Falcon."

"To Garrett!" their voices rang out before they lifted their bottles. Garrett noticed that they all had his favorite, lemon-lime. Touched, he took a long swallow. The citrus flavor stung the insides of his cheeks, the fresh smell reminding him of Heather.

Looking around the excited, chattering crew, he realized she wasn't the only person he'd miss. He had fit in here, too. These guys had become like brothers. Some annoyed the crap out of him—like Hopson. Others, like Dean, he considered friends. Would it be the same in the Majors? Without realizing it, this small team had turned into family. The thing he'd looked for all his life.

And now he had to leave it and Heather. But not before he saw Levi. Made sure the boy knew he wasn't mad at him. Most of all, he wanted to clear his name before he left. With the truth out, Mr. Lettles would keep the boys enrolled and give Heather's camp another chance. She'd worked hard. Didn't deserve to see it ruined. Plus, the group home kids thrived here, despite Levi's setback. Garrett would miss the kids and wanted to ensure this good work continued—without him, he thought with a pang.

He threw back another long swallow. Funny how he'd forgotten the first rule of being a foster kid. Never grow too attached to locations or people. The minute you let down your guard, it all fell apart.

But he was an adult now. He could make things right.

"Gotta go, fellas. I'll stop by before flying out."

A chorus of protests followed him as he raced to the parking lot.

Minutes later, he pulled up to the group home. He still hated this place, but he'd go in for Levi, for himself and for Heather.

"I'm afraid Mr. Lettles is in a meeting," said the receptionist after she'd kept him waiting for over twenty minutes, making hushed phone calls with her back turned.

"Then tell him Levi has a visitor," he growled, out of patience, and stalked to the elevator. The foster director wouldn't put him off any longer.

When he got off on Levi's floor, a security guard and Mr. Lettles waited for him. Boys stopped playing and gaped at the adults.

"I'm afraid you'll need to leave, Mr. Wolf."

"That's not an option. I'm flying to Pittsburgh tonight and plan to see Levi before I go. I'm not leaving without saying goodbye."

To his surprise, Heather hurried out of the other elevator. "I heard from your receptionist that Mr. Wolf was on premises."

Garrett ground his teeth. At least he knew one of the people the receptionist had called while she'd kept him waiting.

Mr. Lettles pointed at Garrett. "I was about to have him escorted out. Perhaps you can persuade him to leave on his own?"

Garrett eyed the beefy security guard. He had the guy by a few inches. He could take him, but he wouldn't fight in front of children. He eyed the boys, and one of them, a friend of Levi's, hurried away down the hall.

"Garrett, Levi doesn't want to see you," Heather sighed, her soft brown waves loose around her sweet face.

"How do you know? Have you asked him?"

Mr. Lettles straightened his tie. "He's been on quite a bit of pain medicine since last night. He's fairly groggy."

"But lucid enough to accuse me of giving him alcohol?" Garrett asked evenly, keeping his frustration in check. Barely.

Mr. Lettles's concave chest rose and fell. "We will certainly question him again when he's more alert."

Levi's friend raced their way, skidding on stocking feet across the tiles. "Levi's awake and wants to see Garrett."

Garrett arched a brow. "Any objections?"

Heather and Mr. Lettles exchanged a look. At last, the director nodded. "But only for a few supervised minutes."

Together, they entered Levi's room, the security guard shuffling to a back corner. The boy was alarmingly pale and looked small, despite his height, as he reclined on a mound of pillows, his arm in a sling.

"I'm sorry, Garrett," he croaked.

Garrett grabbed a cup of water from the nightstand and held it to Levi's mouth. After Levi took a quick drink, Garrett set it down.

"It's okay, Levi. Just tell us what happened."

The boy's eyes welled. "I had a custody hearing the day after your game. It always freaks me out to see my mother. I wanted to talk to you about it, but you were too busy." His voice turned bitter, and Garrett felt a deep pang of guilt. He'd let down Levi as he had Manny.

"I'm sorry. I had interviews and other things

going on, but I should have put you first." He peered at Heather. Her red cheeks told him she recalled their night in the dugout together. Would it make a difference? Get her to soften toward him a little?

Levi sniffled. "When we went on that bike trip, I saw the bottles in the back of your trunk. My mom drinks, and sometimes she sleeps for days. Says she's sick. I thought if I got sick, I wouldn't have to go to court. On my way to the bus, I stopped by your car and got in your trunk with your spare keys. The bottles fit into my backpack so no one noticed."

His words rushed faster and faster, ending in a full-on wail that had Heather pulling tissues from a nearby box to dry his cheeks.

"Well," Mr. Lettles exclaimed. "That sheds a different light on things. My apologies, Mr. Wolf."

"Accepted." Garrett shot him a brief look before he sat on Levi's bed. He gripped the kid's good hand. "Look. You made a mistake. One I hope you learned from. But the earth didn't crack. The moon didn't fall. Last time I checked, the sun still rose. Life goes on, and after things like this happen, we become better people."

"I love you, Garrett," the boy whispered, then fell back against the pillows.

"I feel the same way, buddy. That's never going to change. I'm leaving for the big leagues tonight. But I'll be calling and visiting. You and I are family now. Got it?"

Levi smiled, his braces flashing. "I knew you could do it, Garrett." His eyelids began to droop. "I'll be watching you on TV." His voice lowered, his words starting to blur together. "And it's okay if you get busy and forget about me. I understand."

"Not a chance. When I do this," Garrett tapped his nose with his right index finger, "that's me saying hello to you."

"Cool," Levi breathed, and his eyes drifted closed. "Cool," he whispered again before his mouth dropped open, his chest rising and falling evenly.

"I shouldn't have jumped to conclusions, Mr. Wolf." Mr. Lettles held out a hand, and Garrett shook it. The man was protecting his charges, no more or less than Garrett would have done. He respected that.

"No harm done," he said, though that wasn't completely true. "I hope this means the group home will continue attending the Falcons baseball camp..."

Mr. Lettles nodded vigorously, and Heather's face softened.

"Of course. We'd be glad to," Mr. Lettles said.

Garrett took off his cap and rested it on the pillow beside a snoozing Levi. "Guess I'd better get going." He glanced at Heather. She looked impossibly beautiful as she clutched her purse against her stomach, her eyes somber. "I've got some packing to do."

"Let me walk you out." Mr. Lettles put a hand on Garrett's back, friendly now.

Garrett stepped away. "No need. I'd like a word with Skipper if you don't mind."

After waving goodbye to Mr. Lettles, he and Heather shared a tense, silent elevator ride. Out in the parking lot, they paused by his car.

With people strolling on the nearby sidewalk, he didn't dare reach for her. It took every bit of his willpower to keep his arms by his sides.

"Please say you forgive me, too, Heather."

"I'm grateful that you came here and cleared this up. And I don't blame you for what happened with Levi. I believed you from the start." Despite her words, her tone was off. Not forgiving. Not loving. Her sneaker slid through the gravel, her downcast eyes tracking it. "I can forgive you for keeping alcohol without telling anyone—even me. But I can't trust you again. Won't take that chance." Her chin trembled slightly. "The most painful years of my life were spent watching and worrying that someone I cared about would relapse. Looking for the warning signs, uncovering hiding spots." She sighed and glanced up, her eyes full of regret. "You may be right. You may never have opened those whiskey bottles. But I don't have it in me to have faith in you again, as much as I wish I could." She touched him lightly on the arm. "I'm sorry, Garrett."

He grabbed on to the car door behind him, reeling. Despite their incredible week together, her promise to believe in him, she was still letting old insecurities get in the way.

Still, he hadn't told her about the alcohol. This was his fault. His screwup. Big time. The hugest mistake of his life. She'd never believe in him again and he didn't blame her.

"How do I fix this?" he asked, unwilling to accept defeat. Not when it came to Heather. He loved her too much. There had to be a way.

"You can't," she said quietly. "Without faith in each other, what do we have? We both need to move on. You're going to the big leagues. A much better place for you. Take care, Garrett."

She slid into her car and drove away. He watched the corner where her car had turned long after it'd disappeared.

Leaving her behind meant the next place could never be better.

CHAPTER FOURTEEN

THREE WEEKS LATER, Garrett warmed up in the Buccaneers' bullpen.

"That angle's off again, Wolf," warned the pitching coach. He snatched off his hat and scratched his balding head. "Get that arm closer to three quarters. Remember. We've got to get more movement. Pitches can't be straight here. They'll get hit."

Only it wasn't working. What he'd gained in ball movement, he'd lost in control. His original problem. He was a far better straight overhand pitcher. Heather had seen it. Helped make his pitch even stronger. Yet this guy tinkered with him like all new coaches did, making changes the way a dog marked its territory. And this was the Major Leagues. What Garrett wanted didn't count. He had to do what he was told.

Garrett wound up, his arm feeling unnatural as the ball flew from his fingertips.

The practice catcher shook his head. "Ball."

Garrett stepped forward to the mound's edge, caught the return throw and strode back into position. He brought his glove to his chest just as the distinctive crack of a smash hit sounded from the playing field.

All of the men looked up, watching a streak of white bullet across the park and into the distant stands. The Hawks fans erupted in thunderous cheers while the Buccaneers coach groaned.

"Looks like you're going in, Wolf. That was a three-run homer. We're down nine-nothing."

Garrett nodded. With this blowout, the Hawks would sweep the Buccaneers in their three-game series. As a mop-up reliever, he went in only when games like this got out of hand. Since it was the bottom of the eighth, he'd be just marking an inning. No one expected him to win. Just finish out the game so that the top relievers wouldn't be used.

The lack of pressure would have been welcome when he'd made his comeback. Now it frustrated him. He could do more than clean up starting pitchers' messes. Heather knew that. Smythe too. But here in the Majors, he was just another arm. One that saw play for only a few innings a week. If he was lucky.

He didn't feel lucky.

Missing Heather was a constant ache, a tear in his heart he couldn't heal. Thinking of her ripped him open every time. He had to get over her, but without alcohol to numb his thoughts, she was a constant presence, haunting him with what might have been. Had she moved on?

At the manager's wave, the pitching coach opened the door and ushered Garrett onto the field.

Boos and catcalls rang out as he jogged to the hill. Buccaneers fans dressed in gold and black streamed up the aisles, getting off this sinking ship. He wished he could join them. Pitching an unwinnable game was the last thing he wanted to do. But maybe it was fitting. He was living an unwinnable life—one in which he'd never get the girl or have a professional career he could be proud of. Even worse, it wasn't honoring Manny the way he'd hoped.

He snatched the ball that Greg, the catcher, winged to him. They rarely spoke. He hardly knew the guy. It wasn't how it'd been with Dean. He and the Falcons catcher had spoken the same language, could anticipate each other's thoughts on the field. Now, he simply followed the catcher's calls or caught heck for it later.

Most new pitchers started at the bottom like this. But with a stacked bullpen and an outstanding starting rotation, it seemed unlikely he'd become a Buccaneers starter any time soon.

Keeping his arm at three quarters, he let loose a fastball that ended up in the dirt. Two pitches later, his count was three balls, no strikes. He gritted his teeth when the crowd leaped to its feet. Cheering.

Screw the arm angle. It wasn't working.

He pictured Heather and came straight over the top. Serious heat whizzed by the batter. The next two pitches, right on the corners, got swings and misses.

Strikeout!

Out of the corner of his eye, he caught the pitching coach's glare but ignored it. He was through doing things their way. He had a point to prove.

The next two batters flailed at Garrett's pinpoint throws. Mowed down, they each took their seats back on the pine.

Inning over.

He ambled off the field. Happy with himself for having struck out the side, all three batters whiffed.

His pitching coach loomed at the bottom of

the dugout steps, his face red. He grabbed Garrett's arm and pulled him aside. His teammates craned their necks, and he could feel their expectant stares. The new kid was about to get schooled—good fodder for dugout drama.

"So what happened out there? Looks like you lost your arm angle." His coach's mild words belied his tense face, a vein popping in his forehead.

Garrett hesitated. Should he be the good soldier and apologize for something he didn't regret at all? Or would he take a stand? Say what he really felt? He thought of Heather. She'd never raised her voice, but she always got her point across.

He folded his arms and looked directly into his coach's eyes. "Well, Coach. What happened was I just blew away three batters. And my arm angle was just fine. Thanks."

Garrett held the coach's eye, watching as the man gaped, dumbfounded. Garrett wheeled around, and his new teammates quickly lowered their heads as he took a seat on the bench. Another Buccaneer returned from the field, out on a pop fly. Only one more out and the game was over.

In a moment of blinding clarity, Garrett realized he was, too.

His dream of becoming a Major Leaguer was nowhere close to reality. Personal results didn't matter to coaches who just wanted to implement their own techniques. The way the Majors worked, he could potentially have a new coach every few years who'd want to change things with him again. He would never find the camaraderie he'd had in the Minors. His Major League teammates were settled, had families and were wealthy, more concerned with making money than friends.

The travel was also more grueling in the Major Leagues. As a former foster kid, he should have been used to pulling up stakes a lot. But after his time with the Falcons, he'd learned to appreciate a more permanent home base. He wanted it back badly. More importantly, he wanted Heather.

The Hawks celebrated on field as the last out was made at first. The batter ducked inside the dugout, and the rest of the guys grabbed their gear and headed for the locker room. Where was the outrage? The Falcons would have been embarrassed and mad at themselves for being bombed like that, but the Buccaneers took it in stride. Emotionless.

He followed them into the showers, lost in thought as he washed up.

Should he let go of a lifelong dream to have the life he wanted? At twenty-seven, this late start meant he wouldn't improve much athletically. Not fast enough to become an ace or even a starting pitcher. He'd thought he'd honor Manny's death by proving that he could make it in the big leagues. But now that he'd arrived, he realized that he was only letting himself down. Manny wouldn't have wanted that.

Water jetted across his head as he rinsed off, then headed for his things. When he pulled on his sweatshirt, a four-leaf clover sticker fluttered out of its pocket.

Levi. The boy had given it to him the night they'd clinched the playoffs, thinking he'd need it for luck.

But he didn't need luck. He needed this reminder. Despite what had happened with Levi, he could be a positive role model. Would honor Manny much more that way than with fame or money. Plus, he'd be happier. Especially if Heather would take him back.

He slung his pack over his shoulder and headed for the manager's office. She'd said she'd never trust him, and it'd stung. He'd heard that plenty in life. And this time, he'd definitely deserved it. Despite her childhood, she'd given him more chances than anyone else

KAREN ROCK 363

and he'd let her down. Now he needed to show her that he wouldn't make that mistake again.

Losing her was the biggest mistake he'd ever made. He'd fought hard to overcome his addiction. He'd fight a hundred times harder to win back the love of his life. She was worth far more than the half-million-dollar contract he was about to throw away.

At Garrett's knock, the manager opened his office door, beef jerky dangling from his mouth. He yanked it out and gestured for Garrett to come inside. "How can I help you, son?"

"I've given this some thought and made up my mind. I want off the team."

The older man stopped chewing and swallowed, his eyes wide. "That caught me off guard. I assumed you wanted to increase your role on the team. What's your reason?"

"Personal." Garrett nearly smiled as he thought of the bragging Hopson and posturing Waitman. "Family business."

"O...kay." The man dragged out the word, sounding confused. "You've shown promise, Wolf. The Buccaneers see a future for you."

But Garrett didn't. The only future he envisioned was with Heather. And Levi. And the Falcons.

"I appreciate that," Garrett said. "Most people would kill to be in the Major Leagues, but it's not in the cards for me anymore. I know I can't request being sent back down to the Minors—"

The manager tugged on an oversized ear. "You'd be the first one who's ever asked," He shrugged. "It's a one-way ticket up here."

"Then I'll be resigning effective tonight."

The meat stick thunked to the desk. "You're only twenty-seven. Plenty of years left for a solid career."

"My priorities have changed. But thank you." Garrett stood and extended a hand. "I wish the Buccaneers luck."

"I hope the same for you, Wolf. It's been a pleasure." They shook hands. "Please stop by the main office on your way out to complete the paperwork."

Back in the hall, Garrett's face broke into a grin, a weight off his shoulders. By getting rid of his old dreams, he'd made room for new possibilities.

And they all included the woman he loved.

HEATHER STOOD ON the locker room bench, waiting for the disappointed grumbling to die down. She nudged aside a pair of socks and planted her feet wider, her hands linked be-hind her back.

"Hey!" Valdez put his fingers to his mouth and whistled. "Skipper's got something to say."

She nodded at him, grateful. It'd been a long, contentious battle for the league championship. Losing in extra innings in game five hurt. But there was a lot to be proud of. She searched the crowd for a familiar pair of blue eyes. When would she stop looking for Garrett? *Maybe when your heart does*, a voice inside whispered...

Shoving the persistent thought aside, she forced a smile and looked down at her grim-faced players.

"First of all, congratulations on making it to the finals. I'm disappointed we didn't win, too, but I'm proud of how far we've come, and I know my father would be, as well. Since mid-season, you've turned things around, giving us the best Minor League record in the second half."

A few of the Falcons lost their angry expressions, and others eyed her speculatively. She pushed back her bangs. "Obviously we owe Garrett Wolf some of the credit for jump-starting our turnaround."

Hopson looked at Waitman and shrugged.

"He pitched a great game. Helped us get the shutout to kick off our winning streak."

Heather's eyes moved from one nodding team member to another. "I also heard that he called a players-only meeting that day and motivated you with a pep talk."

Rob swatted the air. "I worked hard for you, Skip. We all did."

A murmur of agreement rippled through the crowd, and Heather's heart squeezed. So she hadn't needed Garrett's help. She'd gotten through to the team on her own.

The thought was swiftly followed by another. Hadn't Garrett said that she'd motivated the guys? Not him. Her old insecurities had drowned him out. What else had he said that she'd missed? Or chosen not to hear?

"Me too!" shouted Valdez. "You came to practice a week after your Dad passed. That took guts."

"Dedication," added Waitman. "You put us to shame."

Hopson took off his hat, and a number of the guys followed suit. "Skipper, we couldn't have had this season without you. Wolf knows it, too. His speech was all about you, anyway. His belief in your abilities as a manager. How you were the only one who'd ever helped his pitching. He said he trusted your coaching ability and so should we."

Heather's lungs seized. Garrett had called the meeting to reinforce her authority. Not take charge. He'd believed in her. What was more, the guys had faith in her leadership, too. She'd blamed her father for not trusting her abilities, but she hadn't trusted herself, either. Garrett's meeting shouldn't have shaken her confidence. She should have known that she was getting through to the players—no matter what he might have added to the conversation. Light filled her, and everything swam into focus.

"You were great out there," she said, speaking over the thoughts whirling through her brain. "I hate to see the season end. It's been a good one. We came together, and next year, we'll be unstoppable."

"You said it!"

"Yes!"

"Falcons are number one!"

Heather smiled at the enthusiastic responses erupting around her. Now that's what she loved to hear.

"To Skipper," shouted Valdez.

A number of the guys whirled hand towels over their heads. "To Skipper!" they roared back.

"Thank you. That means a lot to me." She

wagged a finger and smiled. "Remember this feeling when I hand out your season critiques and lay out your individual off-season expectations. The schedule for tonight's meetings is posted outside my office. See you in a few minutes." She stepped off the bench and put a hand on Hopson's arm. "May I have a word?"

Hopson followed her out into the tunnel, his jovial expression vanishing. He shoved his hat further off his forehead and peered down at her.

"You don't have to tell me," he said. "I know my contract ends this year, and I haven't had the best season. I'm not coming back in February for spring training, am I?"

"Let's speak in my office."

Inside the lit space, she faced him across her desk. "In the first half of the season, as you know, I had concerns with effort issues. That can affect the entire team. During the second half, I noticed a big improvement, and you played to your potential. I expect that next year you're going to start the season the same way you finished this one."

He looked at her, shocked. "What? I'm coming back?"

She nodded, her lips curling. "I've met with Mr. Williams, our Minor League director.

Based on my recommendation, he's decided to invite you to spring training, and you'll be offered a contract contingent on your play. Please keep that last part between us, as technically you'll be a free agent."

His mouth worked for a moment as he struggled to get himself under control. When he spoke, it came out in a rush, relief evident in his voice. "What should I focus on during the off-season, Skipper?"

Heather looked down at her notes, though she knew her plan for him. For each of them. Her team. "You need to get on a weight training program because you're getting older now. Work on building strength and add some daily sprints for speed."

Hopson nodded, the creases in his forehead smoothing. "Got it." He stood and held out a hand. "Thanks for the opportunity, Skip. See you in February."

She shook his hand, smiling warmly. "Enjoy your time off."

When the door shut, she dropped her chin into her palm and stared out the window. Her reflection looked back at her, and she didn't like what she saw. She'd just given Hopson a second chance, yet she'd refused to give Garrett one. He'd been the first on the team to give her his support. His faith had never wavered. So why hadn't she returned it?

Fear.

Plain and simple.

She was afraid to love someone who could hurt her again. But those were childhood issues. These past months had taught her a lot. She was stronger than she gave herself credit for. Despite losing her father, grief she lived with every day, she'd gone on. Had led her team to one of their best seasons in years. Even better, she'd forgiven her mother.

Fear of being hurt shouldn't control her. Hold her back. Pain was a part of life. But joy filled it too. You couldn't have one without the other. Playing it safe meant living half a life, and she wanted it all.

With Garrett.

Time to let it go. Once and for all. Garrett was an alcoholic. Always would be. But she wasn't a young girl anymore and didn't need to be afraid. If he relapsed, they'd deal with it. Together. He deserved the chance, and she should have given it to him.

Only now it was too late, she realized. He was a Major League pitcher. Had moved on to the future he'd always wanted. One that had no room for her.

A KNOCK SOUNDED on her office door, and Heather raised bleary eyes. She glanced at her cell phone. 12:30 a.m. She'd seen her last player fifteen minutes ago. Had Smythe stopped by to discuss his retirement? If so, she hoped they could postpone the conversation until tomorrow, before his party.

"Come in," she called. The door opened, and a tall man with golden hair and blue eyes stepped inside.

Her lungs stalled. She blinked a few times, wondering if her tired eyes had conjured the man she loved.

"Hello, Heather." His deep voice made her pulse leap.

"Garrett," she breathed, struggling to take in that he was here.

He put a hand over his heart and gave a short bow, his lips twisting in an irresistible smile. "In the flesh. May I come in?"

"Of course." She gripped the edge of her desk. It was all she could do not to run to him. His evergreen scent floated beneath her nose, making her light-headed. She wanted to burrow in his strong arms and feel him against her. "What are you doing here? Aren't the Buccaneers playing tomorrow in Florida?"

The tender look in his eyes made her melt.

They'd parted on such bad terms, but seeing him made it all disappear.

"They are," he said. "I'm not."

She scanned the ceiling, as if the answer to this puzzle was hidden there. "I don't understand."

"Let's take a walk. Are you finished for the night?"

"Yes." She grabbed her bag and followed him outside, locking the building behind her.

They strolled in and out of the shadowed shapes created by the moon and trees, stopping near the pond in front of the stadium. A light breeze ruffled Heather's hair, rippling across the water's inky surface. Frogs called to one another from the fringe of rushes, their throaty sound as powerful as the emotions surging in her veins.

Garrett pointed to a small wrought-iron bench. "Let's sit there."

Heather nodded. She didn't trust her shaking knees to take her any farther. None of this made sense. Garrett should be far away. Not here. Especially not with her, given how they'd left things.

They sat side by side, his arm brushing hers and sending warm shivers through her. A frog slipped into the water, and moonlit rings spiraled outward. Stars danced on the undulating water, sparklers that fizzed and popped.

She turned and met his soulful eyes. "What are you doing here, Garrett?"

"I came for you."

His words set off a firestorm within her, making her tremble.

"But your contract?"

"I resigned."

Her mouth fell open. "But playing in the Majors is your dream."

He wrapped a curl of her hair around his finger. "I'm hoping for a better one now. A future for us."

"Garrett. No," she protested, despite the adrenaline rushing through her. "I can't let you do that."

He lowered his eyes, and his hand fell to his lap. "Can't or won't?"

She swallowed hard. "No. I want to. I mean—it's just that your career is so much more important."

"Than you and me?" One of his eyebrows rose, and the expression in his eyes nearly undid her. "Not a chance. I wasn't happy with the Buccaneers. They're a great team. But it wasn't home. This—" he gestured to the stadium "—you—" he cupped her chin and brushed his thumb across her cheekbone "—are home. I should have stayed. Fought harder for the woman I love."

She leaned into his palm, enjoying the rough skin against her soft flesh. "I love you too."

His eyes glowed, his wide smile stealing her breath. "You love me."

She nodded, grinning back. "I should have told you earlier. Wanted to call and tell you…"

He tipped up her chin and searched her eyes. "What else were you going to say?"

For a moment, she worried her words would vanish, but they leaped out instead, fearless. Eager for freedom.

"That I'm sorry for not believing you. I'm done with letting the past dictate my future. Being afraid. I want a life with you, Garrett. Whatever challenges come with it, we'll face together. If you falter, I'll be there. That's my guarantee."

Tenderly, he traced the line of her jaw, making the fine hairs on the back of her neck stand up. "You're the strongest, most incredible woman I know. I'm never going to let you get hurt again. That's my vow."

Heather rested her head on his shoulder, overcome. Had he come back to Holly Springs—and her—for good? He'd called this home. It seemed he meant it. "I wondered if you'd be interested in taking Smythe's job next year. Become the Falcons pitching coach?"

Garrett tucked a stray lock behind her ear, his fingers lingering on her sensitive skin. "I'd like that. I believe in you, Heather. You're a great manager. It'd be an honor to work with you and the camp, if they'll let me."

A deep sigh escaped her. She hadn't realized until then that she'd been holding her breath. "Levi's been bragging about your daily phone calls. He calls himself your second manager. I'm impressed that you've stayed close, despite what he did. I know Mr. Lettles is, too. I'm sure they'll let you work with the foster kids, including Levi."

She felt Garrett's nod. "He's a good kid."

When she peered up at him, his eyes roamed the darkness, his expression even farther away. "You're forgiving and I've been terrible," she said. "You kept the bottles from me, but I shouldn't have accused you of having a relapse, of lying to me. That was fear talking. I didn't want to get hurt again, so I lashed out."

He wrapped his arm around her waist and pulled her closer. "I'm sorry, Heather. I wasn't open with you and broke your trust when you'd risked so much to give it to me. I want you to believe in me again."

"I do. There's always going to be a part of

me that'll feel nervous, that might watch you harder than I should, but I trust that you're going to try. We'll take it one day at a time."

His fingertips grazed her waist, then rose along her rib cage, making her stomach jump. "A part of me will always be tempted to drink. But I'll never stop fighting it. And I won't keep anything from you again. I'll get help if I'm tempted. I'm a flawed man, but I love you with all that I am."

"I'm not perfect, either. I jump to conclusions, make accusations, believe the worst in others, but I'm working on it," she said, meaning it. "I don't want to lose you again."

His arm tightened around her. "You won't. I'll work hard every day to keep us together."

Her heart swelled. "I love you, Garrett."

"I love you, too."

In an instant, his arms encircled her, pulling her against him. His heart thundered beneath hers, and he lowered his lips. She knotted her arms around his neck, pleasure flooding her at the crush of his mouth. When she caressed the back of his head, a shudder ran through him. His deep groan carried in the still summer air.

His hands skimmed across her jittery stomach, then rose to her face, cupping it. Sensation after sensation rolled through her: love, acceptance, forgiveness and a deep sense of rightness. He angled her head, his mouth slanting across hers as he kissed her still more deeply. Her breath slipped away, too fast for her to catch. At last he pulled away, and she snuggled her head in the crook of his neck. Her breath came in fits and starts until it gradually slowed, her nerves calming with it.

When she opened her eyes, he was staring at her with more love than she'd ever seen. Gone were the days of not feeling good enough. His expression said it all.

They weren't perfect.

But they were perfect for each other.

She rested her head on his shoulder, and he leaned his cheek against the crown of her head. He turned her palm over and traced what felt like the number 8 in its center.

"What's that?" she asked, the world around them feeling slow and dreamlike.

"Infinity," he whispered against the part in her hair. "It's how long I'm going to fight to deserve you."

She pulled back and met his eyes, her hands cupping his cheeks. "Sweet man. You already do."

* * * * *

ISBN-13:978-0-373-36703-0

36703

0-373-36703-0

HEARTWARMING
wholesome, tender romances

He was attractive, talented…and way off-limits.

Heather Gadway may have been a world-class college pitcher and a top university coach, but she's a rank amateur when it comes to managing the Falcons, her father's struggling minor-league team. *And* when it comes to managing her aggravating attraction to Garrett Wolf, their talented new ——— it's going to be difficult enough to make it as the first ——— in the league and prove to her overly critical fa——— distractions. No missteps. And certainly —— players. Everything stands between them—incl—— troubled pasts—even as Heather's world falls apart and G—rr—tt's the one who's there to catch her...

⟨ **LARGER PRINT** ⟩

$6.50 U.S./$7.50 CAN.

ISBN-13: 978-0-373-36703-0

50650

9 780373 367030

CATEGORY
WHOLESOME

EAN
(S)

HARLEQUIN®
™HEARTWARMING™

harlequin.com